Your Captivating Love
(The Bennett Family, Book 2)

LAYLA HAGEN

Dear Reader,

If you want to receive news about my upcoming books and sales, you can sign up for my newsletter HERE: http://laylahagen.com/mailing-list-sign-up/

Chapter One

Logan

"How do you feel?" I ask my sister the second she climbs in my car.

Pippa straightens her shoulders. "Free. Finally."

She just signed her divorce papers, so I suppose *free is* the appropriate word. However, *free* does not equal *fine*, which means my top priority for today is taking care of my sister and cheering her up.

This was easy when we were teenagers. All I had to do to brighten her up was to make sure there was plenty of ice cream around, and possibly take her to see a movie. Now that she's thirty, things have changed, but I'm still her older brother, and it's still up to me to find a way to lift her spirits.

"What do you want to do?" I question.

"Ava and Sebastian are having dinner at my favorite sushi restaurant. We could join them."

"Sebastian won't appreciate us crashing his date." Our brother fiercely guards his time with his fiancée.

"Oh, we won't," Pippa says. The corners of her mouth lift up in a genuine smile for the first time today. I narrow my eyes, sensing foul play. In the months since she discovered what a scumbag her now ex-husband is, Pippa has taken up a dangerous hobby: matchmaking. She told our mother her plan is to find the perfect match for each of her siblings. Since there are nine of us, it's an ambitious project. Her first target was Sebastian, our oldest brother. As ridiculous as I find Pippa's idea, he *did* end up with the perfect woman for him.

Our parents have been married for more than thirty years, and they love each other. I can understand the appeal the *perfect match* has to Pippa. I envy our parents too, but as far as I'm concerned, what they have is impossible to find. It was a lucky strike for them, as it was for Sebastian and Ava.

Unfortunately, Pippa seems to be focusing her matchmaking efforts on me now. Unbelievable. I'm the CFO of a billion-dollar company. I can get my own damn woman if I want one.

"Pippa, will anyone else be joining Ava and Sebastian at dinner?" I ask.

"Ava's best friend, Nadine. You know, the one who just moved here?"

Jackpot. I knew this was a setup. I have two choices: put my foot down and tell my sister to find another pastime, or suck it up and go with her plan. The problem: I can't say no to any of my three sisters. I never could, which often led me into trouble in the past. I have a hunch the same thing is about to happen. But even armed with this suspicion, I can't say no. If meeting this Nadine will take my sister's mind off her misery, even if only for a few hours, it's worth it.

"I've heard about her," I mumble.

"Great, let's go then." As I rev the car's engine, I glance at my sister again. Pippa is now borderline ecstatic, which means I'm a dead man.

Nadine, you'd better be fun, or sexy.

Chapter Two

Nadine

"Welcome to San Francisco." My best friend, Ava, her fiancé, Sebastian Bennett, and I clink our glasses.

"I'm so excited. It's finally sinking in that I live here now." I moved to San Francisco two weeks ago; but I've spent most of my time running around getting my ducks in a row, which is why we're just now having a welcome dinner. The place is perfect, with an outdoor bar overlooking the Twin Peaks, and an indoor restaurant. It's elegant but not over the top, which I appreciate.

Ava has told me from the moment I arrived in town that the Bennetts are not snobs despite being billionaires, but I suspected her love for Sebastian made her biased. Upon meeting him and his sisters, Pippa and Alice, I realized Ava was right. They're the opposite of snobs. Maybe it's because they weren't born into wealth.

In fact, Ava told me their family was scrambling to make ends meet when Sebastian started Bennett Enterprises more than a decade ago. Since then, it's grown to be one of the most famous jewelry companies. This family has all my respect. I take meeting them as a good omen that things will be different for me in San Francisco. Better.

"Pippa, Logan, glad you made it in time for a drink," Sebastian says to someone behind me. I turn on my heels and catch my breath. I've seen pictures of the entire Bennett family, and Logan caught my eye from the very beginning. But seeing him in the flesh is an entirely different experience. Dressed in a navy suit, Logan could easily grace a poster for men's cologne. If they hung it on a billboard, I guarantee it'd cause major traffic accidents.

He's hands down the sexiest man I've ever laid eyes on. He has broad shoulders and a muscular build, his high cheekbones emphasizing his dark eyes. His brown hair is ravished as if he just ran his hand through it. All of a sudden, my fingers yearn to touch those luscious locks and his full lips.

Damn.

It's been a long time since a man affected me this strongly. Biting the inside of my cheek, I look away from Logan. The last thing I need right now is to be pining after any man, especially my best friend's future brother-in-law.

"Logan, this is Nadine," Ava says. Without hesitation, Logan shakes my hand. His touch lights a match inside me.

"Nice to meet you, Nadine." Even his voice is sexy. I keep my hand in his a little too long before realizing it's time to break off the contact. I withdraw my hand quickly, giving him a small smile.

"Let's get you two some drinks," Sebastian chimes in. He calls a waitress over and we order. She brings the drinks to us in no time.

We nurse our drinks while standing around a high bar table. I do my best to keep my gaze from Logan and fail often. *Oh, what the hell…* I might be on a self-imposed break from men, but that doesn't mean I can't admire a fine specimen of the male variety when I see one. Let the ogling of Logan Bennett officially begin.

"Let's toast to Pippa's freedom," Sebastian suggests, snapping me out of my daydreaming. Right. I remember Ava telling me Pippa signed her divorce papers today. As we toast, I notice a shift in the siblings' body language. At the word *freedom*, Pippa's smile faltered. Logan and Sebastian both put a reassuring hand on her shoulder.

"If you want us to mess up the guy's face or life, say the word," Logan tells her, and I have the slight suspicion he's only half joking. His grip on her shoulder tightens a notch, and Pippa's smile returns. It's endearing to see them show so much tenderness toward their sister. I'm an only child, so I wouldn't know anything about this firsthand. It must be wonderful to have someone to rely on through the good and bad. I mostly have to rely on myself.

When the going gets rough, I eat chocolate, drink a glass of wine, and then put my proverbial boxing gloves on.

"My brother, always the hothead." Sebastian shakes his head.

Logan merely grins. "Well, someone has to be, since you're so sensible all the time. It's annoying."

"Why don't we talk about your—" Sebastian begins, now smiling too.

Logan interrupts him. "Watch your tongue, Sebastian. We don't want Nadine here to get the wrong impression about me."

I chuckle at their banter. This family is growing on me with each passing second.

"He likes to tell everyone he's the nice brother," Pippa informs me solemnly. "And he *is* nice. Until he thinks someone around him is threatened, and then he's not nice anymore."

"That sounds like very rational behavior," I answer in an equally solemn tone.

"See, smart girl." Logan raises his glass in my direction and pins me with his gaze, igniting every inch of my body. I'm wearing a fitted black dress and a short jacket, which is currently open. Without even bothering to pretend, his eyes travel all over my body, resting briefly on my hips then breasts before returning to my face. I cock an eyebrow. The corners of his lips lift in a smile.

Well, then.

That's when I catch Pippa watching us.

"I'm cold," she says abruptly. Her comment surprises me since it's not cold at all. "I'm going to wait for you all inside." She and Ava exchange looks.

"I'll join you. I finished my drink anyway," Ava says.

"I can't very well leave two beautiful ladies alone. I'll join you," Sebastian adds. "Logan, can you keep Nadine company while she finishes her drink?"

Logan narrows his eyes at his brother and sister while I barely contain my laughter. I overheard Ava and Pippa planning to play matchmakers for Logan and me, but could they be more obvious? They both head inside with Sebastian tailing them.

The second we're alone, the air between us thickens with tension. His mortification with his siblings apparently forgotten, Logan's gaze is smoldering once more. I struggle for words to fill the silence, but being on the receiving end of his attention is a tad more than my mind can process, and definitely too much for my body. My nipples harden beneath my flimsy dress as heat pools in my lower body.

"Wow, that was smooth," Logan comments. "In the interest of starting with a clean slate, I must tell you that my siblings are playing—"

"A matchmaking game? Yeah, I noticed. They've told me a lot about you, Logan." Smiling, I take a sip of my martini.

"All good things, I hope," he says.

"Well, good is relative. Interpretable."

Logan groans, circling the table to stop right next to me. My body buzzes with life at his proximity.

"Also in the interest of starting with a clean slate, please tell me what you've been told. I need to debunk those myths."

"Nothing too bad, don't worry. That you're smart, competitive." With a smile, I add as an afterthought, "And that you have a giant-sized ego."

Logan gives me an I-told-you-so look. "See, that last bit is entirely untrue."

"Is that so?"

"You have my word."

"Mmm... Actions speak louder than words. Time will tell."

"Am I on a probation period of some kind?" He leans toward me, and I take a deep breath. Big mistake. He smells amazing: ocean and sandalwood and inherent masculinity. My knees weaken.

"Maybe," I answer playfully. He laughs, a sound that puts me at ease and makes my heart gallop all at once. Logan Bennett isn't just sexy; this man is sex on a stick.

Logan trains his eyes on me. "I've heard a lot about you too."

"Do I need to prepare my defense?"

"No need. I've heard only good things."

"Really? What did you hear?"

"That you're smart, passionate, and driven."

I grin. "Ava can pitch a person, can't she?"

"She can, and she's rarely wrong."

Ava works with Logan, Sebastian, and Pippa at Bennett Enterprises. My friend is brilliant, and I love her. We met in New York during college, and we've been friends ever since.

Someone knocks into me from behind, sending a sharp pain through my shoulder and hip. An inebriated asshole grins at me, staring languidly at my cleavage. I ball my hands into fists, preparing to apply what I've learned in my self-defense lessons if he makes as much as one inappropriate comment.

"Apologize to her," Logan booms, and the asshole cowers under Logan's gaze; I suspect his impressive height and build also contribute.

"Sorry," the guy says and scurries away. Logan rubs his palm up and down my back in a protective gesture. His touch burns me and, at the same time, a sense of safety grips me.

"I heard you want to open a clothing store," Logan says in an obvious attempt to get over the asshole incident.

"I do. A luxury gowns boutique."

"It's a great idea."

"You really think so?" Aside from Ava, people usually don't react enthusiastically, often countering with "Wouldn't a job be safer?" Yeah, I'm chasing a dream. But if I don't do it, no one will do it for me.

"Yeah, I'm all up for people striking out on their own."

"It's risky, but I've decided not to put it off any longer. It's been my dream for a long time. I've had a few hiccups on the road, and now I've decided to do it."

"Hiccups" is putting it mildly. I've been saving for this ever since college and hoped to open the shop by the time I was twenty-five. Then life happened. My parents lost their jobs, and I moved back home to help them, which depleted my savings. I don't regret it, though. I would do anything to help my parents. After they were back on their feet, I started saving again for my shop.

Then I met Thomas, and things went south once again. I shake my head, steeling myself. I won't think about my ex now; he's in the past, and that's where he belongs. I bounced back after his betrayal, working harder than ever. This time, I'll make it. Logan's staring at me, a mix of worry and curiosity in his eyes. *Damn, am I so easy to read?*

I give myself a mental slap. I have all the reasons to smile, after all. I moved to a new city, close to my best friend. I have a sexy man in front of me, who may or may not be flirting with me. He's completely off-limits, but that's something I'll worry about later on.

"Anyway, I turned thirty a few months ago. If not now, when?" I smile at him genuinely. Oh, God. I just blurted out my age to a man, which I've never done. It's all his fault; I just feel so at ease around him.

"If you want to do something, go for it. If there's anything, we can do to help, tell me. After all, Bennett Enterprises is in the luxury industry too."

"I know." I don't bother to hide the longing in my voice. "Your jewelry is so beautiful. I feel like crying every time I see photos in a magazine."

"They make you cry?" He creases his forehead. "I would've hoped they made you smile." Leaning in closer, he adds, "You light up when you smile."

Right. He's *definitely* flirting. I lick my lips, shifting my weight from one leg to another. The problem is I like his flirty side, and I have no business liking that. Since I broke up with Thomas, I've put up solid walls around me. Apparently, they're not as solid as I thought, or maybe Logan is exceptionally good at dismantling them. At any rate, I will work on solidifying said walls.

Logan pulls back a notch. "Have you looked at retail spaces?" His tone is all businesslike now.

"Not yet. I've been busy finding a place to live. I'll start hunting for a space next week."

"I have a friend who's an excellent realtor. I can hook you up with him."

"That'd be great." To have this practical stranger immediately offer his support is... Wow.

Logan's stance changes from carefree to tense in a fraction of a second. "On second thought, I'll go with you when you meet the first time."

"It's really not necessary." I eye him curiously, trying to decipher the reason behind the change.

"I insist."

"You don't take no for an answer, do you?"

Not taking his eyes off me, he says, "Never."

My skin tingles, my pulse pounding furiously. I whistle loudly, hoping to hide the effect he has on me. "I guess the things I've heard about you are true after all."

"Ah. That didn't earn me points for the ego thing, did it?"

"No, but I'm willing to wait for more proof."

"Very generous of you. This realtor friend of mine is a notorious womanizer. I'd feel much better knowing you're not meeting him alone."

"I can take care of myself."

"I have no doubt. I'm still coming with you," he says.

"Who's to say I'll be safe with you? I just met you."

"Ah, but I have the Bennett name to back me up. Haven't you heard? I'm the nice brother. I'm safe and trustworthy."

To his credit, Logan says this with a straight face, even though mischief flickers in his eyes. Ah, I love a man with humor. Unfortunately, I disagree with him. He may be trustworthy, but he's not safe. A man who can make me laugh with a few words and ignite me with his gaze all at the same time is anything but safe.

"So, I'll be joining you when you meet my friend." His tone is final, and I don't insist. I know how to pick my battles, and I have a suspicion there are many to come where Logan is concerned. "Now, I suggest we join the group inside. I'm starving."

"Okay."

I walk in front of Logan, sensing his eyes on me the whole way. My body simmers with awareness. I'm in big trouble, and I have a suspicion it's about to get worse.

***

Logan

The dinner goes by fast and, at some point, Alice joins us. After dessert, Ava and Nadine inform us they're leaving. To my surprise, this disappoints me.

"Nadine still has a lot to unpack, and I offered to help her," Ava says. "You four have fun."

As the two of them leave, I can't help myself from glancing appreciatively at Nadine's backside. I can proudly say I'm an ass man. I appreciate it in every shape, but Nadine's is perfect. Every part of her is, and I've studied her plenty tonight. Her long, brown hair and tan complexion contrast starkly but beautifully with her blue eyes.

Her full breasts and the swell of her hips are mouth-watering. I was hoping she'd be hot or funny, and I got both. In fact, she's so much more than that, I can't even describe it. She was so full of energy and passion when she spoke about her store that I nearly kissed her... to check if she'd do that with as much passion too.

No sooner are Nadine and Ava out the door than Pippa's stance changes. She gazes at me expectantly, her eyes wide and full of excitement. Sebastian is reading something on his phone, so at least my brother isn't in on the charade. Alice scans the menu, so I'm clear on that front too.

Wait a minute.

Alice is throwing me curious glances every few seconds. Ah, man, Pippa's dragged Alice into this matchmaking thing, hasn't she? I'm a dead man. The problem with loving my sisters is that they're very much aware that I do, and they take advantage of it. The women in our family have us men wrapped around their little fingers. Me, especially. Individually, I might stand a chance of fighting off their plan. When they join forces? No chance in hell.

I was hoping to have Alice on my side tonight. Apparently not. . .

Welcome to the Bennett clan, where alliances change faster than the wind and every sibling thinks they know what's better for every other sibling. There are nine of us, three sisters, six brothers. I'm guilty of plenty of meddling myself. My only hope is that Summer, our youngest sister, isn't in on this too.

When we were kids, the alliances were straightforward. Pippa, Sebastian and I—the oldest trio—versus the younger ones. Things are more complex now.

Pippa breaks the silence. "What did you think about Nadine?"

"I know what you're up to," I reply. "Drop it. I can get myself a woman, thank you very much." I avoid looking at her. I like Nadine a lot, but that doesn't mean I'm right for her.

"We disagree," Pippa says.

"Strongly," Alice adds helpfully.

"You haven't brought anyone for us to meet since you broke up with Sylvia. That was two years ago," Pippa continues. Sebastian remains suspiciously silent. The bastard won't back me up on this.

"That doesn't mean I don't date," I tell them calmly. Pippa's the only Bennett sibling who married, but I came damn close. Sylvia was my fiancée. "I keep my love life separate from my family."

If there's anything the failed relationship with Sylvia taught me, it's that women prefer it this way. I'm honest and upfront with my dates, telling them I'm not up for the long haul, just to have a pleasant time together. We spend a few months together, and I always treat them well, because I believe every woman deserves it.

I was in high school when I decided I wouldn't be an asshole. I made the decision after I overheard a moron saying he wanted to "tap that." He meant Pippa. That's when I realized every girl was someone's sister or daughter, and it wasn't fair to treat them in ways I'd hate anyone to treat my sisters.

I might be an ass man, but I'm no asshole.

So, yeah, I treat my dates right. I take them out, but I don't let them in. It's easier that way. Do I want to keep it up forever? It's tempting. Without too much emotional involvement, no one can rip my goddamn heart out the way Sylvia did. Do I want to be in my sixties and still date around? No fucking way.

I want to build a family, the way my parents did… eventually. And here lies the problem. If I want a family, I need to let a woman in, which I'm not ready to do. That's a conundrum I can't solve. As the CFO of Bennett Enterprises, I pride myself on being able to solve any problem by use of logic. When it comes to my love life, logic hasn't helped one bit.

Pippa's voice snaps me from my thoughts. "You haven't had a serious relationship in a while. It'd be good for you."

"Oh, and you're an expert on that?"

Pippa flinches, her chin trembling. Sebastian glares at me. Damn me and my impulsivity.

"Sorry, that was a dick thing to say." I shake my head. "What happened with Terence wasn't your fault. I'm not implying that."

"I forgive you," Pippa says. "You always put your foot in your mouth."

"Ah, nothing like my sister handing out compliments," I mutter to myself. "Though I do deserve this one. Alice, please don't join Pippa's matchmaking game."

"I have no idea what you mean. I met Nadine a few times, and I like her," Alice says simply. I know on the spot she is honest, and I can see why she likes Nadine. From my brief conversation with her, I could tell she's fiercely determined, competitive, and hardworking. She shares many traits with Alice.

"So there's no chance you'll want to date Nadine?" Pippa insists. "Ever?"

"No." I'm lying through my teeth, and Pippa sees right through me. I'd be more convincing if that woman weren't so damn sexy, and meeting her hadn't been such a shock. Her energy is infectious, her courage to pursue what she wants endearing.

Touching her back sent a jolt straight to my groin. Stepping closer to her, her womanly scent aroused me further still. She smelled like oranges. Nadine has an innate sensuality, unlike anyone I've encountered before.

Which is why I should stay away from her. Ava's the only close friend Nadine has here. Knowing my family, this means they'll embrace her wholeheartedly, and include her in family events. If I were to date her, things would become complicated fast. I only do temporary, and that wouldn't be fair to her. I have a hunch that Nadine has had enough complications in her life; she doesn't deserve one more. I want her to feel happy here.

"Well, it was nice of you to offer to help her with the real estate agent," Pippa says. "The agent is Alex, right? I bet he'll ask her out."

Thinking about Alex makes my blood boil. He's a great agent, yes, but he's a dick to women. He won't lay his paws on Nadine; I'll see to that. *Damn it.* I have no business being territorial with her. She's not mine. But that doesn't mean I'll let anyone take advantage of her.

"I'll make sure Alex won't attempt anything." That's why I offered to go with her to meet him. If I'm honest, I also wanted an excuse to see her again soon. Which goes right against my plan to keep my distance. *Way to go, Bennett. . .*

"How chivalrous of you." Pippa smiles smugly as the waiter brings the round of drinks we ordered. After he leaves, my sister tells me, "Nadine also plans to sell *very* sexy lingerie in her shop in addition to evening dresses."

I spit out my wine. "Now, why would you tell me that, Pippa?"

She grins devilishly. "So you can let your imagination run wild. If you dated her, maybe she'd even give you a private show."

Women in sexy lingerie are my kryptonite, but Pippa has no business knowing that. I don't share these details with my sisters. One of my *dear* brothers ratted me out. My money's on Blake, one of my four younger brothers. That bastard.

I swallow hard. "She wouldn't."

"Yes," Pippa says triumphantly while Alice clinks a glass with her.

"What's going on?" I ask, dumbfounded when even Sebastian laughs.

"You've fallen right into Pippa's trap," he explains.

"You admitted you'd like her to give you a private show," Pippa says.

"I have blood running through my veins, Pippa. And I'm a man." I drop my head in my hands. *Team Logan: 0. Team traitorous Bennetts: 1.* These girls will be my undoing. "You could've given me a warning," I tell Sebastian.

"Why? It's so much more fun seeing you fall right into their trap."

I raise my eyebrows, and Sebastian holds his palms up in defeat. "I didn't have a hand in this. But I'm enjoying the outcome."

"You'll pay for this, brother," I warn him. Alice and Pippa grin. Just by looking at my sisters, I can tell they won't give up their matchmaking plan.

I'm definitely a dead man.

22

Chapter Three

Nadine

I wake up at seven o'clock on Monday, even though we're meeting the realtor at eleven. Logan and I exchanged numbers on Friday at dinner, and Saturday he texted to inform me his friend Alex can meet us today. I'm so excited I can't lie down for another minute. For years, I've been planning, researching, and saving for my dream. Things are about to get real with this meeting, and it's nerve-wracking.

At eight o'clock, my phone chirps. My stomach somersaults when I realize who the sender is.

Logan: Big day. Ready for it?

A huge smile spreads on my face as I type back.

Nadine: Yesssss. Absolutely! I can't wait!!!!!!

Logan: I swear I can feel your energy through the phone.

My smile is out of control now. I might've overdone it with the exclamation marks, but I am so damn excited.

Nadine: Any tips for the meeting?

Logan: Nah, just bring your smile. It's beautiful.

Oh, my. This man is a charmer, and I love it. Taking a deep breath, I remind myself that he's off-limits, and reply as professionally as possible.

Nadine: Thank you for joining me.

Logan: My pleasure.

For some reason, his words send a jolt of heat right through my center. *Way to go, Nadine.* As I shower, I admit to myself there is another reason for my enthusiasm: seeing Logan again, which is silly. If there was ever bad timing to fantasize about a man, it's now. I have to focus one hundred percent on my business if I want it to stand any chance. Still, I'm glad he's coming with me to meet the realtor. Logan's confidence in my idea on Friday was like fuel for my dream; I can use some more of that today. Besides, that man is some serious eye candy. The fact that I don't want to involve myself with anyone right now doesn't mean I can't appreciate his sexy ass.

After I shower, I inspect my business plan for a while then dress in a suit. I still have some time left before I have to leave, so I call my mom. She picks up quickly.

"Hi, Mom!"

"Morning, sweetie."

As always, I breathe a sigh of relief when she sounds happy. For as long as I remember, Mom has suffered from depression, coming in episodes. Sometimes she was happy, and sometimes she wouldn't rise from her bed, or even talk. When I was five, my father left us. We never heard from him again, and sorrow crippled Mom for years. Between the lack of access to medication and the stigma associated with the illness, she could barely hold a job.

Friends and family helped for a while then stopped, saying Mom should "get over herself," as if she was bratty, not sick. Growing up, I worked odd jobs in our small town in North Carolina. I did everything from mowing lawns to carrying mail or bagging groceries. I took care of us the best I could. When I was a junior in high school, things changed. Mom sought out treatment. Then she married Brian, and he's the best man I know.

"Hun, are you there?" Mom's voice resounds.

"Yeah, sorry. I got lost in my thoughts. I wanted to tell you that I'm seeing a realtor today. He'll help me find a space for my shop."

"I'll keep my fingers crossed."

"Thanks. I'm excited, but also scared." This is something I wouldn't admit to anyone but Mom. "What if it doesn't work out?"

"You can always come back home. Jack said you could always have your job back if you wanted to."

I gulp. "Yeah, that's right." Jack is my last boss. He said he'd hire me back in a second if I wanted to.

That's my fallback plan. If I can't make the store profitable enough to be able to take care of Mom and Brian after they retire, I'll return to North Carolina and take Jack's offer. My soul would die bit by bit in that job, but at least I have a plan B.

"I'm sure it'll work out, though," Mom says. "You worry too much."

"Yeah. I'm a professional worrier."

Worrying was all I did before Mom started taking medication, found a stable job, and Brian. It was the first time in forever that I didn't have to worry about going to bed hungry, or about sleeping without heat. It's been more than a decade since Brian entered our lives, and a small part of me still fears he'll bail on Mom eventually, like Dad and the rest of our family did.

I'll never be able to shake off those hard years when I took care of us, when there was no one to count on, and I never felt safe. I learned my lesson... or at least, I thought I did. I let my guard down with Thomas, and that was a big mistake.

"I'll let you know how it goes, Mom. I have to leave now. Say hi to Brian for me."

"Will do."

An unpleasant knot settles in my throat as I leave my apartment. Shaking my head, I push away the negative thoughts, bringing back the smile I promised to Logan.

This better work out. I simply can't fail.

***

A lovely early autumn morning greets me outside. The sky is a beautiful pink, interspersed with stripes the color of amethyst. I take the weather as a good omen. Smiling, I head toward my destination. My smile morphs into a grin as I approach the realtor's office downtown, and an amalgam of smells overtakes my senses: magnolias, cypress, and the occasional whiff of Chanel.

I'm supposed to meet Logan in the park in front of the realtor's office. I arrive with a few minutes to spare and find Logan sitting on a bench. Sweet Lord, he's wearing a suit again, and he is *perfect*. I'm sure he's mouth-watering no matter what he wears, but something about seeing him in a suit and cufflinks turns my knees weak. He exudes power, without losing the mouth-watering factor.

"You're here early," I tell him. He looks up from his smartphone, his dark eyes scanning me, resting on my mouth for a brief second. I wet my lower lip, averting my gaze when heat creeps up my cheeks. I haven't blushed in ages, yet here comes this man, making me feel like a college girl with nothing but his eyes. Rising to his feet, he hands me a small paper bag and a coffee cup I hadn't noticed.

"I bought you a coffee and a chocolate croissant."

"Wow, thank you," I say. "I love chocolate croissants."

Opening the bag, I take out the pastry and bite into it then sip from my coffee.

"I know. I asked Ava."

"That's very considerate of you, Logan." Warmth fills me, and it has nothing to do with the hot liquid I downed. It's been a long time since a man bothered to do something this nice for me. He nods, clearly proud of himself. "Is this part of your plan to show me you're safe and trustworthy?" *'Cause the safe part isn't working.* My body hums in his presence, and he hasn't even touched me today. I hope he doesn't, because I'm not sure I can take it.

"That too, but I thought there's no better way to start this day than by eating your favorite breakfast. After all, today your dream will go from the planning stage to the real stage."

I can't believe he grasps how important this day is for me. I want to hug him but control myself, offering him a smile instead. Logan Bennett isn't just eye candy. He's a sensitive, kind eye candy.

I'm doomed.

I stand in front of him while I nurse my coffee. Logan's eyes travel up and down my body with appreciation, resting on my hips and breasts longer than polite. Something tells me he doesn't do polite, or anything anyone would expect of him. I'm convinced Logan only does what he wants, and I find that incredibly sexy. Still, I wish he'd disguise his flirty look. I've been squirming since I arrived, my chest heaving up and down with labored breathing, and I need to compose myself before we go in.

At five to eleven, we enter the realtor's office. He is all smiles while Logan introduces us.

"Nadine Hawthorne," I say, shaking hands with Alex briefly.

Alex must be in his mid-thirties, and he's an attractive man, but as he gawks at me, his predatory eyes make my skin crawl.

"Have a seat, both of you," Alex offers. "Logan told me a bit about your idea. I need more details. Have you already thought about an area? Do you have any specific requirements?"

I tell him that I'd like the shop to be on a central venue—maybe Union Square or Sacramento Street—and describe the size I'm thinking about. He prods me with more questions, and then shows me pictures of some available spaces on his computer. It's clear he knows what he's doing.

My heart beats faster as I imagine my beautiful shop coming to life in one of those places. When Alex mentions the price range, my enthusiasm plummets. Shifting in my seat, I take a furtive glance at Logan, and then tell them my budget. Alex raises his eyebrows while Logan's lips form a hard line.

"I'll be honest with you," Alex says. "It'll be hard to find something in good shape with your budget, but that doesn't mean we can't try. I have some cheaper options, but I warn you, they'll need some renovations."

"I was expecting renovations. Owners can be persuaded to agree to a lower rent if the place is rundown."

We spend about an hour admiring more spaces on his computer, but nothing fits my requirements.

"Let me do some more research," Alex says eventually. "I can come up with a few options by tomorrow morning."

"Excellent."

"Now, it's twelve thirty. I say it's lunch time. Logan, I suppose you're busy as always, but Nadine, would you like to eat with me?"

I open my mouth to say no, but Logan answers for me. "Actually, I promised Nadine to take her out for lunch. Just the two of us."

The two men engage in a battle of stares, and I'm torn between laughing at Alex and scolding Logan. Amazing how a hot look from Alex makes my skin crawl, but one from Logan has an entirely different effect on me; like making me want to unbutton his shirt, and check if his abs are as chiselled as I imagine, his arms as strong. All very appropriate thoughts to have in a realtor's office, of course. I swear to God, the alpha vibes coming off Logan turn my brain to mush.

Alex backs down. "I'll email you tomorrow, Nadine."

When we're out, I elbow Logan. "Why did you tell him we're having lunch?"

"First, because I was going to ask you to have lunch with me."

My heart bounces at his invitation. Spending more time with him than I thought is a definite bonus… or a dangerous move, depending how you look at it.

"Second, because you should stay away from him. I told you he was a womanizer."

"I wasn't going to go with him, but I don't appreciate you answering for me."

He nods, running his fingers through his hair. It gives him a disheveled appearance, as if he'd just woken up… or did something else in bed. I let out a sigh, remembering how long it's been since I've been intimate with a man.

"I'm sorry, I can be overbearing sometimes," Logan says.

I blink, jerking my head back. What is this? A man who admits when he's wrong? Well, that earns him a bonus point in my books, which isn't helping, because he already has too many points. Not that I'll tell him that. Not yet, anyway.

"Apology accepted. So, where are you taking me to lunch?"

Logan grins. "I still get to take you out? I'm a lucky guy."

"I like a man who's confident enough to admit his mistakes."

Tilting his head to one side, he leans forward slightly. "And I bet you love a man who gives you good food."

"Awfully presumptuous of you."

"Not really. I saw you eat last night and this morning. Your appetite is delicious." He leans in to me until his lips are only inches away from mine. His scent invades my senses, jumbling my thoughts, and I take a step back to clear my head. Logan pins me with his gaze, raising the corners of his mouth in a challenge. This man is intense and, by God, I can't get enough.

"Let's see what you'll feed me, Mr. Bennett."

"You like French food? Besides croissants?"

"I love it."

I remind myself of all the reasons I should keep my distance. For one, he's going to be Ava's brother-in-law. If things between him and me turned weird, that could make family gatherings unpleasant, and I *really* like the Bennetts. The most important reason, though, is that I need to focus on my business. There is simply too much at stake. I can't let anything—or anyone—distract me, much less a man. Last time I did, I lost everything.

I shouldn't flirt back; I really shouldn't. Then I notice Logan's dimples, and I know I don't stand a chance. I'm a goner.

***

After a short drive in Logan's car, we arrive at a cozy restaurant. The inside walls are covered almost entirely in wood paneling displaying intricate carvings. Small crystal chandeliers hang from the ceiling, spreading a warm light throughout the restaurant. Pictures with various French sights hang on the walls.

Our hands touch briefly as we walk to a table. A jolt of need courses through me and my nipples grow sensitive, pressing against my soft, sheer lace bra. I peek at Logan, searching for any signs that I'm affecting him as powerfully as he does me. He seems completely at ease at first sight, but when we sit down, his eyes are darker than before. I draw in a sharp breath, averting my gaze.

Thankfully, the waiter arrives, cutting the tension. We order drinks quickly, but since it's a French restaurant, they boast an impressive list of quiches. I can't decide which one I want. In the end, we order four different types, even though it's just the two of us.

"Tell me about your love for fashion. How did it start?" Logan asks after the waiter leaves. The tension clears from the air, even though I'm quite aware of the continued throbbing in the peaks of my breasts. Logan's eyes are still dark.

"Like most girls, I liked to dress up my dolls. I guess I never outgrew the phase. When I was in high school, I started sewing my clothing. I didn't have a style, and went through several experimental stages until I found it." Sewing was also an escape for me during those hard years. I could pretend I was someone else when I was creating a new piece of clothing.

"I'd love to see pics of that."

"Oh, no, trust me, you don't. Anyway, eventually I realized I wanted to make evening dresses, and I've stuck with that ever since."

"It's a great niche," Logan comments. "High price, low volume."

I laugh. "You sound like Ava. She gave me a lot of insights as I put my business plan together, and she's my very first customer. I'm designing her wedding dress." I've been bursting with pride since Ava asked me to do it. Not only will I be her designer, but also her maid of honor.

"She told me. If you want a second opinion on that business plan, I'd be happy to look over it."

"Thank you. I'll be displaying my designs, along with some well-known designers. If I only sell my dresses, no one will come."

"That's smart."

"Yeah, and also costly. The inventory alone will be a fortune. I can't believe my childhood dream is finally happening."

"Great to see you stuck with it. Did you ever want to give up?"

I remain silent, debating whether I should tell him about Thomas. Except for Ava and my parents, I haven't told many people. Logan seems so easy to talk to, though.

"I almost gave up twice." In quick words, I tell him my story. "I waitressed while studying in New York, and had a nice sum by the time I graduated. The plan was to open a small shop there. But my mom and stepdad lost their jobs, and they needed my help, so I gave it to them. My stepdad had used all his savings paying my college so I wouldn't get in debt. I couldn't afford New York anymore, so I moved back to my small hometown in North Carolina, and got a job there. That was the first time I flirted with the idea of giving up." Remembering that terrible time, I can't help but feel proud of myself. "But I manned up, got a second job—waitressing again—and started saving once more."

"You're tough." He doesn't say this with surprise, but with a mix of awe and curiosity.

"Afterward, I met Thomas, my ex. We were working at the same company. They started downsizing, and they fired him. He couldn't find a job, so he decided to open his own business: a car wash."

"Tell me you didn't give him your savings." Logan's harsh voice makes me flinch.

I smile sadly. "I did. It was supposed to be a loan. Half a year later, I was fired and struggled to find a job. Thomas made it clear he wouldn't support me financially. When I asked him about my savings, he threw in my face that we didn't have a contract. I broke up with him." My eyes burn, all traces of pride gone. Shame overcomes me. "I was so stupid and so trusting," I whisper to myself. Clearing my throat, I add in a strong voice, "That was two years ago. I worked three jobs until I moved here. I'll make it this time, and I won't owe anyone anything."

"I'm sure you will. Let's get one thing straight. You were not stupid. The person you love is someone you're supposed to trust." An endearing fire flickers in his eyes. "If there's something I hate more than people taking advantage of others, it's if they get away with it."

"We're not talking about me now, right?"

"No. My sister recently divorced her leper of a husband."

"I've heard, but I don't know the details."

"I'll give you the Cliff's Notes. He married her for her money. Sebastian and I made him sign a prenup. If they divorced before their tenth anniversary, he wouldn't receive a penny. They divorced before their fourth."

"That's great; it means he walked away with no money."

"No, but he hurt my sister, and the law isn't punishing that."

I'm touched that he cares so much about his family.

"If I run into that asshole again—"

I sit up straight. "Woah, relax, Batman. You can't be the silent protector, making your justice. Sometimes, you have to forgive and move on. Otherwise, you're wasting your energy with people who're not worth it."

It suddenly dawns on me that the scene in Alex's office wasn't a display of manhood, at least not on Logan's part. This man protects fiercely, and loves the same way too. It fills me with joy that I've been the object of his protection.

"Right. I believe we were sidetracked. We were talking about your shop and love for fashion. You didn't study fashion, though, did you?"

"No. It felt unsafe. I majored in accounting. I hope I'll never have to work as an accountant again, but if the store doesn't work out, I'll go back to doing that. My last boss said I'm welcome back anytime."

Logan stiffens at this. "Why not search for a job as an accountant here?"

"An accountant's salary has a greater purchasing power there than in San Francisco." I don't tell him about my plan to look after my parents. Sharing that is too personal.

Logan puts his hand over mine on the table as if sensing my turmoil. If his touch was meant to reassure me, he succeeded. If it was also intended to send my hormones into disarray, he excelled. Being around Logan is consuming; my entire body buzzes with life and need around him.

"You won't fail, Nadine. You have passion, you have drive, and you have a plan. It's by no means foolproof, but it's as close as it gets."

"You sure know how to make a girl feel good."

"Trust me, you haven't seen anything." His voice is low and raspy all of a sudden. "I can make a girl feel *really* good."

I swallow a mouthful of quiche. "Did this discussion turn to sex?"

"Actually, I was thinking about a round of double dessert, but we can talk about sex. It's one of my favorite topics. I'm an expert on it."

I laugh. I cannot help it. "Is that so?"

"I don't mean to brag, but women's opinions have been unanimous on this."

I decide to play his game. "You shouldn't believe everything you're told."

"Oh, I wasn't told. I can tell just by observing a woman how good a time she's having with me."

For someone who hasn't had sex for a long time, his words are like fuel to the fire. I can imagine how his lips would touch mine. I cross my legs to quench the sudden ache between my thighs. I'm already fantasizing about what he could do with his hands on my body, and that's *very* bad.

"We got sidetracked again," I say.

"I'm thoroughly enjoying the new topic." Logan flashes me a smile full of mischief.

Despite myself, I return an equally naughty smile. "Shouldn't you be serious and grumpy all the time? You're the CFO, after all. Chief Financial Officer. I thought grumpiness came with the job description."

"It's required very often when people piss me off, as is the obligatory stick up my ass."

"So I have the privilege of seeing the fun side of you."

"Exactly. I can be Chief Fun Officer for you."

Laughter bubbles out of my throat, my entire body relaxing. "You *are* funny."

"I'm insulted by the surprise in your voice."

"I meant it as a compliment," I assure him.

"I wonder what a real insult would sound like." He winks at me good-naturedly. "Unfortunately, I can't stay longer. I have a meeting in an hour." His eyes don't leave mine as he asks the waiter for the check. Stubbornly, I keep his gaze until my cheeks heat up, and then I break the eye contact.

"What are you doing this afternoon?" he asks as we leave the restaurant. "Do you want me to drive you anywhere?"

"No, thanks. I'll walk around the city, checking out the competition."

"I meant what I said about your business plan. If you want another opinion, I'm happy to help. Also, once Alex sends you locations, I'd like to come with you to see them."

"Why are you so interested?"

Logan stops in front of me, putting his hands on my arms as if it's the most natural thing in the world. I lick my lips.

"I know what it's like to be a founder. If I'm honest, I miss the excitement of those early years. It was fun, mostly because I was building something with my brother. You're doing this on your own in a new city. I don't want you to feel alone here."

His words hit a nerve. Loneliness is something I grew accustomed to after my split from Thomas, and I like spending time with myself. But moving across the country to a place where I only know Ava is a different story. I didn't want to go back to New York. I wanted something new.

"Very considerate of you. You're welcome to join me on the shop hunting, but I have one condition." I hold up a forefinger.

Logan narrows his eyes as we reach his car. "I'm listening."

"I want two croissants next time."

"Feisty. I like you more with every passing second. Call me when you have something." His gaze lingers on my lips for the briefest of moments before snapping up to meet my eyes. "I'll probably see you before that too. My family likes you."

He leans in to me, kissing my cheek. At the same time, he presses his palm against the small of my back, and all my senses explode. The innocent kiss turns into something almost sinful as he lingers with his cheek against mine for a few seconds. His hand at my back feels incredibly intimate, and his smell. *Oh, God, he's too much.* I swear the air between us sizzles. When he finally pulls back, my knees are weak. With a wink, he climbs into his driver's seat.

I look after his car until it's out of sight, gathering my faculties. *Focus on your business, Nadine. Focus.* Repeating this mantra does nothing to calm my racing pulse, though. This man can make me smile, swoon, and have the hots for him all in the span of minutes.

Logan Bennett will be the death of me.

Chapter Four

Logan

I have been known to decide one thing and do the complete opposite, but deciding to stay away from a woman then flirting like there's no tomorrow with her is new even for me. Obviously, I can't control myself around Nadine. When I kissed her cheek, I damn near took her mouth too. I wanted nothing more than to pin her against my car and kiss her blind. That was on Monday. Today is Friday, and I'm still thinking about the non-kiss. Her scent of oranges is branded in my senses now.

A subtle vibration from my smartphone alerts me to a message.

Pippa: Sorry, won't make it to lunch.

My jaw ticks. I'm going to have to eat both portions of Chinese food I ordered to be delivered to my office. Tapping my fingers on my desk, I search through my emails, expecting one from Ava. She was supposed to send me a report half an hour ago. I don't find it, so I text her.

Logan: Where's the report I asked for?

Ava: I left a print copy on my desk, forgot to email it to you. Can't do it now. I don't have access to my laptop.

Logan: Where are you?

Ava: Sebastian and I are meeting the wedding planner.

Right, Sebastian did mention that. My assistant is off for lunch, so I go to Ava's office myself to find the report on her desk. To my surprise, there's someone inside. I recognize her immediately, even though all I see is her back. A smell of oranges lingers in the air. Nadine's staring out the window, giving me a chance to observe her. Fuck, she's sexy, wearing a white, figure-hugging dress, a red jacket on her arm. Her round ass is particularly perfect.

"Nadine."

She turns around, her eyes widening in surprise as I walk into the office. God, she's beautiful. And just like that, my control slides away. The more she talks, the more my resolve to keep my distance from her weakens.

"What are you doing here?" I ask her.

"Waiting for Ava to go to lunch. She was supposed to meet me in her office." Nadine taps her foot, her lips forming a thin line. She's adorable.

"Ava's not in the building. She and Sebastian are meeting the wedding planner."

Nadine frowns. "What?" Pulling out her phone, she dials furiously before pressing it to her ear. "Hi, Ava. I'm waiting in your office. We planned to eat lunch together." There's a small pause, and then Nadine groans. "You forgot?"

I pick up the report, pretending to look through it, disguising my smile. Ava *never* forgets anything. She's an organizational genius. She did this on purpose.

Nadine finishes the conversation in a clipped tone.

"My best friend stood me up. She has a good excuse, though. Wedding stuff." As our gazes meet, I'm confident Nadine doesn't buy the excuse any more than I do. Pippa canceled on me, Ava on Nadine. *This smells of a setup.* "I'll have to join them in a few of those meetings. As the maid of honor." Her eyes light up as she says the last words, and she squares her shoulder with pride. Damn, she's so cute. I'd love nothing more than to kiss that sinful mouth of hers.

A recognition hits home. As Ava's friend and maid of honor, she'll soon become one of our closest family friends. Dating family friends is not a good idea. Daniel did that, and things went wrong, fast. If I date her for a while, even if we break up amicably, it will still be awkward at family gatherings. Nadine deserves to be happy here. I can't mess that up.

"I'll go," Nadine says. "Lots to do."

I open my mouth to say okay, and something else comes out instead. "Stay."

She peers at me from behind her eyelashes with uncertain eyes. Her chest heaves up and down, red splotches appearing on her cheeks and neck. Finally, she looks away, licking her lips. *Jesus.* She's fighting this as much as I am. Who'll give in first?

"I'll grab a sandwich on the way. I have a lot to do," she murmurs. "It's better that Ava couldn't make it. That way, I can check more things off my to-do list today."

"Take it easy, you don't have to do everything at once," I say, remembering how crazy those days when Sebastian and I started out were.

"I don't mind hard work," she responds.

"Of course you don't."

It shouldn't surprise me, but since we've made it big, I've met plenty of entitled people. They expect things to be handed to them. Nadine works hard, and she got back on track after every setback. She's a fighter, and I love that. I respect that.

As I watch her small frame, it's hard to believe she has so much strength in her. I want to hold her in my arms and make sure no bastard ever hurts her again, like her ex. My protective instincts are on high alert. Damn it. I reserve my protective instincts for my family. The women I date are on the receiving end of *other* types of instincts. My limits blur when I'm around Nadine, and that won't do.

"Stay," I repeat. I tilt her chin up and leave her no option but to look at me. She swipes her tongue over her lower lip, and I nearly lose my control and kiss her. "You have to eat. This'll be quick."

As Nadine nods, I realize something. She's lovely, on the inside and the outside. Eventually, someone will ask her out, and that's something I can't live with. The only solution is to ask her out myself, consequences be damned. And there went my resolution to stay away from her. I blame it on that beautiful ass of hers.

You're screwed, Bennett.

***

Nadine

I will murder Ava. First, I'm going to ask her how the meeting with the planner went, and then I will murder her. She did this on purpose. Ava believes my self-imposed dry spell is nonsense, and that Logan's the solution.

Logan is trouble. I know that by the way not only my body reacts to him, but my mind as well. I squirm just looking at him, all strong and tall and *man.*

"We'll eat together. I ordered Chinese for two earlier. It should arrive any minute now." His voice is firm. "Unless you don't like Chinese?"

"I like it." If I'm honest with myself, I *like* being around him. I feel happy, happier than I've been in months. Logan disappears in the corridor, returning with two small bags of takeout food. After I hang my jacket on the back of Ava's chair, I help him put the food and drinks on the table. Our arms brush by accident, and I immediately jump, biting my lip. Great. I've been in the same room with this man for five minutes, and I already want to climb him. How will I survive lunch?

I slump in the chair behind the desk while Logan sits across from me. Having a desk between us should make things easier.

"How come you've ordered for two?" I ask, attempting to grab some chicken with my chopsticks. Just when I think I finally got it, the piece falls back in the plate. There were no forks in the paper bags. Logan's proficient with the chopsticks, which is probably why he didn't bother to ask the restaurant to send us forks too. On a sigh, I concentrate on attacking my chicken again. This will be a long lunch.

"I was supposed to eat with Pippa, but she stood me up," he explains.

Alarm bells ring in my mind. Looks like I have to kill Pippa too.

"What did you do today?" Logan asks me.

I wave my hand. "Boring stuff. Lots of business permits. Very annoying, but I kicked everyone's ass."

"If you need help with anything, tell me. I know people everywhere." He says this with such nonchalance you'd think he was talking about a neighbor.

I roll my eyes. "So, you know everybody in San Francisco?"

"No." Logan shrugs. "But a lot of people know me."

Leaning back in my chair, I point my chopsticks at him. "Are you trying to impress me?"

"Maybe. Is it working?"

I smile, deciding to tease him. "Maybe."

"I see. Do I have to bring up my lady skills again to impress you?" He wiggles his eyebrows.

I swallow, heat rising in my cheeks. "You have a filthy mind, Logan Bennett. It doesn't go with your *nice* brother image."

"It's worth spoiling my image if I get you to blush. You look lovely."

"Logan. . ." I lick my lips, eyeing my plate.

"What?"

"You know what. Stop what you're doing."

"What am I doing?"

I stare at him, tilting my head to one side. "Flirting."

"Glad you're not misinterpreting my intentions. Why should I stop? Am I making you nervous?" A rebellious flash crosses in his eyes. "Uncomfortable?"

"You're enjoying this, aren't you?"

He grins. "Immensely. I don't want to ambush you, though, so let's change the subject. Are you continuing to sew until you open the shop?"

"Yes. I bought some beautiful fabrics yesterday. Back in my hometown, I had to travel to the nearby city to have a decent selection. I love the choices in San Francisco. I could've bought the entire store." As usual when I talk about my dresses, I ramble. "The lighting is bad in my apartment, but as soon as I have a shop, I'll move the sewing machine there."

I remove the straw and lid of my paper cup, and take a sip of water.

Eventually, I get the hang of this chopsticks thing, so I eat quickly and don't speak at all, afraid that if I pause for too long, I'll lose this recently discovered dexterity. The second my plate is empty I rise from my chair, grabbing my jacket, and my almost-full water cup. I need to leave here right away; I still have a million butts to kick today. Logan blocks me on the way to the door. *Oh, boy.* I take a step back as a precaution, but still catch a whiff of his cologne. I swear that thing has pheromones in it. My nipples perk up instantly. *Down, girls.*

"What are you doing tomorrow night?" he asks.

"I'm busy," I say quickly.

"That sounds a lot like a brush-off." He tilts his head to one side, looking at me as if expecting a confession.

I hold my ground, shaking my head. "It's not. I have plans."

"With a man? Are you going on a date?" His eyes are hard all of a sudden, the muscles in his neck pulsing.

"No." I swallow hard. "You're intense."

"Always am."

I press my palm on his chest, pushing him away. Big mistake. Touching his rock-hard chest has the unexpected effect of wiping my thoughts away. Belatedly, I realize my fingers have lingered on him longer than they should have. By the cocky smile on Logan's lips, he's enjoying this greatly. And then it happens. In my haste to put distance between us, I squeeze the paper cup too hard, and the water splashes over my chest.

All over my chest. And I'm wearing a white dress and a freaking white sports bra beneath it, which means my boobs are covered by a thin fabric that immediately gets soaked. So, basically, I'm flashing my girls in Logan's face. *Perfect.* His eyes light up, as if he just found out that Christmas came earlier. I bet he's sporting wood behind his designer pants.

Hyperventilating, I turn around, searching desperately for something to cover myself with. Luckily, my jacket escaped the flood. I grab some napkins from the table and dry myself the best I can. Afterward, I put my jacket on and button it up. Turning around, I notice Logan hasn't moved. He's still staring at my chest, as if he's hoping the jacket will become transparent too. Eventually, his eyes find mine.

"You and I should go on a date," Logan announces.

"Wow, my boobs impressed you that much?"

"What?"

"Were you going to ask me before I soaked my girls with water? I want the truth."

Logan cocks an eyebrow. "Is my answer going to change *your* answer?"

"Maybe," I answer playfully.

He narrows his eyes. "Are you setting a trap?"

"Maybe," I repeat.

Logan whistles. "Okay, full disclosure. I decided to ask you out when I stepped into this office. So, yeah. We should go on a date."

I laugh. I cannot help it. "Most people put a question mark at the end of the sentence when they ask that."

"I'm not most people. Besides, why ask a question? You risk receiving an answer you don't want to hear."

"I see. So, your solution is to boss people around?"

"You're stalling." His gaze pins me down.

"Logan—"

"Nadine."

Taking a deep breath, I say, "I need to concentrate on the shop and making a life here for myself. I don't want to date anyone for a while."

Logan clutches his heart theatrically. "I'm offended. I'm not just anyone. I thought we established that."

"I'll pretend you are."

"Ouch, that hurt." Tilting my head up, he adds, "You like me."

"You're getting ahead of yourself. What makes you think that?" I ache for him everywhere, but he can't possibly know that.

"Your nipples were very happy to see me even before you soaked them."

I groan at that. I have to remember to wear perfect-coverage bras when I'm around Logan. Or when I'm about to meet Ava. I'm sure this won't be the last setup she pulls on me. *Mental note: Logan is not only sexy and stubborn, but also blunt.* I shouldn't ask him a question unless I want to hear the goddamn honest truth.

Looking up again at Logan, I catch him licking his lips. I whip my thoughts together. "It's not a good idea. I have a lot on my mind; I'm not much fun."

"I disagree."

"Shocker," I murmur.

"I love your energy and your will to go after what you want. You're fun and open, and with the risk of sounding like a total man, you're sexy as hell. "

I laugh again. God, I love that he puts me at ease no matter what we're talking about. My mother often says, "When you find a man who makes you laugh without even knowing why, marry him." I wonder what she'd have to say about Logan. She'd probably like him. Hell, that line of thought will lead me nowhere.

Shaking my head, I chuckle. "I can't think of anything but the shop right now. I simply have too much at stake. You understand that, right?"

He steps aside and points one arm at the door, as if telling me I'm free to go. His eyes say something different, though: *You'll be mine.*

"I perfectly understand what I have to do." He doesn't take his eyes off mine. Raising his other hand, he twirls a strand of my hair between his fingers. Then he pushes it behind my ear, his fingers lingering at my earlobe for a few brief seconds. My skin simmers at his touch, and I catch my breath. "Convince you."

Chapter Five

Logan

What has been seen cannot be unseen. The image of her gorgeous breasts is branded in my mind. I think about Nadine the entire afternoon, and the next day. Every man with blood in his veins would find it hard to control himself in her presence. Being near her yesterday was intoxicating. Even now, I'm still high on her laughter. I could hear that woman laugh all day long. In fact, I want to be the reason she laughs. She deserves to be happy, especially after having so much bad luck.

She doesn't trust me, though; I saw that yesterday. I have no idea if it's just me, or men in general, but I'm going to earn that trust.

My phone rings as I enter my office—Pippa's calling.

"Hello, sister."

"What are you doing tonight? I thought we could meet up at Alice's restaurant after work. She has a new chef. I hear the tiramisu is to die for."

"I can't tonight. I'm meeting the senator."

"Oh. That made you sound very important."

"News flash, Pippa: I am a very important person."

"You're also my brother," she states, as if that somehow nullifies what I said. No matter what I do, my siblings still treat me as just their brother. To be honest, that's great. I wouldn't want it any other way. There are plenty of people kissing my ass as long as it fits their agenda, but when I'm with my family, I can be myself. They're honest, and we stick together.

"What about tomorrow?"

"Free."

"Great. I'll move this to tomorrow."

"Sure. Will Nadine be there?"

The thought of seeing her again makes me smile. Her fierce determination stirs something powerful in me. I'd love to listen to her talk about anything, all day long, which is saying something, since I've never been this interested in a simple conversation with a woman before. There's something about Nadine's excitement—it's contagious.

"Of course. Now, before you go all 'I can find a woman on my own' on me, this isn't about you."

I couldn't be happier that Nadine will be there, but I'm not about to share that with my sister, and give her the satisfaction of knowing that her little matchmaking game is working. I'd never hear the end of it. Besides, it's good to be the one with the inside information for once.

"She's all alone here," Pippa continues. "We'll make her an adopted Bennett if you don't want to date her."

Adopted Bennett my ass. "Adopted Bennett" is a term my family uses to refer to close friends. Platonic friends. I have other plans for Nadine. Her mix of vulnerability and strength makes me want to hold her in my arms, and not let her go. Her mouth begs to be kissed, and hell, I'd kiss that sinful mouth of hers into oblivion. I wonder if she tastes as sweet as I imagine, how her full breasts would fit in my hand. Asking her out on a date felt right, even though we clearly both have doubts. Repeating to myself all the reasons why dating her isn't a good idea obviously wasn't working, so I had to do something about the attraction between us.

"See you at dinner, Pippa."

This gives me the perfect occasion to show Nadine I don't give up.

***

The next night, I arrive at Alice's half an hour too late. My family's not in the main section of the restaurant, but that's not a surprise; there's a smaller section adjacent to this one, and Alice closes it when we have a family dinner. As I give my jacket to the coat check attendant, Nadine arrives, flushed and panting.

"Hello, stranger," I tell her.

"Logan." She smiles brightly. "Long time no see. Space hunting with Alex took forever."

I stiffen. I'd forgotten all about Alex. "How did it go?"

Her smile falters. "Not too great. I have appointments to see locations the entire week, so fingers crossed."

I help her take her coat off and *damn*. She's wearing a black strapless dress. I run my fingers over her shoulders and down her arms as I remove the jacket. Goosebumps form on her skin under my hands, and I linger with my fingers a beat longer than necessary, enjoying her softness. The second the attendant hangs our coats, I gesture for him to leave. He's gone the next second. I'll give him a fat tip later. Nadine's back is still turned to me.

"You look great tonight, Nadine," I whisper in her ear from behind.

She draws in a shaky breath. "Thank you."

Her neck is bared to me, and I'm so tempted to kiss her there, and watch her reaction to it. No one can see us here, but hungry as I am for her, I don't want to scare her off. So I step back and ask, "Did Alex behave?"

"Oh, nothing more than a few kisses." Swirling around to face me, Nadine laughs, tilting her head to one side. My wrath must register on my face, because she immediately adds, "I was joking, Logan."

"Not funny."

"That was very funny. You got all caveman for a second."

"You have no idea how much of a caveman I can be." I step closer to her, leaning forward until our faces are inches apart. She licks her lips, avoiding my eyes. "Did you think about what I said last time?"

"A little," she answers.

"Logan, Nadine, there you are," Alice interrupts. "Come on, or Pippa'll eat the entire tiramisu before you even get a chance to taste it."

"I've never been a fan of Tiramisu, sister," I say, not looking away from Nadine. "Pippa and Nadine can have all of it."

Finally, I step away. Like the gentleman I am, I let Nadine walk in front of me. That way, I have a perfect view of her sinful curves and deliciously round ass.

As we walk into the room, I drop my voice, so only Nadine can hear me. "You can do a lot more thinking over the tiramisu."

***

Nadine

Logan offers to take me home after dinner is over. I shiver when we step out in the cool evening air. I grin as we walk to the car.

Once inside the car, I tell Logan, "Your family is hilarious."

I loved spending time with them. It felt like I've known them forever. Their warmth and friendship are so much more than I've hoped for.

"My family likes you," Logan says. "I like you."

Though still maintaining a playful tone, Logan's voice has dropped an octave. The way the words roll off his tongue makes my entire body sizzle. *Get a grip on yourself, Nadine.* I can't lose my head. There's one thing I must concentrate on: my shop. I have to make it work.

Suddenly, I'm aware that we're alone in this space. Resisting him in the restaurant was easy. All I had to do was remember people surrounded us. Inside his car, though, things have changed. Succumbing to his charms seems inevitable.

I'm saved by the radio announcer saying it's midnight, as we arrive at my place.

"Oh, I can't believe it's this late. I have to wake up early tomorrow. You don't have to walk me to the door," I add when Logan exits the car too.

"I'd ruin my gentleman reputation if I didn't. Besides, this isn't a nice neighborhood."

When we arrive at the building entrance, I fully intend to say good night, but Logan asks, "Are you meeting Alex again tomorrow?"

"In the afternoon, yes. I want to hunt for some places by myself in the morning."

"Take care with him. Don't trust him."

"You're acting awfully territorial."

He snaps his gaze to mine, stepping closer to me. "I am."

"You're not even bothering to deny it."

"You like that about me, don't you? That I don't pretend to be someone I'm not?"

He lowers his head until our eyes are on the same level, our lips too.

"I do," I admit. "But you and I. . . It's not a good idea, Logan."

He narrows his eyes as if considering his words. "Let's be honest, okay?"

I nod.

"There is attraction between us." His tone is firm, yet as he places his hands on my shoulder, the touch is gentle.

I lick my lips, dropping my eyes to the ground. "Yeah."

"So we—"

"Logan—"

"Nadine."

"I need to concentrate on my business for a while. I won't have much to offer to a man." Before I lost my job, I remember Thomas's constant complaints that I was working too much, and when I came home, I was too tired to be any fun. Of course, he didn't seem to mind my hard work when he asked for my money. I can't believe I stuck with him for as long as I did.

"If anyone's made you feel that way—" He takes a deep breath as if needing it to calm himself.

Weightlessness overcomes me at his indignation on my behalf.

"You've been dating the wrong men, darling. That's not how it's supposed to go."

"How is it supposed to go?" I *hate* the weakness in my voice.

"A real man will take care of you, spoil you, and fight alongside you for your dreams."

"That's the definition of the ideal man. I thought we were being honest, Logan."

"I am. Let me take you out on a date. If it's good, we'll go on a second one. If it's bad, you can tweet about it. I'm betting I'll get a second one."

I chuckle.

"Nadine, I'm not saying we should jump with both feet into a relationship. We're two adults who like to spend time with each other. We can have a lot of fun together, and if we feel things are moving too fast, we can always re-evaluate, and step away from each other further down the road."

"Is this a very corporate way of asking me to be your friend with benefits? Jump in your bed when the sun goes down, disappear once it's up again?" My stomach dips unpleasantly.

His face grows hard. "I'd never do that. That's no way to treat a woman."

I'm waiting for the punch line before I realize he means it. "Sorry. Didn't mean to offend you."

"I meant that we can take things slowly, no pressure, no expectations."

"Just fun?" I ask.

"Just fun. We've already established that I'm the Chief Fun Officer. Is that a yes?"

Oh, what the hell. One date won't be the end of the world. At any rate, if I keep pretending Logan and I can be platonic friends, I might explode and kiss him squarely on the mouth next time I see him, which will probably be another family gathering. I bet Pippa'd be thrilled.

Here goes nothing. "Yes."

Logan nods. "When?"

"You're fast." I half expect him to pull up the calendar on his phone and schedule me in.

"Don't want to give you the opportunity to change your mind."

"I might," I confess.

"How does tomorrow sound?"

"Okay."

Logan pulls away. "I'll pick you up at seven. I'm leaving you for tonight."

I stand in front of the door to the building, watching him stride to his car.

Before climbing in, he looks at me over the hood and says, "You know what's more annoying than having siblings who think they're always right?"

"What?"

"Siblings who're actually right. You and I. . ." He gestures with his finger between him and me, leaving the sentence hanging.

"Will have a good time together?"

"Good doesn't cover it. It'll be something along the lines of fun and hot. Explosive."

He disappears in the car and takes off, leaving me with a smile the size of Texas.

Chapter Six

Nadine

The next day is very productive. I have so much energy; I'm genuinely concerned my head will explode. It might have to do with the fact that I drank four coffees, or that I'm going on a date with a very handsome man tonight. My money (or lack of) is on the latter. In any case, I shortlist three locations for the shop by lunchtime. They're all in terrible shape, but rent will be cheap, and that will offset the renovation costs. The spaces Alex shows me in the afternoon aren't interesting, so I politely inform him I'll be fine on my own. If I can find a space by myself, I don't have to pay him a commission.

I'm giddy the entire time I prepare for my date, putting more effort in my appearance than I have in a long time. The thought of Logan completely consumes me; everything about him makes me burn and yearn for more. I'm practically counting down the minutes until he'll pick me up. I lay out several dresses on my bed and open my lingerie drawer.

Without thinking, I pick the sexiest underwear I own. Right, why did I do that?

He's not going to see your underwear tonight, Nadine. Well, who knows *what* might happen. The wind can put me in a Marilyn Monroe situation, or... something. After all, the man already saw my boobs. *That doesn't mean he has to see anything more.* I argue with myself some more and, eventually, decide to wear the sexy lingerie anyway, if only because I need to feel sexy. No harm can come from that. I hope.

When I open the apartment door one hour later, my heart somersaults in my chest. Logan is his normal attractive and flirty self, only now he makes even more of an effort than usual to seduce me. His gaze travels appreciatively up and down my body. Licking my lips, I swallow hard. Barely three seconds of our date have passed and already my pulse is ratcheting up. I'll be dancing on a fine line tonight.

"You look sexy as hell, Nadine." His husky tone sends ripples of heat all the way to my center.

"Hello to you, too." Smiling, I wink at him. Then I sashay back inside the room to grab my purse.

"Promise me something," Logan says when I return to him. "You won't worry about anything tonight: the shop, or anything else."

His molten gaze holds mine with determination, and I detect something else beyond heat in his eyes: concern for me, and the promise of fun. I need a pause from my brain, and all the worries it tortures me with. I'm not sure if the fact that he understands exactly what I need scares or reassures me. A little bit of both, I guess.

"It's up to you to make this night so unforgettable that I'll have no choice but to push my worries away."

"That's the sweetest challenge I've ever heard." Leaning on the doorframe, he tilts his head to one side. Unexpectedly, he takes my hand and pulls, bringing me so close to him our bodies almost touch. "If I have it my way, you won't have anything but me in that pretty head of yours."

Catching my breath, I grasp for words, but I can't form even one coherent thought. Fog fills my mind, and the air is thick with sexual tension. Dragging his fingers down my cheek, he adds in a low whisper, "And I approve of the fact that you wear thin bras all the time."

Damn. I forgot about that.

I peer at him from beneath my eyelashes, fighting the urge to lean closer to him still.

"Well, Mr. Chief Fun Officer. Let's go. It's on you to make me forget all my worries tonight."

"You can count on me."

I know before I even step out the door that I don't stand a chance of resisting him. And that is really bad news.

***

"Wow," I exclaim once we're in the restaurant. It's elegant and sleek, the dimmed lights offering an

LAYLA HAGEN

intimate atmosphere. There are small containers with burning incense sprinkled around the room. It's jasmine, which right now seems to be the most sensual smell in the world to me. I think it's just the Logan effect. We sit at a table in the corner and I spot a small dance floor, mentally fanning myself at the prospect of dancing with Logan.

"They have a lot of cocktails." I scan the list on the menu in front of me. "Remind me only to drink one."

"Why's that?"

"My alcohol tolerance to mixed drinks has always been very low, even in college."

"Have wine. Or a martini. You drank that the two times we ate with my family."

I put the menu down. "Do you observe every little detail about everyone?"

"No. Just you." He says the words with ease, but my toes curl. "Back to your martini. . ."

"Cocktails are so much fun, though. But don't let me drink more than one. Trust me, you don't want to see me drunk."

Logan puts his menu down on the table, mischief dancing in his eyes. "This *really* makes me want to see what you do after a few cocktails. Do you spill your deepest secrets?"

I shake my head as Logan narrows his eyes. This is fun.

"Striptease?"

Trying not to laugh, I bring forward my most playful tone. "Maybe."

"I can make you do all those things without alcohol." Leaning forward, he adds in a whisper, "For me." My skin flushes under his gaze. Logan smirks then leans back, my reaction obviously satisfying him. When the waiter stops by, I order a "Seduction on the Rocks." Now it's my turn to watch Logan's reaction with satisfaction. His eyes darken a notch, his lips parting. Great. The next cocktail I order will be "Love All Night Long."

I'm not just dancing on a fine line; I'm deliberately crossing it. But this man demands that I let my inhibitions fall... that I let loose and care about nothing more than his smile. His presence is so intense that it wipes away all my thoughts. What would his lips do? His touch?

He cracks the walls I'd carefully built around myself since my split with Thomas. I should fight, should secure these walls with brick and mortar if need be, but for tonight, at least, I don't want to. I want to have fun, and let this handsome man spoil me.

Sipping from my cocktail a few minutes later, I say, "Tell me an embarrassing story."

"Ah, I've got plenty of those. Any particular topic?"

"I'll leave the choice to you."

"When I was a high school senior, a member of my soccer team was dating Pippa. He was bragging in front of the entire team about how he took my sister's virginity, and being a pig in general. Obviously, I wanted revenge for my sister. But I wanted to be mature and not fight him, so instead I cut a giant hole in the back of his pants before the game started so his boxers would hang out."

"That was mature?"

He shrugs. "He realized what I did and switched our pants. I ended up being the giant idiot with a hole in his pants after all, and I was the captain. Did I mention I had no underwear? So my ass was practically hanging out on the field for all the students and parents to see. Our coach almost had an aneurysm."

I laugh, holding my belly. "You're not making this up, are you?"

"Nope. On the bright side, the sight of my ass ensured I had a hoard of female fans dying to go out with me."

"I'm sure you didn't lack for female fans before either." A knot twists in my throat. He can't be lacking for them now either, can he? He's sexy, fun, and impossibly rich. Surely, women must line up at his door. I can't believe I'm jealous already. *This is fun. Nothing more.* Reminding myself of that fact doesn't seem to be helping, though.

"True." A small smile accompanies this one word, and my insides dip again. Amazing how territorial I feel about a man who isn't even mine.

"You were your sister's self-proclaimed avenger or what?"

"Avenger, guardian, whatever role I needed to fill, as long as I could wear an imaginary hero cape." Pulling a serious face, he says, "Pippa always had a knack for attracting the wrong guys, even though she's lovely."

"Weren't your sisters upset that you were being—"

"Overbearing?"

"I would've said overprotective, but I like a man who owns up to his flaws."

"Trust me, with my family, there's no way not to own up to your flaws. Every time you try to shirk them, eight siblings will happily point them out. Now back to my sister. She didn't catch on most of the time, and when she did, Sebastian had my back, though he never approved of my meddling."

I raise an eyebrow. "So, he never meddled?"

"He did it in his own way, which I didn't always find effective. He likes to *talk* to people. I'm the do-er."

"I see. Was Pippa the only sister you were babysitting?"

Logan remains silent for a moment, his brow furrowed. "I guess. Pippa is the mother hen. She likes to take care of everyone else, often at her expense. She's also very vulnerable. Alice is a lot like you. Resilient, stubborn, and determined. She rarely tolerated my involvement, but both sets of twins were effectively playing bodyguard for her when they could get away with it, and for Summer as well— she's the eternal romantic."

"Sounds as though I'm like Summer too." Although I've tried hard to bury that romantic part of me: the one that dreams of a white dress, of walking down the aisle. It's better not to expect anything. That way, I can't be disappointed, or hurt.

"Is that so?" Logan's expression softens. I try to backtrack, because eternal love is the last thing a man wants to hear about on a first date—or ever, really. Before I have a chance to open my mouth, Logan continues, "You believe in true love, Nadine?"

I lick my lips. "Don't you? Your parents are living proof it exists."

Logan's eyes rove over my face, resting on my lips. Involuntarily, I press my thighs together. "I asked first."

"I used to believe," I confess, lowering my gaze to the glass in front of me.

"And Thomas crushed that."

"Yeah." When I look up from my glass, I find Logan scrutinizing me with an unreadable expression. "Your turn. Do you believe?"

"I'm a man." He drops his voice to a conspiratorial whisper. "I can't own up to believing in true love without my masculinity suffering a downgrade."

Snorting, I grin. His eyes tell me what his lips don't: he *does* believe, and that's good enough for me.

"What does true love mean to you?" Logan asks. His eyes search mine, pure curiosity filling them. No man has ever asked me this, and until now, I never voiced these thoughts out loud.

With Logan, the words come to me easily. "It means having someone I can share everything with. My dreams, my fears. The good days and the bad ones. It means having someone I want to share my good news with first, who's there for me when things go south. I'd ask you what your definition is, but you already told me that'd threaten your masculinity."

By way of answering, Logan threads his fingers with mine on the table. The slight touch electrifies me, an involuntary sigh escaping my lips. Logan's eyes turn darker still.

The waiter brings our appetizer of salmon salad, and we fall into companionable silence. I finish my cocktail between small bites of salmon, and when I'm done with both, I discover with dismay that I'm tipsy. The unfortunate thing is that once I reach this stage, I want more.

"I'll order another drink."

Logan's eyes widen. "You weren't kidding. Your tolerance to mixed drinks *is* abysmal."

When the waiter arrives, I bat my eyelashes at him while ordering another cocktail.

"I become flirty when I'm tipsy," I inform Logan.

"With everyone, yeah. I see that."

"Yep. That's my secret super-tipsy power. I flirt with everyone. I don't discriminate," I affirm with a proud smile.

"Well, that backfired quickly," he murmurs to himself. As the waiter puts the second cocktail in front of me, Logan says, "I wouldn't drink that if I were you."

"Why not?" I challenge, holding my chin high.

"I'm not going to kiss you if you're not sober."

My insides melt and my determination to drink the cocktail dwindles quickly. "So, kissing is on the menu?"

"Depends on you." Logan drums his fingers on the table, and right now, the gesture strikes me as incredibly sexy. A film starts playing in my mind, of Logan drumming his fingers across my skin. What part of me would he touch first? I imagine he'd give plenty of attention to my breasts, caressing them, teasing me. Then his fingers would find my center, and he'd rock my world. Goosebumps form on my arms as if he were indeed touching me. "I want you to be aware and experiencing every sensation when I kiss you."

I drink only water through the main course and dessert. The second unfortunate effect of my tipsiness is that my tongue loosens. "Can I ask you something and you promise to answer sincerely?"

"Sure."

"Do all men expect sex on the first date?"

Logan's lips part in surprise, but he recovers quickly. "No, mostly jerks and amateurs." With a hint of mystery, he adds, "They don't know what I do."

"What's that?"

"Anticipation is key. When you long for something, the release is more powerful."

Heat spears me right through my core. "So, everything before sex is just one long round of foreplay?"

"There is that, and also the fact that intimacy is so much better if you know the person you're with."

His words feel like a caress. "I won't lie; I've had my fair share of sex after first dates, as well as one-night stands. Haven't found either fully satisfying."

"Why aren't you in a relationship?"

He sets his jaw. "Haven't found the right person." He takes my hand, dragging his thumb in circles on my palm. His touch speaks more clearly to me than any words could; it tells me to trust him, that he'd never hurt me. "I think you're sober now."

Grinning, I nod.

"Good. I don't believe in sex on the first date, but I do believe in something else. Dancing on a first date is absolutely necessary."

Logan hauls me onto the dance floor, which is empty except for one other couple. Hooking an arm around my waist, he pulls me toward him until my breasts squish against his hard chest. *Oh, God.* Being inches away from him is too much. He takes my right hand in his, and I place my left one at the nape of his neck. This close, the smell of cologne, soap, and pure masculinity—the smell of *him*— overwhelms me. His scent is more intoxicating than the cocktail I've had. I will get drunk on this man.

"I've got moves, you know," he whispers in my ear.

"Who doesn't for a slow song?" I try to keep my voice even, but my mouth is cotton-dry. Chuckling in my ear, he leads the dance. One step forward, two back; one forward, two back. I've never been much of a dancer but, under Logan's guidance, the movements come naturally; they are fluid, in sync. I involuntarily thread my fingers through the hair on the back of his head, and he leans his forehead on mine. The gesture is so intimate; I don't know what to make of it.

As if sensing this change, Logan says, "I won't hurt you, Nadine. I don't want you to take my word for it; I'll prove it to you." His words reach somewhere deep inside me, beneath the confident air of a woman wearing sexy lingerie. He pulls back a notch, cupping the side of my face with his long fingers. The desire to be alone with him hits me fast and unapologetic.

"I need some fresh air." My eyes dart to the double doors leading to the terrace.

Logan doesn't argue, instead leading the way. Once outside, I shiver, and Logan makes quick work of shedding his suit jacket, draping it around my shoulders.

"Always a gentleman, aren't you?"

"I assure you I don't kiss like a gentleman."

Before I can fully process his words, he closes the distance between us, covering my mouth with his. His lips settle on mine, full and warm. Their touch is enough to send a zing of anticipation through me, setting me on fire. His tongue pushes between my lips, coaxing my own into a dance.

Logan doesn't kiss me as if it's a means to an end.

He kisses me to… kiss me.

I have never been kissed like this before. He worships my mouth, and I know he'd do the same with my body. Without warning, Logan intensifies the kiss. He pushes me against the wall, sucking on my tongue. I burn between my thighs, my whole body alive with need. When I mirror the action on his tongue, I'm rewarded with a groan. He pulls back, dropping his mouth to my neck.

"You taste so sweet," he says. "I could kiss you all night, Nadine."

"Why don't you?" I whisper. "Can I have a second kiss?"

His lips curl into a smile against my neck.

"You're an impatient little thing. No second kiss right now." He lifts his head, looking straight at me. "Remember what I told you about anticipation?"

"Yes."

"I must give you some incentive to accept going on a second date with me."

I laugh. "You sure can negotiate."

"Is that a yes?"

I hesitate for a few seconds, but his consuming presence leaves me no choice. "Yes, Logan, it is. I want to go on a second date with you."

A gust of wind blows, chilling me.

"Let's go back inside," Logan says.

The rest of the evening goes by in a whirlwind. I order a second dessert and listen to Logan's childhood stories, laughing harder than I have in a long time. It's very late when we leave the restaurant, and we're the last ones to do so. Logan drives me home, and I wrestle with myself the entire way—should I invite him in or not?

I'm not ready to take things further tonight, but at the same time, I'm not ready to let him go yet.

***

"You *are* a superhero, cape and all," I say when he walks me to my door instead of just dropping me off in front of the building.

"I'm offended you thought otherwise."

I smile at him, sticking the key in my lock, but the door is stuck. I'm about to push myself into the door when Logan offers, bemused, "Leave that to me."

Stepping aside, I watch him shoulder the door open.

"I suppose I have no option now but to invite you in, do I?" I ask.

"I suppose not."

Stepping inside, I turn on the light. The place looks even more run-down with the small light reflecting from the ceiling. I try not to give my apartment much thought, but it's one of the most depressing places I've ever lived in. It was the only one in my price range.

"I'd offer to give you a tour, but what you see is what you get. A studio with stuff piled up everywhere. It's all I can afford for now."

"Don't apologize, Nadine. Don't forget I wasn't born rich."

I expected to be a basket case having him here, but I'm strangely at ease. Well, except for my galloping pulse.

"I can show you some of my designs," I tell him.

For some reason, his eyes widen.

"I'll just show you pictures, though. I don't want to take the dresses out of their boxes." Logan hunches his shoulders in disappointment. *How did he think I'd be showing him the dresses?*

We sit on the couch, and I instantly become aware of how close we are. I open my laptop and start the slideshow.

"Nadine, these are incredible," Logan says after I show him my newest collection.

"Really?"

"Yes, I mean, I assumed they'd be decent, but they're fantastic. I'm not an expert, but we do work closely with fashion houses for our collection shows, so I know a thing or two. And you didn't attend any fashion school?"

"No degree. I took as many cheap online courses as I could find, and invested in a professional sewing machine."

"You are amazingly talented."

"Thank you." Having someone else besides my best friend believe in me, and acknowledge my talent is empowering.

"What's that?" He points to a folder on my laptop named *Dream House*.

"Oh, just some daydreaming on my part. When I was searching for empty spaces for the shop, I also came across some houses. I saved my favorite one here, even though it'll be a long time before I can afford one. It's good for motivation."

"Show me."

Hesitantly, I do as he says. Showing him my dream house feels as if I'm laying yet another part of me bare.

He smiles while browsing through the pictures. "I see you're the white picket fence girl all the way."

"Guilty," I admit.

"You also seem adamant to have a garden with a very old tree—"

"And large windows in the rooms overlooking the garden." All the houses I loved have those things in common. "One of those rooms would be my workshop. It'd be very inspiring to work with such a view."

"You're adorable, Nadine."

"Thank you." I wasn't expecting that reaction. After pushing my laptop away, Logan turns to face me. As usual, being the sole object of his attention makes me ache for him. He plays with his fingers on the inside of my wrist; the simple movement sets my nerve endings on fire. Carefully, as if he's handling a piece of particularly fragile china, Logan lifts my hand until my wrist reaches his mouth. He feathers his lips on my already sensitized skin, and this sends me over the edge, a moan escaping my lips. He cups my cheek with his other hand and I languidly give in to his touch, craving for more. His fingers trail from my cheek down to my jaw, then around to the back of my neck. Rubbing his thumb against the skin there, he pulls me to him.

This kiss is different than the first one. It's slow and gentle, but it dazzles me nonetheless. When we break off, I struggle for breath.

"I thought you planned to torture me and make me wait for a second kiss until our second date?"

"Changed my mind. Besides, you already agreed to a second date." Logan smiles, his thumb perusing the contour of my lips. "I don't want you to date anyone else while you date me."

My insides melt. I wasn't going to see anyone else anyway; it's not who I am. Nevertheless, teasing him won't hurt. "One date and you're a caveman already?"

"Oh, you've seen that side of me many times since we met Alex."

"True."

I watch him silently. A playful twinkle dances in his eyes, but beyond that is a glimmer of domination, which sends ripples through my body. I decide to play this for all it's worth, because I feel naughty, and it'll be fun to watch him get riled up. "You think two kisses give you the right to exclusivity?"

Logan's stance changes and his jaw ticks. "No?"

"No, but three kisses might."

Logan's tension ebbs away. "I see, bartering for another kiss."

Here, surrounded by darkness and quiet, I become acutely aware of the effect he has on me. Cupping the back of my head, he pushes me even closer to him. Desperate for more body-on-body contact, I climb into his lap, lacing my fingers around the back of his neck. Our groins are dangerously close to one another. His breath on my lips sends a jolt low in my body, and I lean in to kiss him. This one is explosive. He explores my mouth with his tongue at the same time he explores my body with his expert hands. They travel from my neck down to my breasts, lingering there for a sweet moment.

My nipples turn to hard nubs under my bra, throbbing for more of his touch. As his hands move farther down, resting on my hips, I shift in his lap. My soaked thong grazes the already sensitive skin between my thighs, and I moan against his mouth. The movements of our tongues grow faster, more desperate. He pulls me hard against him until my slick flesh collides with his erection. Logan digs his fingers into my hips, groaning. *Wow. Who knew petting with clothes on could be so sexy?*

We pull apart, gasping for breath.

"Nadine." His voice comes out rough and throaty. "I haven't gotten hard from just a kiss since I was in high school."

I giggle, feeling like a wicked schoolgirl.

"Have I earned the right to be your only date for a while?" he asks.

"Yes."

"Great." Smiling at me, he kisses my forehead. "Now, I'm going to leave, because I'm seconds away from losing my self-control."

"Most men wouldn't have a problem with that."

"I am not most men."

"That's right, you're not," I whisper.

"I want to spend time with you, spoil you, and make you smile first."

"Why?" I ask, sincerely confused.

"Because you deserve it. You're fun, honest, and hardworking. I love that. It's refreshing. You've had enough bad luck, Nadine. Time for that to change."

I gulp, moving away from his lap. "Okay."

While I sit on the couch, I take in his ruffled hair, his wrinkled shirt. His breathing is as labored as mine. My control snaps just by *looking* at him.

"How about next Friday for that second date?"

I nod. "Eight o'clock?"

"I'll pick you up."

I watch Logan leave while sitting on the couch, and once I'm alone I grab the laptop. The folder with my portfolio stares at me as a reminder that I must focus on my career, on making the store a success. A man like Logan will never accept being second to anything. It's not in his nature. If I've learned something from his kisses, it's that no matter if he goes fast or slow, he demands everything.

Chapter Seven

Logan

The first thing I do at work the next morning is go to the Creative department to find Pippa. Stepping out of the elevator, I find the team bustling with life and energy. Pippa is at the other end of the room at her desk, holding a crayon in her hand, moving it furiously across a notebook. A look of intense concentration stretches across her features. Ah, I'd recognize that expression anywhere—my sister is in a creative mood. Pippa, like Summer, always had an imaginative spark. Sebastian and I worked with various designers when we first started out, and only when one of them dropped out did our sister step in, showing us some sketches. She was more talented than all the other designers we had.

We have advanced digital programs for designing our collections, but Pippa still sketches everything by hand first. From the numerous incidents in our childhood when I interrupted her from her drawing, I know that now isn't the best time to butt in, but I'll take my chances anyway.

"Hello, sister."

Pippa startles, her shoulders quivering slightly. Furrowing her brow, she shoots me a look I recognize: *You'd better have a good reason for interrupting me.*

"Logan, this is a surprise." Pippa pushes her sketch away.

"I can't visit my sister at her workplace?"

She rolls her eyes. "Like I don't come up to your office enough. You need something, don't you?"

"I do." Pulling a chair from a nearby desk, I sit down. "I'm going to tell you something, and I want you to be quiet until I finish."

My sister's expression changes from attentive to delighted. "You're not here to talk about the budget for the next show, are you?"

"No, even though you, Ava, Sebastian, and I do have to talk it through sometime this week."

"Yeah, yeah, sure." Pippa waves her hand dismissively. She's never cared much about numbers. "What do you want to tell me?"

She'll drive me bananas after I tell her, but there's no way around it. "I went on a date with Nadine." Pippa opens her mouth, but I raise my finger. "No, no, no. I talk, and you're silent. That was the deal."

She narrows her eyes. "I thought you meant something work-related when I agreed. No way am I keeping quiet."

I groan, fully aware I've opened Pandora's Box.

"Why were you pretending to be mad at us for trying to set you up?"

"I wasn't pretending. I *was* annoyed that all of you meddled in my affairs, as though I couldn't get a woman myself."

"Oh, please, Logan. That's what we *do*. We meddle in each other's business, especially when we think the other person needs help. You should know; you do it all the time."

"Are you going to lecture me, or do you want to hear me out?"

After a moment's deliberation, she purses her lips. "Continue."

"We ended up at her place after the date, and she showed me some of her designs. Have you seen them?"

"No."

"They're brilliant. Could we use them for our next collection show?"

Pippa was reaching for her glass of water, but her hand stops in midair as she snaps her head to me. "They're that good?"

"Tell her to show them to you. You have the decision power over this, but I think her designs would be a great match."

Over the years, Pippa chose to work with well-known fashion designers and new up-and-comers alike. "We're already working with a designer for the upcoming show. I can't drop him, but I'll look over her designs, and if they're that good, we can always use them in the future."

"Sounds good."

"Wish I could be bitchy enough to drop the current designer. He's driving me crazy. He practically became a star after we worked with him five years ago, and now he's acting like a diva. Rich people are asses sometimes."

"Pippa, *we* are rich," I remind her.

"Yeah." Dropping her voice to a whisper, she says, "Last week, I woke up in the middle of the night convinced our parents are next door, trying to figure out how to make ends meet this month."

Her words hit me like a punch in the gut. Sebastian, Pippa, Alice, and I were old enough to remember the worst of times. I used to have the same nightmare, but that was more than ten years ago. *Why's she having them now? Ah...* I remember Alice telling me about a therapy session she accompanied Pippa to after the divorce. Apparently, once you feel uncertain in one area, old insecurities and fears start showing too.

Well, there's no reason my sister has to put up with this. Deciding to distract her—even if only momentarily, I offer myself as bait.

"So, back to Nadine. As I said, she showed me her designs last night. . ."

My words have the exact effect I was hoping for. Pippa's frown melts, a grin appearing instead. "Wait a minute. What do you mean she showed them to you? Did she. . . model them for you?"

"No. She showed me pictures."

"Okay, I'm building a little scenario in my head. Did you have sex?"

"Pippa, I'm not discussing my sex life with you."

"Fine, talk to Sebastian about it. Or Blake. I'll get it out of them."

Why did I think that using my date with Nadine as a distraction was a good idea? *I. Never. Learn.* No one's going to save my bacon now.

"Admit it. I was right." Pippa stands up from her chair, swinging her hips in a little dance. I look around, but the rest of the department is not even remotely surprised. I suppose they've grown used to my sister's personal brand of crazy.

"What about?" I ask, though I have an inkling of where this is going.

"About Nadine and you. I knew you'd be perfect for each other since before I officially met her."

"You want to hear me say it, don't you?"

"Yeah."

"Fine, you were right. We're taking things slow, so please don't build any scenarios in your head that take this too far."

"You mean already playing with the idea of the color theme of your wedding is taking things too far?" Pippa asks innocently.

I groan, putting my elbows on her desk. No matter what I say, my sister will go on with her scenarios. I promised Nadine that we'd take things slow, without any pressure, and I intend to keep that promise, even though I felt like going one hundred miles per hour yesterday. Just remembering her sweet, soft lips and her delicious moans as I kissed her is undoing me. I will be patient, though. Nadine is stronger than all the women I've dated in the past, but I want her to trust me completely before I take things further.

"You've sidetracked me," I say.

"Sorry. So, Nadine's designs are great."

"Yeah. You're the creative genius of the company; you have to decide if they'll work for us. Can you ask her to show them to you? Don't tell her I said anything."

"And why is that?"

"Because she doesn't like favors, and I don't want her to think I'm *overbearing*."

"You're sweet right now. Don't worry, I'll let you know as soon as you're overbearing."

Pippa scrunches her nose at the last word. She was the one who announced it was the signature word to describe me.

"I can always count on that."

"Can I ask you something?" Pippa inquires.

"Saying no never stopped you, so go ahead."

She smiles as if I gave her a compliment of the highest order. "Why are you so interested in her success?"

"Because she has passion and determination, and she can't catch a break. If there's anything I can do to change that, I will." Also, if her business fails, Nadine wants to move back to North Carolina. No way will I allow that. Damn it, she's growing on me more than I like to admit, and that is *very bad news*.

"Okay, I'm on it," Pippa says. "I'll figure out how to ask her, and I'll make sure not to mention that you put in a good word for her."

"Thanks. She's proud and wants to succeed on her own. We have someone like that in our family, so I'm walking on eggshells."

Pippa nods in agreement. "We'll pull an Alice again, don't worry."

We both grin. When Alice opened her restaurant, she announced she didn't want to use the Bennett name for any favors. We were already famous by then and had enough money to push her restaurant to stardom, but she made us promise not to get involved. So we promised then immediately broke our word, of course.

Pippa, Sebastian, and I pulled all the strings we could to convince influential reviewers to check out her restaurant. Now here's the thing: said reviewers gave her completely objective opinions. The food was great, so really, she did it all on her own. Still, Alice doesn't need to learn what we did.

"Well, I'll leave you," I say. "What are your plans for the weekend? Do you want to do something together?"

"I'll probably watch reruns of my favorite shows Saturday and Sunday, but Friday night..." She inhales deeply. "I have a date."

I'm so stunned I can't even speak for a second. "With a man?"

Pippa stares at me as if I'm the world's biggest moron. "No, Logan, with a chimp. Of course with a man." She points her index finger menacingly at me. "Don't say anything."

"I wasn't going to."

She raises an eyebrow.

"Okay, I was going to say you're not ready." A number of other remarks are on the tip of my tongue, but they wouldn't earn me any points with Pippa, so I say, "Be careful, and call me if you need anything. Seriously. Anything."

***

Minutes later, I storm directly into Sebastian's office, even though I have a million things to do. Family comes first, so I'm on Bennett duty today.

"Did you know Pippa's going on a date?" I ask him without further ado.

Sebastian doesn't look up from his computer screen. "No, but good for her. It's about time."

"What do you mean 'good for her'? Who is this guy?" I slump in the chair in front of his desk, propping up both feet on his desk. "Do we know anything about him?"

"Well, Logan, since Pippa's the one who'll date him, I don't think we're the ones who're supposed to know him."

Sebastian raises his eyebrows at my feet, but I don't move them one inch.

"I don't want anyone to hurt her again," I say.

"Neither do I, but she's a grown woman. You can't scare off all her dates like you did in high school."

"I didn't scare off *all* of them, just those who were asses. We can ask around, there's no harm in that."

"Except Pippa will cut off our balls if she finds out. I don't know about you, but I'm quite fond of my balls."

"So, what, we do nothing?"

"Exactly."

"Bloody brilliant," I say.

"You're using British slang now?"

"Seemed like the most appropriate word."

"Logan!" His warning tone annoys me.

"Yeah, yeah, I get it. I'll stay put."

"To change the topic, what's this I hear about you dating Nadine?"

I stare at him. "I told Pippa about it before I walked into your office. When did she have time to tell you?"

"Ava told me. She was very smug about it too."

I snort. "I should've seen it coming." Not wanting to talk about this with Sebastian, I switch topics. "Why don't we schedule a budget meeting for this afternoon?"

Sebastian nods. "Excellent. I thought I was the only one working around here today."

"Don't be an ass."

"I'm not. If I were, I'd grill you more on Nadine."

"There's no way I'm sharing any details."

"You're in this deep, aren't you? I'll enjoy watching you fall, brother."

Chapter Eight

Nadine

I wake up panting, my chest heaving up and down as I struggle for breath. Fanning myself, I push a strand of hair away from my sweaty forehead. I had a hot dream. Logan Bennett was starring in it and *holy hell*. This felt so real. It still does. The skin on my entire body simmers, and I ache between my thighs. I blame the hot kiss Logan gave me last night for all of this.

Damn. This felt *too* real.

Grudgingly, I leave my bed and prepare myself for the day. As I decide to skip breakfast, the doorbell rings. I open the door, half expecting to find my landlord in front of it, telling me he's raising my rent. Instead, there's a delivery boy.

"I have a delivery for you, miss." He hands me a paper takeout bag without waiting for my answer.

"I didn't order anything."

He shrugs. "I'm just delivering. It's already been paid for, so you might as well take it."

"Fine."

My heart hammering in my chest, I wait until he's out of sight to close the door then tear open the bag. Inside it, I find two croissants and a note.

Two croissants, just as mademoiselle ordered.
Logan

A sigh escapes my lips, and my stomach flips. Warmth courses through me as I grab my phone and text Logan.

Nadine: Thank you for the croissants.

I hold my breath, waiting for his answer, which arrives in a few seconds.

Logan: Think about me while you eat them.

I've been thinking about him since he left last night, and this is dangerous. Sighing again, I take a bite of croissant. *Oh, they're delicious.* I fiddle with my phone and write back to Logan.

Nadine: Why did you send them?

Logan: I'm spoiling you. It's a mandatory step in "The Bennett Book of Seduction."

I laugh with gusto as I enjoy my croissant, and then decide to tease him.

Nadine: You're trying to impress me, so I don't cancel our date on Friday.

Logan: Nah, I wanted to make you smile.

Damn, this man is perfect. So perfect, in fact, that I'm scared.

Nadine: Careful, Logan. You'll make me fall for you.

Logan: Maybe that's what I want.

Oh. I was fully expecting my last statement to send him running for the hills but, of course, he'd surprise me. I've never met a man this determined, and. . . honest. Time to switch the tone to playful.

Nadine: Our kiss really left a lasting impression on you, didn't it? Or was it my display of boobs in Ava's office?

Logan: Both did. Can't wait to see you again. By the way, if you cancel our date, I'm not above throwing you over my shoulder and kidnapping you.

My knees turn to rubber instantly, and I know what's causing it. The alpha vibes coming through the phone from Logan.

The following week is crazy. I'm running around non-stop, talking to location owners, securing permits, and a million other things. Logan sends me breakfast each morning, and by the time Friday comes around, I'm bursting with excitement at the thought of seeing him again.

Unfortunately, something gets in the way.

"I need to cancel our date," I say breathlessly into the phone.

"Why?" Logan doesn't bother to hide the disappointment in his voice.

"Because I just received the keys to my very own shop, thank you very much. It's in dreadful condition, so I need to start working on it right away."

I'm standing in the shop right now, and it looks every bit as decrepit as it did when I first saw it. But I already bought part of the supplies I need for renovations, so I might as well start.

"Congratulations. I thought you were going to show me your best options."

"I was going to, but the owner of this place called me this morning and told me I had to make my decision today, or he'd give it to someone else."

"I'll come by now."

"You'll try to convince me to go out."

"It's Friday night, so of course I'm going to try to, but I also really want to see your place. Tell me the address."

I dictate it with a grin on my face. He called it "your place." There are a number of people I could've called to tell them about this monumental moment in my life, and yet it's Logan I called first. It wasn't just because I had to cancel our date, but because I knew he'd understand how important this is for me. Even though I have a million things to do, I'm happy he's coming over to share this with me.

I can see past the dilapidated walls and ceiling. Instead of them, I imagine spotlights sprinkled on the ceiling. At least the floor is in great shape; it'll need some polishing, but nothing more. My dream is finally in my grasp. There are three rooms—two in the back, which I'll use for storage, and one in the front, where the actual shop will be.

Logan walks inside the store half an hour later, and I lick my lips at the sight of him. He wears his suit jacket open, and my imagination runs wild thinking about what's under his white shirt. Logan oozes masculinity, no imagination required. Something about the way he owns any room he walks into makes me feel safe when I'm with him, even though he's a danger to my senses.

After a quick inspection of the room, he sets his jaw.

"I know this looks dreadful," I say.

"Dreadful? That's one word. I would've gone with shithole."

"Don't be mean."

"I'm worried about you. It'll be hellish work to get this place up and running, Nadine."

It's been a long time since a man worried about me, instead of the other way around. It feels good. Better than good. Most of all, it feels right—and that scares me.

"It's the only one I can afford."

"Why do you want to start working on it right away? Surely, no renovation crew will begin working this late on a Friday."

I barely keep from laughing as I point at myself with both thumbs and say, "Logan Bennett, meet the renovation crew."

"You want to do it yourself?"

"I have to. No money for a crew. I made a list of everything I need to do." I hand him the list, and he scans it quickly.

"I'm impressed. Do you know how to do all this?"

"Believe it or not, I do. I waitressed for years while in college, and whenever something needed fixing, the owner would make us do it. One summer, he closed for renovations, and I stayed to help. I needed the money, and I gained some extra skills.

After I moved home, a friend of mine had a business fixing up houses, and selling them at a profit. I worked for her during weekends, so my skills are top-notch."

"You're unbelievable."

"Thanks."

"Now, seriously. You'll need a crew to—"

"No money for that. I'll do it myself. It'll take longer than I'd hoped, but it'll work."

"If you want to do all the things on your list by yourself it'll take you three months at least."

"Yeah."

His eyebrows shoot up. "You'll be paying rent three months without making any revenue."

"Logan, stop. I'm aware of all that, but I don't have another option. I'll suck it up and work."

"I probably already know the answer to this, but would you let me pay the crew? I'd be investing in your talent."

I put my hands on my hips. "You want to be an investor? Why?"

"I saw your designs. They're brilliant."

"Yeah, but that would be a conflict of interest."

"How so?"

"We're dating. I can't accept it." Even though I can see in his eyes that his offer is honest, the term "sugar daddy" rings in my mind. I don't want to depend on anyone except myself to see this all the way to the end.

"I thought you might say that. I'll help you with the renovations then. On weekends."

I was expecting a lot of things from Logan, but not this. Ava told me how hard he works, and that he saves his precious spare time for his family. Now he wants to give that up for me. I recognize this for the significant commitment it is. Who is this man, and why didn't I meet him at a more appropriate moment in my life? Say, one year from now, when I'll have all my affairs in order?

"It's very sweet of you, but you don't have to do this, Logan."

He smiles. "I know. I want to." He closes the distance between us with a few strides. When he's close enough to me that I can smell the woodsy scent of his cologne, he adds, "You said 'we're dating' like it's a regular thing." He wiggles his eyebrows. "That's a big statement for you, considering I nearly had to blackmail you to earn a second date."

"Well… " My voice fades as Logan's eyes turn darker, zeroing in on my lips.

"I made an impression last time, didn't I?" His voice is low and breathy. My body immediately responds to it, desire billowing in my center, coiling through my veins.

"You're a good kisser," I say matter-of-factly.

"Good? I never settle for good, Nadine."

"I might consider upgrading that to excellent," I tease. "Depends on you."

"I do love your challenges. Now, back to helping you renovate. I want one thing in return."

"What's that?" I already know I'll agree to anything he says. It's the side effect of inhaling his intoxicating scent. It must contain pheromones; I'm sure of it.

"The promised second date. Tonight."

"You're playing dirty."

"I've been accused of doing that to get my way."

"You always get your way, don't you?"

Leaning in to me, he whispers, "Yes."

"Okay, but we'll have to go somewhere that a dress code isn't required." I point to my jeans and black cotton T-shirt. I have rags I plan to use for the renovation work in the back, but nothing else. "If we go to my apartment to change, it'll take forever."

"Fine by me."

After I grab my purse, we step outside and I lock the door to the shop.

"I can't believe I found a space on this street. The location is perfect."

I glance around the area with a huge smile. "Perfect" doesn't begin to cover it. This is a posh shopping area. A designer shoes and bag store is next door, and a high-end restaurant across the street. I've researched statistics, and there is plenty of foot traffic here. Parking opportunities aren't as good as I'd hoped, but they'll do.

"The only downside is that it's a million miles away from my apartment."

Logan puts his arm around my shoulders as we walk to his car. The gesture isn't sexual at all, but it still makes my heart race. No, his caress speaks of safety, caring, and familiarity. Without thinking, I cuddle closer to him. Glancing up, I let out a slight sound of surprise. The sky is clearer than I've seen it since I arrived, and it's the first time I can appreciate the multitude of stars sprinkled above me. They resemble tiny diamonds.

"Actually," Logan says, opening the door of his car for me. Once I'm inside, he continues. "The location is the best part. It's two blocks away from where I live. I foresee endless opportunities to convince you to stay overnight."

With that, he closes the door. Wiping my palms on my jeans, I try to calm my heart. It beats even faster than before. What does Logan have in store for us?

When he climbs in the driver's seat, I immediately try to fill the silence. "I don't know why I'm surprised you live downtown."

"Yeah. Sebastian lives in a quieter neighborhood. I'm all for the hustle and bustle."

"So, where are we going?"

"Dancing. Thought you should see my wild dancing skills, since you thought I could only go slow. I can do slow, and I can do wild." He guns the engine. "It's mind-blowing either way."

"Are we still talking about dancing?"

"I am." Glancing sideways at me, he adds with a smirk, "Are you talking about something else?"

"No, not at all." Heat creeps into my cheeks, but I'm counting on the darkness to hide it. "I feel guilty for not working tonight, but I'm happy we're going out. You're the first person I called."

"I'm glad to hear that, Nadine."

***

Midway through the drive, Logan's phone rings.

"Pippa," he mutters, putting it on loudspeaker. "Hi, Pippa," Logan answers.

"You told me to call you if I need anything. You seemed to mean *anything*, but can I still hold you to it?" Pippa speaks in a low voice, and there is commotion in the background.

Logan's grip the wheel tighter. "Of course."

"Good. Can you pick me up from my date? I'm at Ember. It's on—"

"I know the restaurant."

"How fast can you be here?"

"Twenty minutes, tops."

The call ends.

"What was that?" My head spins as I try to make sense of it.

"My sister wants a rain check from her date."

"Wow, you have a code or something?"

"No, but I told her to call me if she needed anything."

Logan sports a killer expression afterward, so I don't ask for more details. We arrive in front of the restaurant exactly twenty minutes later, and he texts Pippa to let her know we're here. Ember is similar to the high-end restaurant across the street from my shop, except larger. Through the floor-to-ceiling windows, I have a perfect view inside. Elegant black and white furniture fills the interior, the only patches of color coming from the guests' clothes. Pippa walks out the front door before I finish inspecting the restaurant. Wearing sky-high black stilettos and a fitted red dress showing off her gorgeous curves, Pippa is by far the best-dressed person around. She looks like a woman on a mission. And right now, her mission seems to be fleeing the scene, though I believe she had an entirely different goal in mind when she dressed up for the night.

"Drive," she instructs after she sits in the backseat.

"Your apartment?" Logan asks Pippa, hitting the gas pedal.

"Yes."

Logan drives in silence. He opens and closes his mouth a few times, glancing in the rearview at Pippa. Eventually, he asks, "Pippa, are you... Did anything happen? Did he do something?"

"Nothing happened, I just panicked. Turns out I wasn't ready to date after all."

Seeing her sad expression in the rearview mirror, I finally realize what this was about. I've heard about Pippa's divorce and, unless I'm mistaken, this was her first post-divorce foray in the dating world. I sigh sympathetically, and that's when she seems to realize I'm in the car too.

"Crap," Pippa says. "You two were on a date, weren't you? I'm sorry. Why didn't you tell me, Logan?"

"It's no problem," I assure her.

"You told me to call you if I needed anything, but. . ." Her voice fades. "I didn't call Sebastian because I knew he and Ava were at the theater, but it didn't occur to me that you two were as well."

She looks out the window as her words fade. I've only met Pippa a few times, but she always had an air of exuberance that was contagious. Now there's no semblance of that girl.

"I had a mini-panic attack," she continues. "Poor guy didn't know what hit him. Come on, Logan, you're dying to say 'I told you so.'"

Logan huffs. "I'd never say that."

"Well, you were right. I'll put dating on hold for a while."

More silence follows, and then the car comes to a halt in front of what I assume is Pippa's building.

"Are you sure you want to be on your own?" I ask her. "You can go out with us, or I can stay with you and have a girls' night in." She seems to need company.

"Yeah, thanks, but I'll read a steamy romance, and drink a glass of wine. You two have fun. That poor dude probably has blue balls; no reason for me to cock-block the two of you too."

I flush while Logan says, "Really smooth, Pippa."

"I'll try dating again… eventually. It's never too late to start fresh, is it?" Pippa asks, hope and desperation warring on her expression.

"It's not," I respond. "I have a degree in it."

Pippa gives me a sheepish smile that tells me she already knows my story. I'm wondering if Ava or Logan is to blame. Pippa exits the car, blows us both kisses, and heads to the entrance of her building; her steps slow, her shoulders drooped.

Logan looks worriedly after his sister.

"Wow."

"Yeah, wow," Logan says. "I wasn't expecting her to call. Pippa, like Sebastian, is very self-sufficient. Rarely asks for help, rarely lets her guard down."

"Will she be okay on her own?" I ask.

"Not really. If she called, it means she needed company. She would've taken a cab otherwise. But I have no idea how to fix this. Pippa'll kick us out if we go upstairs."

"You can't fix everything, Logan."

"Thank you for offering to have a girls' night in with her."

"Sure. I thought she could use some girl fun."

Logan scrutinizes me with an unreadable expression, caressing my cheek with the back of his hand. The contact electrifies me, cutting my breath short. I lean into his touch, hungry for more. When it comes to Logan, it seems I always want more.

"You're not in the mood for dancing anymore," I state.

"No, sorry."

"It's okay. Neither am I."

"We can still have a drink downtown."

I check the clock. "Logan, it's very late. I don't want to blow you off, but I have to start work early tomorrow, which means I have to get up super early since the commute from home to the shop lasts forever."

To my surprise, the corners of his mouth lift. "I'll make you a dangerous proposition."

"I'm all ears." I have no idea what he has in mind, yet my body already sizzles with anticipation.

"Spend the night at my place."

I let out a long whistle. "That line was even smoother than Pippa's."

"I don't mean for sex." Logan laughs with gusto. I'm surprised at how relieved I am to see some of the tension his entire body held earlier bleeding away. The recognition of how important this man's happiness is to me hits me squarely in the chest. We agreed we'd have fun together. Caring for him is dangerous.

"I have a spare bedroom. You can sleep there, and you won't have to wake up so early. We can walk there if you want to; it's that close. You can sleep longer. What do you say? Extra sleep?"

"Nooooo, the words 'extra sleep' are magic to me. Now I can't say no."

"I was counting on that. Say yes, Nadine."

Swallowing hard, I nod. "You weren't kidding when you said you foresee endless opportunities to convince me to stay overnight, were you?"

"You have no idea."

***

We stop by my place first then drive to Logan's. His apartment is not at all what I imagined. When he said he likes the hustle and bustle, I conjured what I believed to be a bachelor's pad in my mind, complete with a pool table in the living room. Instead, he owns a spacious—but not extravagant—two-bedroom apartment, decorated in shades of white and brown. It's masculine yet warm and welcoming. The first thing that strikes me is the sheer number of paintings hanging in the living room.

"Gifts from Summer," Logan explains.

"She's very talented." I mean it as I lose myself in the swirl of colors and shades. Continuing my inspection of the living room, I detect my favorite item within seconds: a fireplace.

"Wow, I can't believe you have a fireplace. I love them! They make me think about Christmas." On the mantelpiece is a group picture of the entire family. It's an old photograph; Logan doesn't look to be more than twenty. Sitting between Pippa and Alice, he has an arm around each of their shoulders, hovering protectively over them. There are nine siblings in the picture. I already met all of the girls, but I still have four brothers to meet. The two twin sets. From what Ava told me, I'm unlikely to see the first twin set, Christopher and Max, because they live overseas, expanding Bennett Enterprises. But Daniel and Blake, dubbed the party brothers, are in San Francisco. I can't wait to meet them.

"I can start a fire if you want to," he says.

"I'd love that."

"In the meantime, I have some takeout menus on my fridge. You can call either and order whatever you want. My fridge is empty."

"You don't like to cook?"

"I do, but I don't like to cook only for myself."

"Will I get a chance to taste your cooking skills?" I ask, remembering Ava telling me that Sebastian likes to cook naked. Maybe Logan likes nudism too. *Goddamn it, Nadine. You really can't keep your mind out of the gutter, can you?* I've only just entered his apartment, but I can already picture him walking around naked. Clearly, I can't trust my judgment around Logan, and that's dangerous on so many levels.

"If you come here often enough, you will."

"Ah, I see. You're trying to find more incentives for me to sleep over."

"Cooking is an incentive, got it," he says brightly.

The thought of him naked is an even bigger incentive, but I'm not about to own up to that. Not yet, anyway.

While Logan starts the fire, I busy myself scanning the menu. Half an hour later, there's a burning fireplace, and Thai food on plates in front of it. Logan and I sit on the floor, close enough to feel the heat from the fire. Closing my eyes, I inhale the scent of the wood—pine.

"What's that smile for?" Logan asks.

I realize I've been lost in dreamland for a while.

"I love your apartment," I say. "It's very homey."

Halfway through dinner, Logan rises to his feet. "I remembered I have a bottle of champagne. I'll grab it."

"What are we celebrating?" I call after him as he disappears from my view.

When he returns, he hands me the glasses, pops the cork off the bottle, and pours the fizzy drink in the glasses.

"What are we celebrating?" I ask again.

"That you got your key."

"Oh." My stomach drops a tad. "I'd rather we celebrate after the opening."

"No." Logan takes my feet in his lap, making me lose my balance for a split second. "It's important to stop and celebrate little milestones too. It helps you recharge and have energy even when you still have a lot of work ahead of you."

I smile. "You always say the right thing."

"I've been in your position. I don't want you to be overwhelmed."

Which is exactly how it is, but with Logan next to me, I don't feel like I carry the weight of the entire world on my shoulders.

Clinking my glass against his, I tip it back, tasting the bubbles. The fireplace, the champagne. . . God, this man makes it hard for me to remember why keeping my walls up around him is a good idea. His charm disarms me. I take in the sight of his glorious body, the ridges and lines of his toned chest visible underneath the thin, white shirt. Desire stirs between my thighs and my breathing becomes more labored. Just when I thought this night couldn't get any better, he starts massaging my feet.

"Oh, this is heaven," I murmur, closing my eyes. His hands work wonders on my tired feet. *God, why does this man have to be so amazing?* I feel so many things when I'm around him. Right now, I'm spoiled and safe—which scares me. Not many people have made me feel safe.

When I open my eyes, I find him staring at me hungrily, his eyes dark with lust. *Oh, my.* I take my feet away, sipping from my champagne glass.

"I'm sorry about cutting our date short tonight," he says. "Pippa—"

I hold my hand up to silence him. "Don't worry. You never have to apologize for that. Family comes first, I understand."

Logan's eyes cloud. Instinctively, I scoot closer to him, looking for a way to soothe him.

"That's probably the best motto to describe me. It's always been like that."

"It *should* be like that."

"So, it doesn't bother you?"

"Why would it?"

"It did bother plenty of women I've dated. They felt they came second after my family, and weren't happy with it. I had a fiancée, Sylvia, a few years ago. She broke up with me over this. Summer needed help with one of her first galleries, and I was spending most of my free time with her, which meant I had to cut back on a lot of the time I spent with Sylvia. I told her she could hang out at Summer's with me.

"She didn't have to do anything, just be there, but that proposition didn't go over too well. I felt guilty for leaving her alone too much, but one night she came clean and told me she was leaving me. She said she had filled her long hours alone with the pool boy."

I barely suppress a gasp. Logan's tone is neutral, as if all this means nothing to him, but the deep lines in his forehead tell another story.

"She threw it in my face that I practically pushed her to do it, and if I continued, I'd have to settle for the idea that any woman I'll be with will find someone on the side to fill the time when I leave her to hurry to my family's side. She felt she always came in second place for me."

I stare at him, absolutely stunned. I can see on his features that the betrayal still hurts, and hell, I can't blame him. I'd be hurting too. I search for appropriate words. My first instinct is to name-call the vixen, but that wouldn't be the best course.

"Anyone who believes they're in competition with your family is not worth your time."

Logan's lips curve up, and the smile reaches his eyes. I breathe a sigh of relief, surprised again, by how important this man's happiness is to me.

"Sorry for bringing Sylvia up. Exes talk doesn't make for an exciting date conversation, even if this is a pseudo-date."

"For the record, this date is realer than many others I've had."

"I wanted you to know this is who I am. That'll never change. When my family needs help, I'll be there for them."

I lace my hands at the back of his neck. "I wouldn't want you to change. This is one of the things I love most about you."

Logan licks his lips. "What else do you *love?*"

Uh-oh. It's about a million days too early to drop the L-bomb, no matter the context, so I switch gears to a playful answer. Playful, but true nonetheless. "Your ass in a suit. It's round and perfect."

"Wait until you see it out of a suit."

"I'm trembling already."

"You should, because I can't wait to see your sweet ass out of those jeans, and I will. Tonight."

His words drip with so much authority and power that I instantly soak the fabric of my thong. There's something insanely sexy about a man who knows what he wants and goes straight for it.

Logan pulls me closer to him, and just when I think he'll kiss my mouth, he dips his head, planting his lips on my neck. I gasp in surprise and delight. He curls an arm around my waist, yanking me up from the floor and pulling me closer. As if it's the most natural thing in the world, I open my legs, planting them on either side of him before sitting on his lap, our groins inches apart. *How on earth did I end up in his lap again?*

Instead of questioning this further, I lean into his kiss, and things heat up quickly from there. With every stroke of his tongue, I want more. His hands roam across my back and thighs. Needing to be closer to him, I slide forward, until our groins touch. I moan, and Logan groans a low sound deep in his throat that makes me crave even more. As the kiss grows wilder, I can't keep my body still. I fidget and squirm, and then realize we're practically dry humping.

"Touch me." The second the words leave my mouth, my face flames white-hot. The shame only lasts a bit, need overpowering it.

"I am touching you," he teases.

"Please."

"Nadine." My name from his mouth sounds primal.

He flips me on my back and I yelp in surprise, afraid I'll fall. I cling tightly to his neck as he lays me on the carpet, looking at me briefly before diving in for another kiss. When his hand touches the button of my jeans, my entire body squirms in anticipation. A new wave of want hits me as he unzips them. Pushing my jeans down, Logan pulls back. Even though I still have my top and (tiny) thong on, I feel completely naked.

"You're beautiful." His hoarse voice does things to me. When he leans forward once more, he rests on one forearm, his other hand reaching down to my inner thighs. He traces his fingers first on one, then the other. I quiver beneath his touch and reach for his fly, but he shakes his head.

"Tonight is just for you."

"But won't you. . ." I glance at the bulge in his pants and need no further proof that he is just as aroused as I am.

Feathering his lips over mine, he mutters, "Trust me, giving you pleasure is the most exquisite thing."

"Logan. . ."

"I want to show you how you can only receive things, and how good it can be."

He pulls my thong between his fingers in one thick line of fabric and rubs it against my wet folds.

"Holy—Ah!" I arch my back. "Logan."

"I love watching you like this. You flush so beautifully." He leans in to kiss my collarbone, then up my neck. He releases the fabric, so my thong covers my mound again. Pulling back, he gives me a heated look, dropping his eyes to my lips, my breasts, and between my legs.

"I love to see you soaked for me."

"So much stalling," I say in a breathy voice. "Whatcha gonna do about it?"

"First, I'm going to tease you some more."

That wasn't the answer I expected. Logan spreads my thighs farther apart and runs his fingers up each of my folds, over my panties.

"Fuck." The feeling of the slick fabric over my sensitive skin is too much. I lick my lips, pushing into his fingers.

"Greedy girl."

"Logan."

Finally, *finally*, he slips his hand underneath my thong, pressing his palm against my sensitive clit. I arch against him.

"Tell me, beautiful. What do you want?"

"You know what I want." My thighs are quivering with need.

"Do you want me to slip one finger inside you?"

"Yes."

With exquisite slowness, he inserts one finger.

"Oh, God," I gasp, my inner walls clenching around him. He makes a 'come here' motion that prompts my skin to prickle all over my body. When he slides in a second finger, I'm a goner. He starts moving his fingers in a maddening tempo until exquisite pleasure ripples through my body. I come hard against his hand, chanting my release against his lips.

"That was... Wow," I say.

"You are amazing."

"You deserve all the accolades. I didn't do anything."

"Oh, you did more than you know."

Licking his lips, Logan then plants a gentle kiss on mine. I want to pull him to me for more, but he says, "Nadine, my self-control already hangs on a thin thread. If I kiss you again, I'll lose it, and when I make love to you, I want to be able to take my sweet time with you." My breath catches. *When*. Not *if*.

"This doesn't have anything to do with anticipation, does it?" I narrow my eyes at him, as I get dressed.

"Maybe it does," he says playfully. "Let me show you to your room." He takes my hand as he leads me through the apartment. The bedrooms are adjacent and, in the doorway, Logan says, "Think about me while you sleep."

"I didn't bring anything to sleep in," I realize. "Just fresh clothes for tomorrow."

"I can give you a shirt."

Two can play this anticipation game of his. Deciding to be naughty, I say, "I'll sleep naked. Think about *that* while you sleep."

Chapter Nine

Nadine

I wake up with a big grin in the morning. It takes me a minute to realize why I'm not in my bed, and why I'm smiling.

Logan.

I rise from the bed and head straight to the bathroom. I use his shower gel to wash; it smells like him, and I imagine that Logan is in here with me. God, the things he did with his hand last night… To take my mind off the heated moment—because otherwise, I'll be frustrated the entire day—I do what I love most in the shower: sing obnoxiously at the top of my lungs.

After I step out of the tub, I dress in the clothes I brought yesterday and head to the kitchen, a delicious smell guiding me. To my astonishment, I find the table set and plenty of food on it.

"And here I was, thinking you not only sleep but also eat breakfast naked," Logan says. Holy wow. I've only seen Logan wearing suits. Now he sports a pair of washed-out jeans and a simple white T-shirt.

Casual looks good on him. In fact, more than good. The fabric molds to his skin, showcasing his to-die-for body even more so than his work shirts. The jeans hang low on his hips, giving me a glimpse of his gorgeous V-shaped side abs. Today will be excruciating.

"You wish," I respond when I finally remember how to speak. My mouth waters as I inspect the food. And even more when I inspect Logan. I make an effort to concentrate on the food; otherwise, I might be tempted to rip off his T-shirt, and then we won't leave the apartment today. *Priorities, priorities. Right, back to food appreciation.*

"Where did all this come from? Your fridge was empty last night."

"I had someone buy breakfast for us and some other things. Come on; eat up. Long day ahead."

I sit at the table silently, wishing I'd have the words to tell him how much this means to me. No one's ever made me breakfast. When I was a kid, I prepared my own and made sure Mom didn't starve herself. After my mom got back on her feet, she always left for work before I woke up, so I ate by myself.

"You can still back out of helping me."

"No chance. By the way, I'm sure you are a woman of many talents, but your singing skills are terrible."

It completely slipped my mind that he might hear me. "Oh, well, I can't wait to show you my other talents." I wink at him.

"What might those be?"

"I won't tell you yet. A girl's got to have her secrets."

Logan narrows his eyes. "Will you be naked when you show me those skills?"

"You perv."

He holds up his palms in defense. "I can't help it. Someone teased me right before I went to sleep. Gave me the biggest case of blue balls since I was in high school."

I burst out laughing, shaking my head.

Inspecting the full table, I ask, "Why is there food for five people?"

Logan tilts his head to one side. "We'll do a lot of physical work today, so we need a good breakfast."

"Logan, you don't have to help me. I'm sure you can find better things to do on a Saturday."

"Not at all." He surprises me by rounding the table and hugging me from behind, his teeth grazing my earlobe. "I can't wait to see you sweat. I might even be rewarded with small, delicious grunts. From all the hard work, of course."

Goosebumps form on the skin on my arms, and Logan chuckles. I wonder what he'd do if he knew about the goosebumps on my inner thighs, and the slickness between them. I fantasized about him the entire night, waking up panting, and this *so* isn't helping. But before I can decide on the best way to tease him, his phone rings.

"I'm helping you. It's not negotiable. Consider it a gift for me, fulfilling a guilty pleasure."

I consider it the nicest thing anyone's ever done for me.

He moves away and answers the call. While I chew my food, I can't help overhearing bits and pieces of his conversation, even if he's a good few feet away from the table. Most of it doesn't make sense, but when I hear the word *billion*, I almost choke on my croissant.

Most of the time, it's easy to forget who Logan is—CFO and stakeholder of a multi-billion dollar company. This man rubs elbows with the most important people in the country. This same man chose to date little ol' me, a girl from a small town with a big dream, and to spend his Saturday renovating a shithole instead of doing anything else.

After he finishes the conversation, he fills a plate with food and excuses himself, explaining he must send a few emails before we leave. He spends the rest of our breakfast typing on his laptop.

Afterward, on the way out of the apartment, he picks up a toolbox by the door.

"This wasn't here yesterday," I remark.

Logan chuckles. "You're perceptive. I had a driver bring me my toolbox from my parents' house this morning."

"I have tools back at the shop. You don't need to bring it with you."

Logan feigns shock. "Of course I have to. I need my toys, can't play with someone else's."

I do a double take. "You have to stop doing that."

"What?" he asks innocently.

"Throwing around sexual innuendos all the time."

"I have no idea what you're talking about. I was speaking from a technical perspective. Not my fault you have a dirty mind." He winks at me, adding, "Seriously. Every man needs his tools." Then he wiggles his eyebrows.

Right. No innuendo there.

***

When we step into the store, the monstrosity of the task hits me. If I were alone, I might crumble underneath it, but with Logan at my side, it seems manageable.

"First things first," he says. "I suggest we cover the windows with paper."

"Why?"

"It'll maintain an air of mystery. Wouldn't you rather have the people who pass by wonder what's going on inside rather than see all the gritty steps of renovation?"

"Building anticipation, I understand."

"Exactly. You're a fast learner. Let them wonder."

As we cover the windows, I'm thinking there is some merit to this anticipation theory, because even *I* wonder what we'll be doing inside.

Once done, I show him my list. "Let's start with the first two points."

Logan nods. "That's a great place to start."

As we start working, it becomes clear he's a pro at this. I sigh. Seeing him doing physical tasks has me squirming and imagining… things.

"Do you want me to nail this for you?" Logan's baritone voice booms between heavy breaths.

Unfortunately, my brain picks out only the words "nail" and "you," and my imagination goes completely off the rails. *Yes, Logan, you can absolutely nail me.* Only when he asks, "Nadine?" do I realize he's waiting for my answer.

"Yes, please," I say breathlessly. "You are excellent at this stuff. How come?"

"There was a lot of physical work to do at my parents' ranch when we were kids. There was almost always something to renovate, and Sebastian and I helped Dad. After Sebastian left for the city, I did most of the work. Even now, my dad likes to do stuff himself. I go out and help because the old man is stubborn and doesn't understand that he's not supposed to fix the roof at sixty, so I go and make sure he's okay. That's why I have a toolbox there."

Every other man in his position would send someone over to help his dad. Not Logan. I want to hug him. But if I do, I'll kiss him too, and the whole thing will escalate quickly. There's enough sexual tension as it is. Who knew there could be anything sexy about sweat and dust?

As I hear Logan breathe hard, and even occasionally grunt, I can't help but sneak glances at him then admonish myself. I have to pay attention, or accidents might happen. More than once, I find my concentration sliding as I ogle him instead of doing my task.

My prediction comes true not five seconds later, when I accidentally spill water on Logan's shirt, soaking it. Now, here's the thing. I'm not a clumsy person, not at all. But being around Logan seems to change that. He's a danger to my mind, and my senses.

"If you wanted to see me shirtless, all you had to do was ask," Logan says with a lazy smile. "It wasn't necessary to get me all wet."

I lick my lips as I watch him remove his shirt, laying it on a radiator. *Holy smokes.* Now this… This is beyond distracting. The man is a work of art. My vision roams over his chest and abs, over the V-shaped dent pointing downward. With a wink, Logan goes back to working as if he didn't just make my ovaries explode. He could wear his jacket, but why would he? Teasing me is more fun. Also, if I'm honest, he'd be too hot if he wore it. Taking deep breaths, I follow suit, concentrating on my tasks. Over the next few hours, I do manage to do that, save for the glances I sneak every now and again. I think I'm doing an excellent job of not being obvious until he says, "Like what you see?"

"You're great eye candy," I offer. He holds up his right hand as if saying, *Not my fault.* Except it is, it's entirely his fault for having a body made for sin.

"You'd better use both hands to fix that board," I warn him.

He wiggles his eyebrows. "I can do great things with just one hand."

I gulp, remembering the way he touched me last night. "I completely agree."

For the next hour, I keep my eyes focused on the task at hand, though my mind travels to dirty land again.

"You're dirty," Logan says unexpectedly. I blush, wondering if he can truly read my mind, before I realize we're both covered in a thick layer of dust.

"So are you." I drink in the sight of his muscular frame again. Then I notice he's watching me.

"You have an unfair advantage," he says, pinning me with his dark eyes.

"What do you mean?"

"I'm half-naked. You're not."

I lick my lips. "Lucky me."

"Let's get some of this dust off you."

Before I realize what's going on, Logan disappears in the back, returning with a glass full of water. He picks up one of the brand new brushes, and dips it in the glass. I follow his movements as he grabs my hand, turning it wrist up. Logan runs the soaked brush over my skin in one light touch. The patch of skin between my legs slickens instantly, and I involuntarily press my thighs together.

"Oh." The word slips past my lips in a moan. How can one simple swipe turn me on like this? As if it's the most natural thing in the world, Logan pushes my shirt up until my strapless bra is visible. Tugging with his teeth on his lower lip, his hand pushes it downward until my breasts spill free. His Adam's apple dips low in his throat as his eyes lock on my girls.

"You really are very talented with just one hand," I say.

"Thought you needed some cleaning here too." His voice is rough. God, we're both so turned on, it's a miracle we can see straight anymore. When Logan touches one of my nipples with the brush, I see stars in front of my eyes.

"My nipples are especially dirty, huh?" I manage to ask.

"Especially." His breath catches as I dip my fingers in the water then torture him, running my hand all over his chest, descending lower and lower until I reach the fly of his pants. Logan's nostrils flare, as if he's having trouble breathing. His eyes are locked on my breasts.

"Now what?" I inquire.

"Now, back to work," he says.

The bastard. Why does he have to be such a tease? I'll have my revenge.

We work for another three hours before I give in. Every muscle in my body hurts from the exertion, not to mention sexual frustration. Facing the paper-covered windows, I tilt my head to the right then to the left, squaring my shoulders in an attempt to relieve some of the tension.

"Tense much?" Logan whispers in my ear, startling me. I hadn't heard him come up behind me.

"Mmm. A little."

He presses his fingers on my spine, pushing them farther up. The second they slide from my shirt onto my bare skin, I shudder. Before long, both his hands massage the base of my neck and shoulders. They are rough and calloused—all man, yet at the same time, they glide effortlessly against my skin. He presses on the exact pain points as if he has a degree in massaging.

"This is good. Oh, Logan."

"Stop those sounds, Nadine." His voice is equal parts desire and torment.

"Why?" I ask.

He groans in my ear, and it's the sexiest sound I've heard all day. Involuntarily, I flatten my back against his chest, and my hips follow. That's when I feel his hard-on against my ass. Logan drops his hands from my shoulders, wrapping me in his arms. I still.

"Because I was planning on taking you out to dinner then making love to you at home, in an actual bed. I've clung to that thought all day. It was a good plan." He drops his head in the crook of my neck, his hot, labored breaths singeing my skin. I've never felt more wanted.

At the same time, I've never felt safer. I had no idea a man could awaken both feelings inside me, much less at the same time, but Logan is unlike any man I've ever met. "You know what the best thing about plans and rules are?"

"What?" I'm shocked to discover I'm trembling in his arms. It's more of a light shiver, but it's impossible to miss.

"Breaking them."

Logan flips me around, pressing his lips on mine. I grin against his mouth, before giving in to his kiss.

"Let's move to the shower," he says after we pull apart. For a few seconds I'm confused, still lost in the bliss of the kiss. Then I understand—there's a small shower in the shop's bathroom. I'm planning to eventually remove it since it'll have no use for my buyers. But for now, for Logan and me, it'll have an *excellent* use.

I nod fervently. "Let's go." My fingers tremble and, when he takes my hand, I notice his do the same. We both have so much sexual tension bottled up, we're charging the air around us. Once inside the small bathroom, it becomes unbearable.

"I want to see you naked, Nadine."

We take each other's clothes off in one minute flat until I remain in only my thong. The sight of his muscular body takes my breath away. I'm too turned on even to talk, but he isn't.

"You're so sexy."

He hooks one thumb in my panties, but instead of taking his time to push them down, he rips them apart. I smile, content to feel his desperation.

"Sorry about that." His voice comes out as a growl.

"I'm not."

"I can't wait to hear you beg, Nadine."

"I don't beg," I reply.

Cupping my jaw, he tips my head up to him. "You *will* beg me. I promise."

I quiver under his molten gaze, but don't find it in myself to argue. Instead, I'm looking forward to Logan keeping his promise.

I turn on the water as we step into the small shower. I put some shower gel here when I brought my supplies for the renovation, so I could freshen myself up during work. Now I've found an even better use for it.

I pour shower gel in Logan's palms and mine, and run my hands all over his torso. His abs are even harder than I imagined. His skin seems to heat up under my fingers.

"Touch yourself," he says. My eyes widen, but I obey. "Touch your breasts. They're gorgeous."

I run my fingers around my nipples. Damn, they're so sensitive that they hurt. Logan lowers his hand to his erection, wraps his palm around it, and strokes himself up and down. The sight is too much for me; my body burns, yearning for him to touch me.

"Change of plans. I want you to touch me," I say.

"Demanding girl." Letting go of his shaft, his hands find my breasts and he touches them expertly. But he's teasing me, the bastard. He circles the skin around my nipples, without actually touching them, driving me crazy. Two can play at this game, so I set out on a mission: make him lose control. I grip his erection, running my palm up and down then up again, rubbing my thumb across the head. Logan takes a breath through gritted teeth.

"Oh, fuck. Nadine," he grunts out my name, taking a breath through gritted teeth. While I continue to stroke him, he parts my knees with his legs, exposing me. Dropping one hand between my legs, he runs his finger across my folds, up and down. He mimics my moves on his erection, driving me craaaaaazy.

"Need. Touch." My voice is low and breathy. "Inside me. Now."

"No full sentences," he murmurs. "I like that. You know what I'd like more? To hear you beg."

Gathering all my faculties, I force myself to say a full sentence. Now, both my hands are fisting his hair. "If you're not inside me in two seconds, you'll be sorry, Logan Bennett."

"Menacing. Sounds sexy. Still not what I want to hear."

He flicks my nipple with one hand and pinches my clit with the other. My hips buck against his, and his erection rubs against my inner thigh.

"Fuck, fuck, fuck. I need to be inside you right now, woman."

I chuckle. "Really? I'll tease you some more."

Abruptly, he flips me around, my ass brushing his crotch in the process. We both gasp.

He nudges his knee between my legs, parting them once again. Then he slaps his erection against my slit, setting my body on fire. I swallow hard, my knees threatening to give in.

"Please, Logan. I need you. I beg you."

"Grip the shower railing." His voice comes out as a growl. "You'll need to hold on to something."

He steps out of the shower briefly and retrieves a condom from his jeans, putting it on. He glances at me once, smiling devilishly, before entering the shower again. I grip the railing as he instructed while he peppers my back with kisses. The chaste pecks make me shiver. I grip the railing tighter when I feel him poised at my entrance.

"You're so wet, Nadine. I love this."

He slides the tip of his erection inside me then pulls back out. He repeats the in-and-out movement a few times, only with the tip, touching a spot inside me that makes me hungry for all of him. Nibbling at my earlobe with his teeth, he says, "You're tight, babe."

"God, Logan. Please. I need all of you inside me. Now."

"Your wish is my command."

He enters me slowly, inch by inch. As I take him in, my inner walls clench around him with delight and protest.

"Fuck, you're big," I say, leaning my head back.

He kisses the exposed side of my neck. He pulls out then slams back into me hard. Logan makes love to me in a maddening rhythm, flicking my nipples with his fingers.

"This is so good, Nadine."

Feeling his hot breath against my earlobe is amazing. Feeling him inside me is almost too much to bear. My entire body is on fire, desperate for release. Logan drives into me even harder, dropping one hand to my clit.

"I'm so close," he whispers, circling my clit until my legs buckle. I grasp the railing even harder, moving my other hand behind me to grip his neck. A crushing pressure forms inside me, threatening to undo me. *Oh, God.* I will come so hard I might pass out. When he starts widening inside me, my thighs quiver.

"Logan—"

"Now!"

I come harder than I ever have, tremors overcoming me as we both ride our orgasms out. Afterward, Logan holds me in his arms until I calm down, kissing my shoulder gently.

***

"Let's wrap this up for today," Logan says as we dress. His shirt is finally dry, and he puts it on.

"More than agree. I can't even feel my body."

Logan grins, running a hand through his hair. "Now, that's not only because of the work, is it?"

I fold my arms over my chest, enjoying the banter. "Not sure. I do recall doing something equally exerting that was also fun."

Logan puts one hand on the side of my ear. "What else could be at fault for it?"

"You're going to make me say it out loud, aren't you?"

"Yeah. That big ego you keep hearing about? I need to feed it with something. So, tell me."

"Can't remember. I guess I need to be reminded."

"Challenge accepted." He kisses my forehead. "I want us to head home first."

"Let's go," I say.

"Let me check something before we leave."

"Okay." He goes to the front room while I remain in the bathroom, freshening up. When I join him in the front, he's pacing around the room, sporting a frown.

"What's wrong?"

"I have bad news. The floor is rotten."

"No." I freeze. "The owner said there was no need for ground renovations."

"He lied so you'd sign without bringing a specialist to check the place. I was rather suspicious when he told you to sign right away. In all my years of business, whenever someone gave me an ultimatum, there was something fishy going on."

"I checked the place, but it didn't even cross my mind that he was lying to my face."

"I can have your contract canceled, and I can make that moron very sorry, just say the word."

"No."

Logan narrows his eyes. "That wasn't the word I expected."

Massaging my temples, I calculate a few things. "Even with this roadblock and his lie, this is still the best deal I can find. The location is excellent and…"

"Fine, keep the location," Logan hisses through gritted teeth. "I can still make the asshole sorry."

"I'll give him a piece of my mind when I see him. Please, don't get involved, okay? I can handle this."

Logan still shoots daggers with his eyes, but I hold his gaze until he nods. "I know this is a setback."

"Setback" is an elegant way of saying I'm screwed. Depending on what caused the rotting in the first place, and how far the damage extends, this will delay my ability to open the store for a few weeks, if not a month, even with Logan helping. That means another month where I only have costs with the rent and no revenue. One step forward, two back. Story of my life. Can't catch a break. If there's an asshole within a hundred-mile radius, I'll find him and let him scam me. I might as well take this as the warning sign it is: I should concentrate on my business one hundred percent.

"I'll be all right" is all I say out loud. "I always am, eventually. I'll figure something out." *Like how to survive on even less money.*

"We'll figure something out together, okay?" Cupping my cheeks, he kisses my forehead. "Let's go home now."

"I really should sleep at my place tonight. I don't have anything to change into for tomorrow."

"We'll go to your place so you can pack some things, and then we'll go to my apartment, okay?

Nadine, let me take care of you. I don't want you to be alone. Besides, I still have a challenge to fulfill. I must remind you why you're sore. Can't very well do that if we're not in the same place. Or do I have to use the 'extra sleep' card again?"

I laugh. "Great. Now you have an even stronger card than extra sleep. Extra sex."

Two thoughts war within me. One is that I should keep my distance from him, go back to my apartment, and draft out a fight plan for the next few months, taking this setback into account. The other thought is that I can't possibly face being alone in my crappy apartment when the alternative is spending the night with this amazing man. Under Logan's stubborn gaze, the second trail of thought wins. I'll stop overanalyzing this and just enjoy it, for however long it lasts.

"Let's go."

* * *

We take a short trip to my apartment. I intend only to grab clothes for tomorrow, but Logan makes me pack for several days.

Once we return to his apartment, he instructs, "Go into the bedroom and strip."

"Well, that was straightforward." I can't help smiling the entire time I undress in his bedroom. I expect him to burst inside any minute now. Instead, he tells me to step out of the room and come in the bathroom. Sex in the tub. That sounds very appealing. Opening the door to the bathroom, I can't believe my eyes. There's a bubble bath waiting for us.

"I prepared a hot bath for you." He emphasizes the word you, while his eyes travel hungrily up and down my body. "Relax in it while I make you dinner."

"Logan, I... Wow."

"Told you I'd take care of you."

Feeling my eyes beginning to sting, I turn around, pretending to concentrate on the bathtub. I'm used to taking care of others, not the other way around. Logan's setting the bar pretty high for any man who'll come after him.

When I slip inside, I relax almost instantly.

"This is perfect." I sink deeper in the water, watching Logan. His hair is wet, and he smells of mint shampoo or shower gel. "This could even make me forget that I'm only having you to myself for half a day tomorrow."

"I can—"

"Don't you even dare mention canceling on your parents."

He said that he usually visits his parents on Sunday afternoons, and I don't want him to change that for me. "Now, go and leave me alone. You're disturbing my relaxation juju."

He smiles. "Fine."

"Are you sure you don't want to join me?" I ask seductively.

"Nope. I'll get my share of you later. I'd like to make it to the bed with you this time around." He winks before leaving.

I enjoy the bubbles and wonder if I'm making a mistake by spending time with Logan. He's wonderful, of course, but my track record with men is proof that I should thread carefully. *Should I stay over today too?* I run my hands over my thighs, remembering how he made love to me. This man is talented in bed—or, well, in the shower. The things he made me experience were out of this world. He's a true charmer out of bed too. He's slowly winning me over—helping me, making me laugh, and spoiling me. Oh, what the heck. Why should it be a mistake to give in to a man who treats me like a princess? I can let him rock my world, even if it's just temporary.

By the time I finish with the bath and step out into the living room, I decide not to overthink this. I will simply let this amazing man woo me.

I find him in the kitchen. He changed into a fresh pair of jeans. These, too, hang low on his hips, fueling my imagination.

"Whatcha cooking?" I ask him.

"Tenderloin beef with mango salsa."

"Wow, this sounds fancy."

"Nothing but the best for the lady. I must impress you enough so you won't have second thoughts about staying over tonight." He glances at me from the corner of his eyes.

"I was thinking about that in the tub. How did you know?"

He turns to me. "I could tell you were afraid this is moving a little too fast."

"Is it?"

He smiles. "Maybe, but who cares? As long as we're happy, I don't see what the problem is. I'll be honest. I don't know where this will lead, but let's not worry about that. Being around you makes me happy. Being inside you makes me even happier."

I roll my eyes at him. "You're such a man."

"And proud of it. Do I make you happy?"

"Very," I admit. "You spoil me."

"Glad you approve, because I plan to spoil you a lot more."

We fall into silence and, as I watch him proficiently cook, an unwanted truth slips out of my mouth. "No one's cooked for me in years, even before I moved to college."

"How come?" he asks with a frown.

I fold my arms over my chest, preparing to back out of the conversation because I haven't talked about this to any man I've dated. Instead, more truth slips past my lips.

"Mom was sick all the way into my high school years." *I can tell him the whole truth, can't I? He won't judge.* "She suffered from clinical depression, but didn't receive treatment until I was a high school sophomore. They were desperate years. I felt like the adult in our house most of the time."

His grip on the panhandle tightens. "Your dad?"

"Left when I was five."

I don't feel overwhelmed, the way I always do when I remember those hard years. Instead, I'm relieved. I tend to loosen my tongue when I'm around Logan. I trust him more than I've trusted another man, and that scares me.

"Now I understand," Logan murmurs, pushing the pan away from the stove before turning his attention to me.

"What?"

"Why you don't accept help easily."

"I do—" I catch myself. "I really don't, do I?"

"Nope." He smiles brightly, his delicious dimples making an appearance. "You don't trust people will stick around, or follow through on their promises. But don't worry, I'm more stubborn than you are."

I appreciate his light, playful tone and that he isn't prodding me with more questions.

"Let's eat. I'm starving."

"Sure. Can you give me some plates? They're in the cabinet behind you."

I take out the plates and, when I turn around to Logan, I catch him in a compromising position.

"You're checking out my ass, aren't you?" I ask him.

"Guilty." Grinning, he adds, "In my defense, you have a fine, fine ass."

After dinner, we start kissing in the living room, never making it to the bedroom.

This man will turn my world upside down.

Will I survive it?

Chapter Ten

Nadine

Waking up in Logan's bed instantly brightens my morning. We only eat a quick breakfast then head to the store.

"How long can you stay today?" I ask on the way there. "Until you leave for your parents' house?"

"Oh, I don't have to go anymore." Logan peers at me cheerfully.

"What? No, Logan." I come to a halt, elbowing him. "Sunday is your family day. I don't want you to miss it."

"I'm not going to miss it. Now, move your delicious ass or we'll be late, and last I checked, you had a million things on your to-do list."

"Don't mock my to-do list. It's the only thing keeping me afloat. And coffee. Let's not forget coffee."

"I don't even get an honorary mention?"

"I'll consider putting you after coffee."

Logan's mouth forms an O. "You've wounded my pride."

"You're distracting me from your family thing. What did you do? Why don't you have to go?"

"Hurry up, you'll see."

Closer to the store, he adds, "Remember what I said about not overthinking our relationship?"

"Yeah."

"Good. Hold on to that, because I'm about to introduce you to my parents."

"You—huh?"

I sneak glances at Logan as we walk, but he doesn't show signs of wanting to continue the conversation. I focus on the birds chirping all around us instead, wondering how they can be so energetic and cheerful in the morning. I've always envied them.

When we arrive at the store, I see exactly what Logan meant. His entire family plus Ava is camping in front of my shop, carrying toolboxes and wearing rags.

Ava and Pippa wave at me.

"We arrived a few minutes too early, but the shop across the road has excellent coffee," Ava says.

"The cupcakes are also yummy," Pippa adds.

My cheeks turn red. Now I understand why Logan was in a hurry.

"Let's get introductions out of the way, shall we?" Logan says. "Nadine, this is my mom, Jenna, and my dad, Richard." I shake hands with his parents.

Logan looks exactly like his father; they have the same tall, muscular build and dark eyes. His mother is small and there's something very feminine about her, even though she's wearing a pair of jeans and a

T-shirt. Alice is her spitting image. "You already know Pippa and Alice." Both of them smile at me. "This is Summer."

Summer is a beauty. To her sides are two of the brothers I haven't met.

"And these are—" Logan begins.

"Blake and Daniel," I finish for him. He frowns as everyone walks into the store, except for the twins and us.

Blake cracks a smile. "Ah, we don't even need an introduction."

"Our reputation precedes us," Daniel says.

"You've met?" Logan asks doubtfully.

"Ava showed me a family picture," I say.

"And out of the gazillion Bennetts in it, she remembers us," Blake says. "You have fantastic taste."

"I beg to differ," Daniel says. "She would've had great taste if she went out with one of us. Instead, she chose Logan."

The twins grin and, even though their appearance is nothing alike, their grins are similar. Daniel winks at me, and I decide to play this for all it's worth.

"There are some delicious male genes in this family," I affirm, and Logan growls.

Seemingly satisfied with having gotten their brother riled up, the twins enter the store.

"Delicious genes, huh?" Logan asks, encircling my waist.

"Easy, caveman. You're so territorial. They're your brothers; we were messing with you." After a pause, I add, "What is everyone doing here?"

"Well," Logan starts, "remember how I told you I have a family thing today?"

"Yeah."

"And you needed major renovation help, so I decided to ask them if they'd like to join us here. That way, you have a renovation team, and I spend the day with you *and* them. Everybody wins."

Biting the inside of my cheek, I look inside the store as the family mills around. "I'm not sure how much of a win it is for them. I mean, I'm sure they had way better plans for their Sunday."

"Nadine, relax." He takes my hands in his. "My family loves to help. I've told them about you and—"

"When did you tell them about me?" I ask suspiciously.

"While you were in the tub last night. Also, I told them about the rotten floor. We're going to fix it."

"Thank you for doing this," I tell him. Mentally, I calculate how much time this one day will save me.

As if reading my mind, Logan says, "That'll cut your work time."

"Yes. Maybe I can even open before Christmas. Ohhh, I can't wait to decorate my store."

"You have a miles-long to-do list, and the first thing on your mind is Christmas decorations?"

"Hey, a girl needs to have her priorities straight."

"Indeed."

"How can I thank you for doing this?"

"Mmm, I can think of a few ways. I'll whisper them to you tonight when we're alone. Now, let's work."

Once inside, Logan says, "Listen up everyone. Nadine will tell you everything that needs to be done, and then we'll divide the work among us."

I tell them everything as quickly as possible. While I list the tasks, the Bennetts exchange glances, pointing at each other, already dividing everything among themselves. I have a feeling they've done this before. While I'm certain the older siblings had to shoulder a lot of the physical work at the ranch, that need wasn't there anymore when the twins and Summer grew up. Yet they all look ready to work. I can't believe my luck to have them on my side. After taking a punch at every turn, this seems almost too good to be real.

"You don't worry, Nadine," Mr. Bennett tells me. Putting a hand over my shoulder, he adds, "We'll take care of this together. Everything will work out."

I blink, staring at my hands, my eyes stinging all of a sudden. *What must it be like to grow up with a dad—a family—you can count on?*

"It's a good thing we each brought a toolbox," Sebastian says, pointing at the twins and his dad. "That way, there'll be no waiting time."

"You each have a toolbox?" I ask, my eyebrows raised.

"Men and their toys," Pippa says. "Don't try to understand."

"I brought no toolbox, just my humor," Summer chimes in. "I can't hit a nail to save my life, but I can crack jokes."

"You're not wiggling your way out of this, little sister," Pippa admonishes her. "You're here to work, not entertain."

"I'm happy to do work if you find something that won't put me at risk of cutting my fingers," Summer retorts.

Within seconds, Pippa finds Summer a job cleaning the back room. "No danger of harming yourself here, Summer."

I was expecting Summer to protest, but she happily nods. "This place will be kick-ass," she remarks.

"Thank you. I have great plans for it."

"Let us know if there's anything we can do to help," Alice offers. "I opened a restaurant, and Summer regularly has events at galleries. We have some experience."

"That's very kind of you to offer."

"Girls have to stick together." Alice winks at me.

Pippa looks at her with disbelief. "Since when is that your creed? You always wanted to be one of the boys when we were young."

"I grew up," Alice says, throwing her hands in the air, though I have a slight suspicion there is more to it than she says. By the way Pippa looks at her, she thinks so too. Not wanting to see Alice cornered, I step in.

"You had in-family gangs?" I ask.

All three girls roll their eyes. "When you have so many siblings, there's no other way. We had cliques," Pippa says.

"Pippa stuck with Sebastian and Logan," Alice says. "The twins each had their group. I was gravitating between everyone."

"And absolutely everyone loved me," Summer chirps. "Being the little sister has its perks."

"Oy," Sebastian calls from the front. "How about we don't make a working clique and a non-working clique? No one's allowed to slack. Come on."

With a smile, Summer heads to the back room. Pippa, Alice, and I start working on the walls while the twins and Logan take care of the rotten floor.

***

Logan

"I haven't worked this hard in years," Daniel complains as we work on the floor.

"Great. You should be reminded what hard work feels like now and again," I reply dryly. Blake and Daniel have lived the high life ever since our family started making money. When we set up the company, Sebastian and I decided to give every family member shares, so Blake and Daniel receive a good income without being involved in Bennett Enterprises. That's not to say they don't work… occasionally.

They do small projects of their own from time to time. Fun projects. One's more likely to find them partying on a yacht rather than working. The Bennett work ethic seems to have skipped these two. Sebastian says they'll get their shit together *eventually*. I say if we'd cut their monthly allowance, *eventually* would become *right now*. Yeah, I'm all for tough love. I should cut them some slack, though; they didn't hesitate to show up here today, and they'll always have my back. Family comes first for them too, just as it comes for me.

"Don't be a dick," Blake says.

"I'm not."

"I meant Daniel," Blake continues, winking at his twin before addressing him directly. "Nadine must be very special to him if he made us all bust our asses on a Sunday."

"She is," I reply.

Daniel shakes his head, moving on to patching up a portion of the floor a few feet away from Blake and me.

Nadine's with my sister on the opposite side of the room. I smile, seeing how well she blends with my family. I knew they would embrace her, but I wasn't sure how she'd react. I remember Sylvia scrunching her nose every time I mentioned my family, coming up with excuses to slip out of family gatherings. Thankfully, Nadine is nothing like her. In fact, she's unlike any woman I've dated. When I passed her and Summer earlier, my sister was telling Nadine how stressful the next gallery show would be. Instead of politely giving her sympathy, Nadine offered to help her in any way she could, even though she has a lot on her plate.

During our second date, she didn't hesitate to try to cheer up Pippa with a girls' night. Nadine always puts everyone else first. That's why that bastard ex of hers took advantage of her, but she didn't become bitter or hateful, which makes me admire her even more. Finding out about her childhood made many things click. This woman is a fighter, but even fighters need to rest. It's time someone took care of her, and I'm up to the challenge.

Right now, watching her from across the room, I know my relationship with her will not be like the ones I've had since Sylvia. I don't want superficial, and I'm not so sure about putting an expiration date on it. That last part scares the crap out of me.

Blake's staring at me.

"What?" I ask aggressively.

"I know that look," Blake says. "I patented it."

"What are you talking about?"

"That look says, 'I feel too close to this woman. It's time to panic and do something stupid.'"

"That might be your way, but not mine."

"Maybe. But you've still got that look," Blake continues with a proud smirk. "If you screw things up with Nadine, I'd be happy to take your place."

"Did you just make a pass at my woman?" A vein pulses in my neck as I grip the cloth in my hand tighter. "'Cause brother or not, I'll rearrange your face."

Blake breaks into laughter. "Relax, man. I wanted to prove a point."

"If I were you, I'd make that point quicker, or I'll punch you. So you realize I'm serious."

"You always were all 'shoot first, ask questions later.'"

"Point, Blake."

"The point is if you find a woman, and you can't stand the thought of losing her, keep her."

I loosen my grip on the cloth. "If you're an expert, why aren't you fighting for a woman?"

He shrugs. "'Cause I haven't found that woman yet."

I swallow a sardonic remark. Maybe I can learn something from my little brother, just this once.

***

Nadine

After Summer finishes cleaning the back room, Ava and I take over.

"This place will be beautiful once it's finished," Ava says.

"I can't believe this is finally happening."

"I'm so proud of you for sticking with your dream, even with all that happened."

Her words tug at my heartstrings. "I can't believe I have a roomful of people helping me."

"The Bennetts are lovely."

"I can't believe they're doing this for me."

"Well, technically they're doing it for Logan. But they all heard plenty about you, trust me. How *are* things with Logan, anyway?"

I drop my voice to a whisper, even though it's just us back here. "It feels like I've known him forever. He's... I had no idea men could be like him."

"You have to thank Mrs. Bennett for raising them the way she did. They're one of a kind."

"He's made me think about things I wanted to forget. Like love..."

"It's the Bennett effect, trust me," Ava tells me. "On our first date, I was daydreaming about the initials in my signature if I carried Sebastian's name."

"This man could get me pregnant by just looking at me," I sigh dramatically.

Ava elbows me so hard I nearly drop my bucket. "He did more than look at you, didn't he?"

"Yeah."

"Do tell," Ava beckons.

"Don't," Pippa says, having just entered the room. "I'm all for finding out the dirty details, but Mom's ears are finer than a rabbit's. She can hear gossip even through walls. I don't know about you, but I always thought moms had to be kept in PG-13 territory."

Ava and I burst out laughing.

"Why don't we do a girls' night out instead?" Pippa suggests.

"Sure. I have a ton of work, but I'm sure we can find some time," I reply. Also, I love the idea of having a group of girlfriends.

"Letting steam off is important. Though, by the sound of things, my brother's helping you plenty."

"So, you can hear through walls too?" I ask.

"Maybe," Pippa answers with a smile. "Or maybe I like to eavesdrop." Then Mrs. Bennett casually enters the room, asking us if we need any help. With a grin, I assure her we're fine.

After she leaves, Pippa asks no one in particular, "How is it that being around her always makes me feel like a teenager?"

"That's the effect moms have," I reply, thinking fondly of my own.

For the next two hours, everyone works hard. Except for Summer who, after finishing the tasks Pippa entrusted her with, has found herself with nothing to do. She brought everyone coffee from across the street, followed by sandwiches. After pumping coffee and food into each of us, she proceeded to talk everyone's ear off. Her current victim is Alice.

"Summer, I love you," Alice says, "but for Heaven's sake, how can you talk so much?"

Summer gives her the stink eye. "I spend hours alone each day. I love my art, but paintings don't talk back. So shut up and listen to me."

Alice rolls her eyes, but she continues to listen to Summer's rant, and even shares her opinion whenever Summer pauses for breath.

"I swear she's the most talkative of us all," Blake says.

"And she has no filter," Daniel adds. The twins are helping Pippa and me.

"Well, I will say she's the only one who calls you man-whores to your faces," Pippa says. At Daniel and Blake's stricken expressions, she adds, "Oops, I guess I just did too."

"I'm not. . ." Blake stutters. "I mean, lately, I haven't. . ."

"Dude, there's no need to pretend with Pippa," Daniel says. "She knows who we are. Good thing she also loves us, faults and all."

"So, what do you think?" Blake asks Daniel while eyeing Alice and Summer. "Should we save Alice before she turns deaf?"

Soon enough, Daniel and Blake gather around Summer. Alice inconspicuously leaves, winking at me.

***

We make a lot of progress. It's pitch dark outside when we finish, and I offer to buy everyone dinner, even though money is tight. It's the least I can do. They refuse, bringing up some very dubious excuses. I suspect it's because they want to leave Logan and me alone. Everyone leaves, except for Logan's parents and Blake.

"Nadine, I can come by this week and help," Mr. Bennett says.

"It's not necessary."

"Please, humor this retired man. I have nothing to do all day, and my wife refuses to let me repair the damn roof. I feel useless."

I glance at Logan to make sure I'm not crossing any boundaries, but he's smiling at his father. I nod. "Thank you."

"You're doing me a favor," Logan tells me as his parents bicker over Mr. Bennett's stubbornness.

"But you said you don't want your dad to do dangerous construction stuff," I reply.

"Trust me, there's nothing dangerous here. If he stays at home, he'll want to repair that damn roof." Dropping his voice to a whisper, Logan adds, "I had a brilliant idea. I can have someone repair the roof while he's here."

"Actually," Blake says loudly from across the room, "I'll join you and Dad, Nadine. I have some time off," he explains at my questioning glance.

"Thanks."

After the three of them leave, I stretch and say, "Why is your family doing all this?"

Logan pulls me into a hug, kissing my neck. I love being in this man's arms. No place in the world seems safer. "Because I asked them to, and we always back each other up. As opposed to Sebastian and Pippa, who are the epitomes of self-sufficiency, I ask for help when I need it."

I push him away with a smile. "So, that makes you perfect, doesn't it?"

"Oh, I have plenty of defects. Wait till you discover them all."

"What have you told them to convince them?" I insist.

"That I believe in you and your dream."

"How is it that you always have the right words?"

"It's all documented in my secret book of how to charm a woman." He pulls me into a kiss—dirty, raw, and perfect. I fist his hair, pressing my torso to his. His hard chest feels amazing against my breasts. A groan reverberates in his throat, masculine and dominant. It sends a jolt of heat between my thighs. *Damn, this man can kiss.* His strong hands cup my ass, sending more heat to my tender spot.

Then he pushes me away. "Come on, let's grab some dinner on the way home. I'm starving."

"We can buy a sandwich. The coffee shop is still open."

Logan snickers. "I need more than a tiny sandwich. I'm a big boy."

Naturally, my mind immediately goes to the gutter at the words "big boy." I sigh, remembering his lovemaking in the shop and later on his couch yesterday. "Mmm. You are a big boy indeed."

"I didn't mean *that.*" Logan throws his head back, laughing.

"I didn't realize I said it out loud." Blushing, I lick my lips.

"I'm not complaining." A boyish glint dances in his eyes. "So, I'm big?"

I narrow my eyes. "You know you are."

"I like hearing it." Tipping his head to me, he drops his voice to a conspiratorial whisper. "All men do."

"When they're teenagers, surely?"

"Nah, pretty much always. Let's go. I have great plans for us tonight."

***

We buy pizza with the intent to eat it after we arrive at the apartment, but end up eating it on the way. Turns out I was starving too.

"You shower first, I'll go after you," Logan says the second we enter his home.

"Why are we showering separately?" I ask. "Your shower is way bigger than the one at the shop. I foresee a hundred possibilities for sexy times in the shower."

"I foresee endless possibilities for that, and we'll try out all of them. But I want you in my bed tonight. If we shower together..." His voice is husky and full of promise, sending a shiver down my back. "Now, be a good girl and go."

Showering alone is torture, but I take the opportunity to make myself as flawless as possible. Afterward, I wait alone in Logan's bedroom. Unable to stay put, I walk from one side to the other, inspecting it. We were both exhausted when we entered it last night and fell asleep. This morning, we were in a hurry, so I haven't had a chance to look around. The massive bed with a leather headboard dominates the bedroom. Everything is clean and organized. Even though he told me he has a maid, I'm sure he's the one organizing his things. I suppose one doesn't achieve as much as he did without immaculate efficiency.

I never thought this particular trait to be sexy, but when it comes to Logan, it is. God, everything about this man is a turn-on. I feel his presence in the room before he speaks and turn around to face him. I have a towel wrapped around me. He's wearing absolutely nothing.

"Drop your towel, Nadine."

His voice drips masculinity and sex appeal. It has such a powerful effect on me, almost as if he touched me. Holding my breath, I do as he says.

He groans. "You have such a beautiful body."

I open my mouth with the intention of returning his compliment, but only an "Oh" comes out. His eyes turn darker.

"Lie on the bed."

Once again, I do as I'm told. In a fraction of a second, Logan is next to me, and he settles on his knees between my legs.

He puts his forefinger on my mound. "I want to kiss you here, Nadine."

"Yes."

"I've wanted to taste you all day."

Running his fingers across one inner thigh then the other, Logan nudges me to open even more for him. Resting on my elbows, I drop my thighs completely to the sides, exposing myself to him.

"So beautiful," he murmurs, his lips merely inches away from my swollen flesh. When he blows a cold puff of air on my heated center, I yelp in surprise. He drags his fingers up and down my folds in a slight caress, and I fist the sheet with both hands to keep from buckling against him. He lowers his head, swiping his tongue in a slight touch over my folds.

"Oh, God, Logan." Closing my eyes, I shudder.

"So sweet." Finally, he places his mouth, hot and firm, on my sensitive flesh. First, he focuses on my clit, his lips nibbling and sucking it expertly.

"Holy fuck," I cry.

I swear to God, I'm going to grab his head and make love to his face if he doesn't give me my release soon. But I know he's not going to be that merciful with me. He presses his lips harder on my clit, and I'm certain I'll explode. Then Logan puts one finger inside me, torturing me even further.

"Logan," I pant, pressing my feet deeper into the bed. When he inserts another finger, stretching me, pleasuring me, I squirm, my entire body sizzling. I touch myself, rolling my nipples between my fingers, hoping to quench the fire. Instead, I'm intensifying it.

I cry in protest when Logan unhitches his mouth from my clit.

"You're so fucking sexy." His eyes focus on my hands, which are currently torturing my nipples while his fingers torture my pussy. He curves his fingers inside me, and I nearly pass out.

"Come on, Nadine. I want to feel you clench around my fingers."

"I want your tongue," I manage to say. Logan's eyes darken instantly.

"Your wish is my command."

He pulls back his fingers, leaving me cold and empty for a split second before his tongue fills me. His thumb flicks my clit as his blessed tongue slides in and out, in and out, in motions so precise they bring me close to climax in a few seconds.

I lose my control. Instead of fisting the sheet, I curl my fingers around his hair. My hips are about to leave the mattress when Logan puts his hands on them, forcing me to stay put.

"Don't move," he commands. "Just feel. Feel all of it, and let me see and hear you." He plunges his tongue back inside me. Every nerve ending zaps to life, awoken by the lash of his tongue, the sinful power of his words. I ride the wave of pleasure, giving myself to the release with complete abandon.

"*OhGodOhGodOhGod.*"

My legs jerk violently as I come, Logan's name on my lips.

"This was gorgeous," Logan says. His voice is rough, and lust clouds his eyes.

Still panting, I push myself to a sitting position. Logan is on his knees before me, his erection inches away from my face. *Yumm.* I could lick him. Instead, I decide to tease him.

I fist his shaft from the tip and slide my hand to the bottom, then play with his balls.

"You like them?" He wiggles his eyebrows. "They're my real jewels."

I snicker. "Proud of them, aren't you?"

"Very."

In a fraction of a second, Logan overpowers me. I'm beneath him, and he kisses me. It's passionate, yet gentle.

"I love doing this with you, Nadine. It means more than it ever did... before." Uncertainty flickers in his eyes. "I don't know how to explain this better, but... Do you understand?"

I run my fingers through his hair, his words warming me. "Yes. It means more to me too."

"Good. We'll see where this takes us. I just ask you one thing. Trust me."

I don't hesitate. "I do."

He presses his forehead to mine and kisses me again, his mouth warm and reassuring, his arms hovering protectively at my side. Right now, encircled in his arms, I'm happier than I've ever been. He appreciates every part of me. With every inch of my body he claims, I surrender a piece of my soul. I trust him, and that truth is both reassuring and frightening.

Abruptly, Logan says, "On your knees and turn around." I do as he says with my heart in my throat. "Now, put your hands on the headboard." His commands make me ache for him even more, if that's possible. With my back to him, I can't see or anticipate what he'll do next. I can only feel, and that makes everything so much more intense: the waiting, the guessing, the desire. I hear the sound of a wrapper being ripped apart, and Logan rolling the condom on.

He's suddenly behind me, his skin radiating heat. He places one palm on each of my buttocks, spreading them slightly. He dips his tongue between them. Just one short lick.

I fist the sheets, biting into the pillow. *Holy wow. What was that?*

He dips his tongue again, and a white-hot shiver races through me. The sound of my muffled cry fills the air. When he drags his tongue across the crease of my ass, my thighs almost give in, wetness rushing to my center. I'm panting, nearing a climax again, and he isn't even inside me! I lift up, taking my hands away from the bed, so I'm only on my knees.

Logan plasters his chest to my back and smooths his hands across my waist and ribcage, up to my breasts, rolling my nipples between his fingers. I cry softly when I feel his erection between my thighs, slapping his length gently across the seam of my sex, rocking back and forth over the slick and sensitive flesh, torturing me.

A master of anticipation, that's what Logan Bennett is. My hands grip the headboard, the delicate flesh between my thighs becoming even slicker. He drops one hand to my hip, driving into me. Pleasure whips through me as he pushes himself in and out, in and out, igniting me. He lifts my ass slightly then enters me even deeper. So deep, in fact, that his jewels slap across my clit. *Oh, my.*

Gripping the headboard even tighter, I meet his thrusts with fervor and desperation, tearing deep groans from his chest. Drops of his sweat drip on my back, from his forehead presumably. I find it incredibly sexy. Closing my eyes, I revel in the sound of heated flesh as it slaps together. Logan puts his mouth on my shoulder, grazing the skin with his teeth. His grip on my hips tightens, his nails digging into me as he takes me with ferocity.

"My sweet Nadine, what are you doing to me?"

Instead of an answer, I sigh out loud, arching my back, my body ripe for release. Logan drops one hand between my thighs, his fingers finding my clit, applying the sweetest pressure on it. My inner muscles clench around him as we both come apart.

Afterward, we lie next to each other, sweating and panting, when I suddenly burst out laughing.

"No idea why you're laughing, but I like the sound," Logan says.

"I'm so happy." There's nothing more to it.

Turning to one side, Logan pushes himself up on an elbow, facing me. "So, you liked what I did to you?"

I purse my lips to hide my smile. "Maybe."

"Maybe?" He feigns offense, widening his eyes.

"I don't remember it all that well." I love naked banter.

"My headboard does."

"What?" I push myself up on my knees and gasp. My nails have left deep scratches in the leather. "I can't believe I scratched your headboard. I ruined it."

"You didn't ruin it. You left a testimonial of how brilliant I am in bed." He laughs seductively. "You can tease me all you want about my skills. The headboard bears the truth."

"I'm so sorry. I'll buy you another bed or headboard. When I'm not so broke."

"No way. I'm not changing this headboard."

"We should try your floor," I joke. "Nothing to ruin there."

Logan pulls me under him. "I'd say we go in the shower now. Plenty of promises to fulfill. We can visit the floor later."

"Sounds perfect to me."

Chapter Eleven

Nadine

On Monday morning, I wait for Blake and his dad inside the store with apple pie. They both devour it upon their arrival, and then we work. The two men are definite pros, and the best part is they don't snoop.

The no-prying part only lasts until noon, however, when a delivery boy brings me flowers. It's a gorgeous bouquet of red roses. They come with a note, but I barely have time to gaze at it when Mr. Bennett and Blake walk up to me, staring at me expectantly.

"I don't mean to meddle," Blake says with an expression that tells me to expect lots of meddling, "but in the interest of our family, I have to ask, are those flowers from my brother? I must protect his honor if they're not."

"Yes, they're from Logan," I say. Blake smiles smugly, but Mr. Bennett nods and returns to work.

LAYLA HAGEN

Blake lingers and mutters, "Nothing good in store for me. If Sebastian and Logan get hitched, my sisters will have ideas for the rest of the male members of our family too. Max and Christopher are older than me, so hopefully they'll focus on them first."

I barely resist laughing at his quasi-monologue. Blake winks at me and goes to finish his task. I don't return to my work right away, admiring the flowers instead. Butterflies flutter in my belly, and there's a knot in my throat as I lean to smell the roses. I retrieve my phone with shaking hands.

Nadine: Thank you for the flowers.

Logan: Welcome. **You said there's nothing beautiful in your shop right now, so I thought I'd send you something beautiful**.

My heart somersaults at his words. I did say that sometime last night. I can't believe he was paying attention. Logan Bennett, super-busy CFO, took the time to do this for me.

So this is what dating a *real* man is like. I remember Ava telling me how special Sebastian made her feel, but I didn't understand. Now I do, and it frightens me. How on earth will I piece myself together if things between us don't end well? Especially since I'll have to face him at any family events Ava will invite me to.

Men don't stick around. Sooner or later, when the going gets rough, they leave. Dad did. Thomas did.

Mr. Bennett interrupts my thoughts. "Everything all right, Nadine?"

"Yeah, I just got lost in my thoughts for a bit."

"Can you help me with these shelves?" he asks.

I nod.

"Those are some beautiful flowers my son sent you," he comments while we work with the shelves.

"Yes, he keeps spoiling me. Your son is the most thoughtful man I've met."

Mr. Bennett nods. "He's always been this way. I could tell since he was a kid that he's the most sensitive of them all, and much too protective for his sisters' liking." A nostalgic smile spreads across his face. "After Sebastian left to work and he became the oldest brother in the household, he took his role even more seriously. Since Sebastian started to help us out financially, Logan felt the need to look after his siblings in every other way he could."

Oh. I didn't think there was something that could make me care for Logan even more, but it seems I'm in for surprise after surprise where this man is concerned.

***

The next weeks are hard. Blake and Mr. Bennett show up every day at the shop, and the entire clan joins us on Saturdays. Logan doesn't flaunt his wealth, but there are subtle hints everywhere. His fridge is always stocked with food, and the apartment is always clean in the evening, no matter the level of mess I leave behind when I head out in the morning. He also insists for a company driver to take me to my apartment and pick me up in the morning whenever I sleep there. I fought him on this in the beginning, even though he said it'd be for my safety because my neighborhood isn't among the safest in San Francisco. After witnessing an ugly fight on the way from the bus station to my building, I stopped protesting.

I make sure I sleep at my apartment at least two times a week, but I'm still at Logan's place most of the time. He says it's convenient for me, which it is, but I'm worried. If he needs his space, he's not getting it. Men can be very protective of their "men space." I have completely invaded Logan's space. He insisted I bring a lot of clothes here, which I have. While I'm sure he counted on having to make space for me in his bathroom, I'm pretty sure he didn't count on finding my stuff everywhere. And I do mean *everywhere*. I stare at the open fridge incredulously. My eyeliner is inside it. *Wow.* I have no idea how it got there, but I snatch it quickly before Logan can see it. Heaven knows what else he found. Yeah, safe to say I don't have an ounce of Logan's organizational talent. Quite the opposite.

On the morning of the fridge-eyeliner incident, I bring up the subject of *space* to Logan. We've just finished breakfast—I'm proud to say I managed to rise before him three times this week and prepare breakfast—and we're about to head out.

"I'll sleep in my apartment for the rest of the week."

Logan stops in the act of knotting his tie. "Why?"

"To give you some space," I say with nonchalance.

He tilts his head to one side, smiling. "Why would I need that?"

I shrug, my stomach twisting. "All men do."

Logan waltzes toward me, cornering me against the wall. He places his hands on either side of my head, trapping me in between.

"I don't," he says.

"But—"

"I like waking up next to you," he interrupts me. "I like knowing you're here when I return late in the night from a meeting. If you weren't here, we'd only see each other on weekends. I need you, Nadine."

"You do?"

"Yeah." He cups my cheeks, kissing one eyelid then the other. He pulls back, watching me. "I'm not your asshole of an ex or father."

I drop my eyes to his shoulder. "I know that."

"I don't think you do, but that's okay." He raises my chin until my gaze meets his. "You'll learn. I'll show you."

My eyes sting with the onset of tears. I blink quickly, looking away. His words brought out raw emotions and old insecurities. And he's also reassured me; he'll be patient with me, and that means more to me than he can imagine.

"So, what else do you like about me?" I ask with a big smile. "Besides waking up next to me."

"Let's see. Your awful singing in the shower."

"Stop it, it's not that bad."

He continues as if I haven't spoken. "Finding your stuff everywhere."

My mouth forms an O. "Surely not *everywhere*." *Please, dear God, don't let him know about the eyeliner in the fridge.*

"I might have seen your eyeliner in the fridge."

"Right, I changed my mind." I narrow my eyes. "I don't want to hear what else you like about me."

"I can show you what I love about you."

Without waiting for an answer, Logan covers my mouth with his in a breathtaking kiss. His lips nip at mine hungrily, his tongue expertly exploring my mouth, coaxing whimpers of pleasure out of me. I kiss him back with the same passion until we're both breathless. Logan's grinning when we pull apart. His good mood is infectious.

We leave the apartment holding hands, and I have no more thoughts of going to my place for now, though I'm still worried. In my experience, when things seem too good to be true, that's usually the case.

***

Since my organizational skills don't improve over the next few weeks, I decide to spoil my man with a bath one night in November. I buy candles and bubbly gel, preparing everything in time for his arrival.

When I hear him open the door, I say out loud, "I'm in the bathroom."

A few seconds later, Logan pokes his head in. His eyes register all my romantic setup, but his expression is apologetic rather than happy.

"Sorry, I have a last-minute meeting. I needed to grab something from home. Don't wait for me, I'll be late."

"Are you sure you can't join me for a little while?" I pout.

Logan shakes his head.

"Okay." A plan already forms in my mind. I have to up the stakes and be more convincing, show him what he's missing. With Logan still here, I drop my clothes bit by bit, watching him while I do so. I step in the bathtub, making a "come here" sign with my forefinger. I am *so* hijacking this meeting of his.

"I want one kiss before you leave."

"Nadine, you'll be the death of me." His tone is so husky that warmth pools between my thighs. He bends to kiss me but I pull back, lowering myself in the bathtub, lying on my back so my body is visible only from the shoulders up. I run my hands up and down my inner thighs, making sure Logan sees I'm moving my arms.

"Nadine, are you touching yourself?"

"Why don't you reach down here and find out?"

Sweat breaks out at his temples. "Jesus, you're not letting me out of this, are you?"

"No. It's your fault. You're very sexy in this suit. I want you to take it off."

Logan shrugs off his jacket then removes the cufflink of his right wrist, rolling up his sleeve. When he dips his hand in the water, he goes straight for my sex, cupping it. My hands are just playing on my thighs.

"You were tricking me."

"It worked." I close my eyes and lean my head back, resting it on the edge of the tub. Logan runs his fingers up and down my folds, teasing me. "Now *this* is the best way to relax."

"Look at me." His commanding tone sends shivers through me, despite the warm water.

Opening my eyes, I watch him panting while he pleasures me with his expert finger.

Abruptly, I rise on my knees, splashing water around. "I need to touch you."

"I have to go," Logan says, but his stance remains unchanged. That's my cue that he won't resist me. Careful not to make him *too* wet, I undo his belt, lower his zipper, and push his pants and boxers down, freeing his erection.

Taking a deep breath, I move my lips across his length, watching his eyes as I do. As he fists my hair, I feel powerful and wanted at the same time. I test his boundaries and his will by speeding up just a bit.

"I won't last, Nadine."

I don't stop; I only increase my pace.

"Fuck." Logan throws his head back, grunting out my name again and again. Abruptly, he pulls away. He grabs a condom from a nearby shelf, rips the foil, and slides it on.

"I need to be inside you," he grunts. Lowering himself to my level, he kisses me hard. I tangle my hands in his hair, pulling him in the water with me. I only realize what's going on when I hear a giant splash of water and see Logan step into the tub, still fully clothed.

"Logan, your suit—"

"I need you. Now."

Without any other words, he lowers himself into the water and pulls me in his lap. I'm hungry to touch his skin, but for now I settle on tracing the contours of his muscles through his shirt. Logan slides into me, stretching me inch by inch. My tight passage pulsates around him, welcoming him.

"Being inside you feels so good," he murmurs. When he is inside me all the way to the base of his erection, I start moving up and down, enjoying seeing him coming undone, and knowing I'm causing him pleasure.

He rests his head back on the edge of the tub, and I lean in for a quick kiss on his neck. He rolls my nipples between his fingers, his eyes watching my breasts bobbing as I slide up and down, straddling him.

He takes a nipple between his lips, suckling at it while he slides two fingers between us, reaching for my clit.

"Logan." I say his name through gritted teeth as his thumb circles my clit.

"I want to see you come, Nadine. You blush so beautifully."

I pick up the pace like a woman possessed.

"Fuck," I murmur.

"Yeah, that's right. I love to see you all wild like this."

"You make me wild."

Logan cups my jaw with his free hand, making me look straight at him. "You're mine, Nadine."

My eyes widen at the glint of dominance in his. His words ooze masculinity and, in this split second, I'm certain they alone could bring me to climax. But Logan doesn't rely on his words only. He presses his thumb straight on my clit, not moving it anymore, just applying pressure. I will lose my mind for this man.

"Oh, God," I cry as he thrusts his hips forward with ferocity, kissing me as my sex twinges around him. We both come at the same time, crying our releases into each other's mouths.

We stay huddled together for a few minutes, drawing ragged breaths and sharing chaste kisses, both smiling. Then I rise to my feet, allowing him to do the same. He discards the condom and, as I'm about to step out of the tub, Logan grabs my arm, gently pushing me against the wall adjacent to the tub.

"What are you doing?" I inquire. The dominant glint is still in his eyes, turning the tension between us scorching hot.

"I want to see you come again."

Oh. This man has a very sinful mouth.

"Logan, I don't think I can—"

"You will. Just enjoy this."

I can almost taste the sexual tension between us. It turns my mind foggy, my body needy. I relax, allowing him to work his magic on me. He nudges my legs open with his knee and drops his hand between my thighs. Running his fingers up and down my folds, avoiding my clit, he reduces me to shudders.

"I thought you didn't have time," I tease, licking my lips.

"I'll always make time to pleasure you. Besides, you'll have another orgasm in less than two minutes. You're still sensitive."

"I am—" I begin, but my words fade as Logan presses his thumb on my bundle of nerves, sliding his fingers inside me. Instinctively, my hips thrust forward as my back flattens on the tiles. They're cold and, coupled with the intense heat inside me, the feeling becomes too much. Everything is too much—the knowledge that he takes pleasure in giving me pleasure, and having his hands on me. Inside me is a better description. His fingers do wonders thrusting inside me again and again, finally curving and touching my sweet spot while his palm presses on my clit.

My release is brutal. I writhe and moan, fisting his hair and pulling him into a kiss.

He holds me in his arms until I calm down, and reality slowly slips in.

"Oh, wow. I'm sorry for your suit."

"No, you're not." Logan grins. "You've wanted this since I came home."

"Yes," I admit. "But in my fantasy, you weren't wearing your suit. Though it *was* hot."

I drink in his disheveled appearance. There's something incredibly sexy about making a man like Logan Bennett lose control this way.

"You should go change," I tell him.

Giving me a quick kiss, he rises, arranging his clothes. When he steps out, he drips through the entire bathroom. To my astonishment, he returns a few short minutes later.

***

Logan

"You haven't changed," Nadine says.

"Not the suit, but I've changed my mind. Scoot over."

"Are you—"

With a loud splash, I jump in the tub with her again, my clothes still on.

"I canceled the meeting. And this is the very first time I've done that."

"You're saying that so I feel special."

"You are special to me."

I grip her hips, pulling her into my lap. Her knees are at my sides, her sex pressing on the zipper of my pants. Cupping her cheek with one hand, I give her a quick smooch before lowering my lips to her neck, then down her chest.

"Logan."

I trail my lips up once more, reaching her ear. I'm hard again. "You make me want things, Nadine."

"What kind of things?"

"Things I didn't want to want. Like waking up next to you every morning, and wishing neither of us went to work so we could spend time together. I don't care if we're making love, eating takeout, or renovating your shop. Even watching you sleep makes me smile. The more time I spend with you, the more I want."

I pull back, searching her eyes. Different emotions are warring in their blue depths, reflecting the same torment taking over inside of me. The desire to throw all caution to the wind and jump into this relationship with both feet competes with the fear of heartbreak and disappointment.

"We'll figure this out together. I'll do the right thing by you, no matter what. You deserve it."

Despite the heat of the water, Nadine shivers. This was supposed to be just fun. We agreed to it. If I'm honest, though, I knew deep down that it'd be so much more than that right from the beginning. Everything about her is consuming. I trace her lower lip with my thumb.

"You're a wonderful man, Logan," she murmurs. "We said we'd take things slow."

I nod, smiling. "Yeah." We're not taking it slow, and we both know it. Neither of us says it out loud, though. We're accomplices on this journey of restoring each other's broken hearts. "I promise—"

"Don't make me any promises, Logan," she interrupts. "I don't want to pressure you into anything."

"Okay."

"Actually, I changed my mind. I do want you to make me one promise." She pauses as if expecting me to say something. "Why aren't you surprised?"

"I have three sisters. I know all women are bipolar."

She throws her head back, laughing loud and long. God, I love her laughter, and I love being the reason for it. "That's one hell of a research-based conclusion there, but I fear you're right."

"So, what was that promise you wanted?"

"That you'll never lie to me."

"I promise."

She nods, her shoulders relaxing. "Have you found an antidote to your sisters' bipolarity?"

I don't hesitate. "Chocolate. If that fails, I keep my distance, but it almost always works. I have the best chocolate shop in San Francisco on speed dial."

"What if it's late at night?" she asks playfully. "Surely they're closed."

"Not for me."

"Oh, right, I forgot. You're Logan Bennett. You can make everyone do what you want with a few words."

"Except you. I actually have to work to convince you."

"I'm afraid that won't change, Mr. Bennett." Her voice is serious, but her expression betrays her. She's on the verge of bursting out laughing once again.

"I like it, Ms. Hawthorne. You keep me on my toes. That makes me crazy for you."

We're both laughing now.

She taunts me, moving her ass right over my erection. I open my mouth, but a groan comes out instead of words.

"Do you have trouble speaking, Mr. Bennett?"

I growl then kiss her mouth. She pretends to fight me off, but I grip her wrists.

"You little fighter. Even in your sleep, you fight. You kick me when I touch you at night."

"I do not do that," she says horrified.

"Yes, you do. Every time I try to touch you in your sleep."

"You shouldn't touch me when I'm asleep, you pervert."

"Unfair accusation, coming from someone who's currently dry-humping me."

"Wet-humping is the right term, since we're in a tub full of water. Are you complaining?" She pushes herself up briefly, but I grip her hips and pull her against me. Hard. Her clit collides with my erection, and Nadine gasps, her body quivering. She grasps the edges of the tub, her chest heaving up and down with labored breaths. I gave my woman a mini-orgasm.

"Why don't you get out of this shirt?" she asks after regaining her breath.

"You don't like it? I was under the impression you loved my shirts. You wear them inside the apartment all the time."

"I've also stolen some of your socks," she adds. "They're so comfortable." Licking her lips, she runs her hands over my soaked shirt. She wants me naked. "Shirt. Off. Now."

"Nah, I'm good," I tease. "It's wet anyway."

"You'll ruin it."

I chuckle. "You just want to see me naked."

"I always want to see you naked, but in the bathtub, it's a normal state of being."

I kiss her slowly, drawing whimpers and moans out of her.

"Thank God you didn't have your smartphone in your pocket when I first dragged you in the water," she says.

"I had it in the back pocket of my pants."

"No way."

"Lucky I have a spare one."

"I ruin everything. Your headboard, your phone."

"Don't forget the shirt," I add in a low voice.

"What? I didn't ruin your shirt."

Gesturing to it, I challenge her. "The night's still young."

Within the next few minutes, I find out Nadine's not only good at sewing clothes.

She excels at ripping them apart too.

Chapter Twelve

Nadine

Thanks to the Bennett clan, I'm able to open the store ahead of schedule, and as the opening day approaches, my nerves stretch thinner. I'll be opening four weeks before Christmas, and I've already decorated the shop. It's warm and welcoming, even if there's still work to be done. I send Mom a picture after I finish decorating, and she replies with a smiley face. God, I really want this shop to succeed, so I can bring Mom and Brian here. My stomach churns at the thought of going back to North Carolina if I fail. I dread this outcome now even more than I did before I moved, and I know why: Logan.

The Friday before the opening, he puts his foot down. I've been in the store the entire day, cleaning and polishing everything. Despite the fact that everything is in place ready for customers on Monday, I still feel it's not ready.

"There's nothing for you to do here anymore. You need to go out."

"But I'm opening the store in three days," I protest. "There must be something left to do. I just don't remember it." I tightly clutch the rag I've been using to clean the dust.

Logan gently puts one hand on my arm, tilting my chin up with the other.

"You've worked non-stop lately. You don't sleep well, and you don't eat much. Nadine, you're exhausted. You need a break."

His concern fills me with joy. I can't believe he noticed all those things about me. He's right, of course. I don't sleep well, often waking up several times a night, remembering yet another task I must do and jotting it quickly on my phone, so I don't forget it. Logan's a light sleeper, so more often than not I also wake him. Then he'll wrap his arms around my waist, pulling me to him. Feeling his body cocooned to mine calms me every time. It gives me a sense of security.

But now, I'm in crazy mode. Surely, I have forgotten to do something. Logan seems to be reading my thoughts. His eyes narrow and just like that, he's done being gentle.

"Do you like ballet?" he asks.

"Yes. I love it, but—"

"We're going out. It's not negotiable." Snatching the rag out of my hand, he throws it on the counter. With nothing between us, he closes the distance and kisses me silly. I respond in kind, grabbing his hair, pressing my breasts against his steely chest. His cologne is intoxicating, his kiss even more so.

"You're a caveman; you know that?" I mutter after we pull apart.

"I never pretended not to be."

"You recommended yourself as a gentleman, when we first met. Turns out there's as much 'cave' as there is 'gentle' in you, Mr. Bennett."

"I call that well-rounded, Ms. Hawthorne." He grins, and I can't help but smile back. "Let's go. If you don't agree, I'm not above throwing you over my shoulder and walking into the theater. You need a break, Nadine. You're going to get one whether you want it or not."

How can I say no to his dark, piercing eyes? They're full of concern and lust. It's a sexy look on him but, then again, every look is sexy on Logan. I'm tempted to argue some more, to see if he'd actually throw me over his shoulder. I suspect he would, which sends jolts of heat down my center. I choose the peaceful way.

"Fine, what ballet are we watching?"

Logan gives a triumphant fist pump in the air. "The Nutcracker. Pippa, Blake, and Daniel will be there."

I smile, threading my fingers at the back of his neck. "Oh, that's fun."

"We have to be there in two hours."

I pout. "That doesn't give me much time to prepare."

"Wear one of your dresses," he says. The huskiness in his voice sends ripples down my back.

"I'll grab one, and we can go to your apartment to change."

I've brought the dresses I designed to the shop this week and arranged my favorite ones beautifully on dummies. The expensive designer dresses are still back at my place.

I grab a dress from a hanger, and we head to his apartment. Dressing up doesn't take me long, but I spend enough time on hair and makeup to make Logan impatient. I don't hold back, smearing on red lipstick and styling my hair in a wild, voluminous do. The daring hairstyle matches the dress, which is long and fashioned out of black silk. It doesn't show cleavage unless you stare straight from above, but it *is* backless.

When I step into the living room, Logan whistles. "Damn, woman! You're making me seriously reconsidering going out." I twirl once and take a slow bow, giving him full view of my cleavage. He lets out a heavy breath.

"After taking forever to prepare, you can be very sure we're going out." I accentuate every word with a shake of my finger.

"Is that so?"

"Yeah. I want to show off the dress." He strides to me and I take a few steps back, knowing his proximity will cloud my judgment. Predictably, I hit the wall, and Logan loses no time in trapping me between his arms.

"I can think of a better use of this dress than showing it off." His eyes darken as he speaks. Lust and masculinity pour off him, and it's turning my knees to rubber.

"What's that?" I murmur.

"Taking it off." His fingers linger at the hem of my neckline, the callused tips barely touching my skin. I shudder, licking my lips. "I wouldn't be gentle. It begs to be ripped off you."

"No chance. I worked months on this dress."

He chuckles. "Fine, I don't need to take it off at all."

Before I have a chance to process his words, he turns me around, pressing himself against my naked back.

"You're so beautiful, Nadine." Pushing my hair to one side, he kisses the back of my neck. "So sexy. You look fantastic in this dress." His hot breath across my skin accompanies every word. *I want this man. Now.* He touches my bare back with one hand, pulling my dress up with the other, grazing my inner thigh in the process. Almost involuntarily, I push my ass back and let out a moan. Logan's hard for me already.

"Condom," he murmurs. "Wait."

He leaves the room briefly, returning with his zipper open and his pants pushed slightly down, having already rolled the condom over his erection. He settles himself behind me again, cinching my dress up to my waist and parting my legs. God, I'm dripping for him.

"You're so wet already," he whispers, as he slides my thong to one side.

I lose myself in the sea of sensations and emotions as his big hands and hungry lips explore me. Logan more than touches me—he worships me. Every part of me. He nibbles my earlobe, moving the tip of his erection around my clit, his length pressing on my slit. He circles my clit with his tip again, and again, until my knees wobble.

"I need you inside me now," I say between moans. "I want to feel all of you."

"Oh, you will. You will feel me so deep inside you that you'll pass out from pleasure." His promise still on his lips, he thrusts inside me.

"Logan." My legs tremble in earnest now as I take him in, stretching around his length. In this position, he's deeper inside me than ever before. I give myself to him completely as he makes love to me hard and fast, grunting out my name as we climax.

***

Logan holds my hand when we enter the venue, minutes before the showing is about to begin. I'm still blushing from our sexy episode before we left his apartment. We exchange furtive glances every few seconds.

The venue is packed, but we find Pippa, Blake, and Daniel almost immediately, chatting animatedly near the entrance. Women throw the twins appreciative glances.

"So, the theater is one of your pickup places?" I ask jokingly.

"It can be." Blake answers. "But tonight, we have a date with our sister." In unison, the twins each take Pippa by an arm.

"Nadine, what are you wearing?" She inspects me from head to toe. "It's gorgeous. I'm going to steal that."

"It's one of my designs."

Pippa's mouth opens, her gaze slipping to Logan for a brief second before returning to me. "Girl, I'll come by on Monday the second you open and ravage your stock."

"Can't wait."

"Seriously, I'd love to see some of your other dresses too."

"Sure, I'd be happy to." My heart soars with excitement at her appreciation. As we go into the box for the performance, Pippa whispers something I don't catch to Logan, and both glance at me with a quizzical expression, like they're sharing an inside joke.

Before we take our seats, Logan whispers to me, "I'm very proud of you." He pinches my ass for good measure, doing that thing again when he makes me feel like a girl and a woman all at the same time.

I'll never get enough of Logan, and that scares me even more than the opening on Monday.

***

Two hours later, we leave the box, chatting animatedly while making our way to the exit. We're almost at the door when Pippa comes to an abrupt halt, turning white. The men stop too, but they are far from pale—all three of them are red in the face. Blake even clenches his fists.

A man in his late thirties with brown hair and green eyes stops in front of us.

"Pippa, what a surprise." His tone is glacial. Next to me, Logan stiffens. The man surveys the party, stepping in front of me.

"I'm Terence Lancaster."

Suddenly, I understand everyone's reaction. He's Pippa's ex-husband, also known as asshole extraordinaire, ranking even above Thomas. He holds out his hand to me. I shake it shortly, not wanting to add to the tension.

"Coming with your brothers to the opera, Pippa? Couldn't pay a man to join you?"

Pippa pales even more at his words. If I hadn't already disliked Terence on principle alone, now I hate his guts.

"Let's step outside and you make that remark again," Logan says. "I don't want to spoil the carpet here."

"You always did have a temper," Terence tells Logan.

"So do we," Daniel says. He and Blake both have their hands in fists at their sides.

"You can't talk to our sister like that," Blake booms. Several people passing by throw us alarmed glances.

Terence rolls his eyes, though I detect a flicker of fear in them. "Where is Sebastian?"

"You're out of luck today," Logan says through gritted teeth. "Sebastian is the sensible one keeping us from knocking your teeth out, and he's not here tonight. Step outside."

"Stop it," Pippa says. "All of you. Terence, leave."

To my astonishment, Terence gives a mocking bow and heads for the door, clearly fearing the brothers. Not ten feet away, a blonde appears from a narrow corridor, taking his arm.

"Sorry to make you wait, love. There was a line to the ladies' room."

Pippa spares the pair one glance, but in the split second it takes for her to register that Terence and the blonde are a couple, the fire leaves her eyes. Discreetly, I squeeze her hand. She squeezes back then takes a deep breath, turning to her brothers.

"What the hell is wrong with all of you?"

"What do you mean?" Blake asks.

"Terence is a jerk," Logan adds unhelpfully.

"*Now* you're overbearing, brother," Pippa tells him. Turning to her two other brothers, she adds, "And you two, don't piss me off. I can't put the Terence episode behind me if every time we meet him, someone causes a scene."

"Why are you mad at us? He was rude to you," Daniel says. Next to him, Blake still has his hands fisted.

"I can handle myself." She pulls herself to her full—and quite impressive—height. "Now, if you'll excuse me, Nadine here is my favorite person tonight, so I'd prefer to spend the evening in her company. The rest of you can do whatever you want, away from us."

"Pippa—" Logan begins, but his sister holds her hand up, shaking her head. Blake opens his mouth then closes it again. I can almost see the wheels turning in Logan's mind. Should he call the sweets shop he has on speed dial? Or is it one of those rare instances where chocolate isn't the answer? Finally, he holds up his hands in defeat. The man has excellent preservation skills. Daniel pulls his brothers away with an apologetic expression, and the three men leave.

Stunned by the turn of events, I gaze at Pippa expectantly.

"Well, tonight didn't go as expected," she says.

"Are you in the mood for an impromptu night out?" I suggest.

"Not really." We wait a few minutes inside the building, until most of the ballet viewers exit, and then we leave too. Outside she adds, "But I don't want to go home either."

"Hey, I have an idea. Why don't we go to the shop? It's done, and I can show you some dresses."

"Great." She smiles, and I'm relieved to see that it reaches her eyes. "Make sure to show them to me before we down the bottle of wine."

Perplexed, I observe her tiny purse. No way does she have a bottle in there. "Which bottle?"

"That one." She points to the small souvenir shop across the street, which has wines on display. "While I buy it, why don't you call up Ava and ask her if she wants to join us? I'll call my sisters."

"Done."

I watch the sky while I speak to Ava. There are almost no stars in sight today, clouds hanging low and heavy. This is a good night for wine. Pippa returns with a bottle just as I finish the conversation with Ava.

"Alice and Summer are coming," she announces.

"So is Ava."

"Well, I call that a party."

Chapter Thirteen

Nadine

Pippa and I arrive at the store first. Once inside, I turn on the lights.

"Wow." Pippa sits in one of the armchairs near the entrance, holding the bottle in her lap. In the front of the store is a small waiting parlor for husbands or friends accompanying the customers. It consists of a small table and two armchairs. Then there is the central area, where the dresses and lingerie are, and two changing rooms. The back room serves as my storage area. Ava, Alice, and Summer arrive a few minutes later. The girls wear jeans and T-shirts; we obviously pulled them away from a cozy night in. Upon closer inspection, I discover each brought a bottle of wine. Either they didn't receive the memo that we already have a bottle, or they're taking this girls' night thing too seriously. *Four bottles for the five of us. This will not end well.*

"I love the Christmas decorations. This place is great." Summer peeks around appreciatively.

"Your dad and Logan helped a lot. I don't have more chairs, though."

Pippa waves dismissively. "No problem. Summer can sit in my lap, Ava in yours."

"That still leaves me out," Alice remarks. "You didn't even have one sip of wine and you already can't do math?"

All of us burst out laughing, which is just as good because there was a slight tension in the air since the girls arrived. They all found out about Terence's scene tonight. Thank God for the wine.

"I'll sit on the floor," I say, lowering myself to the carpet, careful not to damage my dress. Ava and Alice join me, leaving Summer and Pippa in the armchairs.

As Pippa prepares to open her bottle, a realization strikes me. "Ugh, I don't have any glasses."

"I bought some on the way." Alice retrieves a stack of paper cups from her bag.

"Paper cups and wine. How very Bennett of us," Pippa says with a smile. "Nadine, you've had dinners with us, and we even worked on this shop along with you." She holds the bottle in front of her as if she's speaking into a mic. "Let's not forget you're sleeping with our brother," she adds as an afterthought. I blush violently. "But you aren't truly a Bennett until you've had wine with the girls."

Truly a Bennett... Her words hit me hard, squarely in the chest. God, I'd love to be part of this family, but I can't let my mind wander that way. Logan and I agreed on fun and having a good time, both making it clear it would be temporary from the very beginning. At the time, I was relieved there was no permanency to *us*. Now, the thought of "temporary" suffocates me. Then again, so does the idea of "permanent." Logan's not ready for that, and neither am I, mainly because I don't believe in permanent. Men don't stick around forever.

"From paper cups," Alice insists, snapping me back to the present. "That detail is crucial."

"Yeah, it's a tradition," Summer says, "mostly born out of the fact that we decide to have impromptu nights out at the worst of times, so we never have glasses and end up buying paper cups."

"You often have gatherings like this?" I smile at them, and Ava chuckles.

Summer purses her lips. "Only if our brothers piss us off or if we're celebrating something."

"I have an idea." Pippa points at me. "Can you bring out some dresses before we start drinking?" Turning to the other girls, she explains, "Nadine designed the dress she's wearing herself. She's crazy talented. I suggest we each try one."

The others nod enthusiastically, and I know I have what each of them needs. I disappear between my dresses, and everyone cheers when I return with them.

"Let's try them on," Summer says, rising to her feet.

"I only have two changing rooms, but you can take turns."

In fifteen minutes, everyone's ready. They twirl and laugh, complementing each other. I'm the only one who hasn't joined in the fun, mainly because I'm too busy trying not to tear up. Seeing my designs on actual people feels surreal.

"This is gorgeous," Ava gushes. "I can't wait until you start working on my wedding dress."

"Nadine, I love this dress," Summer announces. "I want to wear this to my gallery show at the end of next week. As a matter of fact, I want all of you to wear these dresses to the show."

"What?" I ask, my mouth suddenly dry.

"Summer is used to our brothers doing whatever she says," Pippa says. "Alice and I usually don't but, this time, I have to say I agree. These dresses are fantastic."

"We'll buy them," Alice says, incorrectly interpreting my expression.

"No, I'll be happy to gift them if you want to wear them to the gallery. That would be excellent marketing."

"We'll buy them," Pippa says firmly.

Ava pulls me to one side. "First rule of business: don't gift your products, not even to friends."

"All right, people, we have our dresses." Alice puts her hands on her hips, mimicking model poses. "I say we change back into our clothes and open that wine."

"Can you shorten my dress a few inches?" Summer's dress is the only one that doesn't fit perfectly since she's so petite. Dazzled by the fact that I made my first four sales, I nod, afraid that if I speak, I'll tear up.

"Okay," Pippa says. "Out of the dresses, in with the wine."

Said and done. Fifteen minutes later, the girls are back in their clothes. Alice pours wine for everyone, and Summer plays some music on her phone. Within minutes, there is an energetic party vibe in the shop.

"Are you designing the bridesmaid dresses too?" Alice asks me.

I turn to Ava. "I don't know. Am I?"

"I don't want to take advantage of you, since you have a lot on your plate. But I'd love it, of course."

"How many bridesmaids will you have?"

"Twelve."

I do a double take. "What?"

"It's our fault," Pippa chimes in. "We have a few cousins who have to be in the wedding and a few of the adopted Bennetts too."

"Will Caroline be one of the bridesmaids?" Summer asks with wide, hopeful eyes.

"Why do you want to know?" Alice teases. "So you can run and tell Daniel?"

Summer purses her lips but doesn't deny the charges.

"What am I missing?" I ask Ava.

"I'll tell you the short version," Pippa answers. "Caroline is one of my best friends and a former adopted Bennett. Then Daniel dated her for a while. Things didn't work out, and now she avoids family celebrations."

"She and Daniel should get back together. He keeps asking about her," Summer states.

"Oh, Summer, you're so young," Alice says. "Men must pay when they mess up, and Daniel messed up."

"What Alice said," Pippa adds.

"Just to be clear, yes, Caroline will be a bridesmaid," Ava tells Summer.

"So, how about those dresses?" Alice asks me.

"Twelve," I repeat, still stunned. "Sure, I'd love to do the dresses."

The sisters start talking about their cousins, brothers, and childhood pranks. Ava and I, both only children, eat up their words and laugh our asses off. After we down the first two bottles, we start to slur our words. I suspect we'll resemble a drunken sorority meeting by the time we finish this. Ava and I are sitting on the armchairs right now, the sisters sprawled on the floor.

"Oh, man, I miss Max and Christopher," Summer says. "Why do they have to be so far away? I'm sure there's some place for them here in Bennett Enterprises."

"There is," Pippa says in a reassuring tone. "But Sebastian trusted them the most to oversee our foreign offices and expand the business there. He was right to do so too. They've done an excellent job."

"I spoke to Max last week," Alice chimes in. "He's eager to return. In two or three years, he'll be back. Christopher too, probably."

Summer pouts, her lips violet from the wine. "That's a long time."

"Aww." Pippa elbows her. "Someone misses her favorite brothers."

Summer stands up straighter. "I don't have favorites."

Alice narrows her eyes. "Then how do you explain that Blake and Daniel think Sebastian is your favorite, and Sebastian and Logan think Max and Christopher are your favorites?"

"Because then they'll all fall over each other to become her favorite," Pippa explains. "Oldest trick in the book."

"I don't know what you all are talking about." Summer crosses her arms. "I don't have favorites, but I can't help if I'm the boys' favorite sister."

"Oh, my God," I interject. "My head is going to explode if I hear *favorite* one more time," I say with a smile.

Alice snorts and Pippa shakes her head, opening the third bottle. Alice, Summer, and Ava decide dancing is in order. Turning the volume up a notch, they start swinging their bodies to the rhythm.

Pippa remains on the floor, and I seize my chance to play the pacifier, crawling next to her. "Are you going to forgive your brothers?"

Pippa sighs, hugging her knees to her chest. "Terence is an ass, and I'm not *that* mad at my brothers. It's just that..."

"What?"

"It's going to sound silly."

"I promise not to laugh."

"Well, they've always been like this. Overprotective, having my back. I keep thinking if I hadn't grown up believing all men are like my brothers—funny, sometimes stupid, and taking their alpha role too seriously, but overall genuinely nice guys—maybe I would have stood a chance."

"Trust me, Pippa, not having assholes for brothers is a good thing. Be happy you have them."

"I am."

She presses her paper cup to her lips before taking a large gulp of wine. "Terence is dating someone else," Pippa says.

"Yeah."

"I mean, I don't love him anymore, but seeing him with someone else hurts. I don't know if it just hurts my pride, or something more, but I felt the ground shake beneath my feet when I saw them."

She hunches her shoulders, a tear rolling down her cheek. Pippa's usually so exuberant that I'm at a loss for words, but I instantly see red. Anyone who makes Pippa lose her spark deserves every misery in this world. I kind of wish Logan and the twins had wiped that stupid smirk off Terence's face.

"It's normal. So, how about forgiving your brothers? Terence was asking for it."

"You sound like Logan," Pippa tells me.

"Well, I'm Team Logan on this."

Abruptly, Summer stops dancing. "We're picking teams? I'm Team Logan too."

"You don't even know what this is about," Pippa says.

"Doesn't matter. I'm Team Logan," a clearly inebriated Summer repeats.

"Me too," Alice says. "Wait, who's on the other team?"

"Terence."

"Ugh." Alice frowns. "I thought we were talking about soccer teams."

I laugh, then fill her in. "No, we're talking about whether Logan's entitled to kick Terence's ass when he's rude to Pippa."

"Definitely Team Logan," Alice says.

"Me too." Ava slumps in an armchair again.

"Putting it like that, he's obviously entitled to kick Terence's ass," Pippa says, sighing. "I'll tell them everything's fine when I see them."

"I want to call Christopher," Summer announces out of the blue.

"Uh, what time is it in Hong Kong?" Alice asks.

"I'm not sober enough to calculate the time difference," Pippa states. Before I have the chance to jump in, Summer's already calling, putting him on speaker.

"Summer, is this urgent? I got out of a meeting to take this call."

"No," Summer replies. "Just wanted to tell you I miss you."

"We also miss you," Alice and Pippa chime in, while Ava and I chuckle in the background.

"Ah, my girls are drunk again," Christopher exclaims. I like him already. "Anyone sober around there?"

"I am," Ava and I say at the same time.

"I recognize Ava's voice. Who's the other sober voice?"

"Nadine," I reply.

"Ah, Logan's girl."

I blush, and everyone turns to Summer. Evidently, she's the one who spilled the beans to Christopher. She grins, not sorry in the slightest.

"Well, Ava, Nadine, take care of my sisters. I have to go back to the meeting. And for God's sake, don't let them drink anymore."

The sisters frown at the phone while Ava and I reassure Christopher. After the call ends, Summer, Alice, and Pippa resume their dancing, while I sit next to my best friend.

"I can't believe you all want to wear my dresses," I tell Ava.

"I always told you how talented you are."

To my astonishment, Ava tears up.

"What's wrong?" I ask.

"My mother would've loved to have something like this."

I hug Ava with one arm. I met Mrs. Lindt one time. Unfortunately, she was in the late stages of her illness. Even so, whenever she spoke about her love for creating clothes, her eyes lit up. Ms. Lindt was one of the few people to tell me to go for my dream. She'd had the same dream when she was young, but she got pregnant and set it aside. She told me she didn't once regret giving her dream up for her daughter but, given the chance, I should go for what I want. I made that chance happen. Now I only have to turn it into a success.

Ava interrupts my thoughts. "I offered before, and you rejected it, but if there is anything you need, a loan or something, tell me."

"You introduced me to the Bennetts." I point at the three sisters, who've stopped dancing. Now they hug each other, singing the refrain of the song playing on Summer's phone at the top of their lungs. They're adorable. "That practically means I owe you for life."

Ava pulls a serious face. "Speaking about Bennetts, how are things between you and Logan?"

"Honestly? I want to pinch myself. He's so…"

"I'd go with self-assured, but I think you're about to say something else."

"Perfect. He's charming, attentive, not to mention sexy, even if he likes to behave like a caveman now and again. And that man cooks like you wouldn't believe it."

"So, you two are…"

"We haven't talked about what we are or aren't. I'm not going to bring up the topic of "defining our relationship" either. I don't want to jinx what we have. I finally found a good thing, so I'm not taking any chances. I'll enjoy it while I can, no matter how long it lasts."

A dull ache spreads through my chest at my words. I miss Logan already.

Someone knocks at the door, and my stomach dips. It must be some neighbors, complaining about the noise. I can't see what's outside because I haven't taken down the paper covering the windows yet. I'll do that Monday morning.

When I open the door, I'm surprised to find Logan, Sebastian, Blake, and Daniel outside.

"Who is it?" Ava appears next to me.

"Bennett overload," I tell Ava.

"Drunken Bennett overload," she replies in surprise. I narrow my eyes and giggle. The boys seem to have drunk at least as much as we did. Sebastian appears to be the soberest, closely followed by Logan. Blake and Daniel are behind them, bickering over who has the more toned abs. Right.

Stumbling inside the store, the boys peek around for their sisters.

"We've come to say sorry," Logan tells Pippa. "Haven't we?" He throws the twins a death stare. Sebastian reinforces the threat by tapping his foot on the floor. Blake and Daniel don't look sorry in the slightest, but they cower under Sebastian's gaze. God, they're all so adorable, I could hug them. I'm very huggy today.

"We're sorry you were there to witness it," Daniel says.

"I'd still kick his ass," Blake clarifies. "But sorry we upset you."

Logan remains silent.

Sebastian groans, dragging his hands down his face. "This apology plan is going nowhere fast. You were supposed to say 'we're sorry.' No additions," he admonishes.

"At least I can always count on them to be honest," Pippa tells Sebastian.

"Especially after they've had a few shots," he supplies. "They might've overdone it."

"So did you," Alice tells him. "Let Blake and Daniel be Blake and Daniel. Logan never pretends anyway; not even you can make him apologize. You're the only diplomat in the family."

"How did all of you end up drunk?" Summer asks.

"Well," Sebastian says. "These three went to drink and plot how to best corner Terence."

"We did," Logan admits.

Blake points at Sebastian. "Then he came and played the big brother card."

"We're getting off topic," Sebastian says. "I wanted to drive everyone back home safely, but they corrupted me to drink too."

Blake squeezes his shoulder. "That's what little brothers are for, Sebastian."

"Cab for everyone?" Daniel asks. "This was my pickup line in college," he informs me. "I'd offer to share a cab with whatever girl was the prettiest, and gave her a night to remember. Pity I was too drunk to remember."

He all but pats himself on the back with that remark. Turning serious, he looks at me and adds, "I also didn't say a proper good-bye tonight. I'll leave in three days to visit a friend in Thailand, and I'll be gone for some time. I hope to see you again when I return. I'll kick my brother's ass otherwise."

It takes me a second to understand what he means. He's unsure if I'll still be dating Logan. *Wow, way to sober me up completely.*

I smile. "I'll be Ava's maid of honor anyway."

Soon, the cabs arrive. Ava, Sebastian, and Pippa take the first one, while Alice, Summer, and the twins grab the second. Logan and I walk to his apartment.

***

Logan's quiet the entire walk, and I wonder what's on his mind. Maybe he just needs to sleep. Except he doesn't seem tired, and he's not *that* drunk. When we enter his apartment, he squeezes my hand gently. I stop in my tracks in the center of the living room. It's pitch dark since neither of us bothered to turn on the light.

"Sorry for the drama tonight," he says in my ear from behind me. My back is turned to him. "And thank you for putting up with my crazy family."

He flattens his chest against my back, reminding me of the moment of passion we shared before we left. He intertwines his fingers with mine, and this simple act feels even more intimate than making love to him did.

"Your family is great, Logan, and I love every single one of them. Exuberant Pippa, spoiled Summer, crazy Blake and Daniel. I have to come up with an adjective for Alice. I even adore Sebastian for making my best friend so happy. I love your parents too."

I search out his warmth, taking his arms and draping them around me. Logan puts his lips to my ear. "Not mad at me for being overbearing?"

"You mean flat-out threatening Terence? No." Fearing I'm setting a bad precedent, I add, "I mean I'd be fuming if you had no reason, but you had a good one."

"I thought you'd be mad at me by default."

I laugh, swirling around. "Why would I do that?"

"No idea. I thought there was something about girls sticking together."

"I got everyone on Team Logan way before you guys arrived."

"You're perfect."

I lick my lips. "No, I'm not."

"Yes, you are." Kissing one eye then the other, he adds, "You're more than perfect."

"Your sisters want to wear my dresses to Summer's gallery show," I tell him.

"That's great. Let's celebrate your first sales."

Wrapping his arms around my waist, he lifts me off the floor. I catch a glimpse of his expression in the moonlight—he's grinning. Logan is genuinely happy for me. My first impulse is to tell him that I still have a lot of work ahead of me before I can celebrate, but I remember what he said about celebrating each step. Right now, that feels exactly right, especially when I can do so with Logan.

"Agreed, but no more alcohol, please."

Logan puts me down. "Fine by me. That's not exactly what I had in mind anyway." He presses his forehead to mine, cupping my cheeks. "I already told you you're perfect, right?"

"Are you trying to charm the pants off me?"

"I would, but you're wearing a dress."

Suddenly, I understand why he's trying to charm me. The bastard. "No, Logan, you're still not allowed to rip apart my dress. A thousand compliments won't convince me."

"I don't have time for that many. I need you," he says with urgency, then devours my mouth. A few seconds later, I'm lifted off the floor again. Logan carries me in his arms, walking blindly through the dark.

"Shouldn't we turn on the light? Can you find the bedroom—"

"Shh," Logan says. "Don't worry, I won't hurt you."

Keeping his promise, he leads us to the bedroom safe and sound. He lays me on the bed, turning on the lamp on the nightstand.

"I want to see you," he says.

Maybe it's the few sips of wine I had, or maybe Logan somehow succeeded in tearing down yet another one of my walls, but a confession slips past my lips.

"If the store does well, I want to bring Mom and Brian here."

Logan nods, urging me to go on.

LAYLA HAGEN

"I... The reason I want to go back to North Carolina if the store fails is not just for me; it's for my parents too. I want to take care of them after they retire."

He hops into bed next to me, lying on one side. Caressing my cheek with his fingers, he says, "We're very much alike, Nadine. Don't worry. Everything will turn out all right."

"I hope so. I'm confident right now. I am very lucky to have run into you and your family."

He kisses my forehead, his lips lingering on my skin while his arms pull me closer to him. At this moment, I realize that I've never felt so cherished in my life.

"I've always considered myself a lucky guy," Logan murmurs against my forehead, "even more so after Bennett Enterprises became a success." Pulling away, he tilts my chin up. "But meeting you, that was my real luck. You mean more to me every day, Nadine. You complete me in the best possible ways. In all the ways." As he holds my gaze, it strikes me that he's right. We're very much alike—we're two people learning to love and let ourselves be loved again. Without taking his eyes off me, Logan starts removing my dress carefully. I undress him too, kissing each inch of skin I reveal.

Logan makes love to me gently, for a long time. Afterward, as we fall asleep in each other's arms, I am sure I never want to let him go.

Chapter Fourteen

Nadine

On Monday morning, I wake up with a jolt, half an hour before my alarm is set to ring. D-day is here. Logan's side of the bed is cold. I wish he were here to hug me good luck, but he had to fly out to London to meet his brother. He'll be gone the entire week, back just in time for Summer's gallery. A bulge of anxiety forms in my stomach, but I push myself to my feet, and force myself to go through my morning routine.

In the living room, I find a croissant and a note on the table.

Wish I could be here for your opening week, or at least kiss you good luck this morning. I did try to hug you when I woke up, but you kicked me good (I'll have the bruise to prove it when I return).

Love,

Logan

The note alone is enough to turn my anxiety into euphoria. I eat the croissant and make myself a coffee. Unfortunately, the coffee turns my previous euphoria into downright dangerous energy. My pulse is drumming in my ears, and my heart beats at a nauseous speed. I walk to the store even though I'm wearing high heels, hoping to walk off some of that energy. No such luck.

Once inside the shop, I wipe my sweaty palms on my jeans, remove the paper covering the glass and turn on the sign on the door, indicating I'm open for business. Right then, my neighbor, the owner of the shoes and bags shop, passes by, offering a thumbs-up. I wave and give her a smile I'm certain came across as manic.

This is *it*. The day I've been preparing years for.

It's a good thing that my euphoria level was out of this world when I entered the store, because with each hour that passes, it dwindles and dwindles. Not one soul steps inside, which makes all of my dread come back. What if this is a mistake? I've invested everything I had into this. To think I might lose everything makes me sick to my stomach. I play with my phone, itching to hear Logan's voice, but he's on the plane. I resolve not to call him when he lands either. I'll sound like a whiny child, and that's not sexy at all.

When Pippa sends me a smiley face, my mood lifts. I remember that I did, in fact, sell the girls four of my dresses, which gives me a great head start. *Yeah*, a vicious voice says in the back of my mind, *to four people you know. They might've been pity buys.*

Luckily, I have the changes for Summer's dress to keep me occupied for the afternoon. Not one single person steps into the store the entire day. When I head to Logan's in the evening, I'm in tears. On Tuesday, I go over the advertising plan I worked on with Ava. She's a marketing genius, but she had to scale her genius down to my nonexistent budget. The plan was to save up the money I earn in the first month of sales, and use all of it for marketing. If today is anything to go by, I won't have anything to save.

In the afternoon, I have my first customer when an elegant woman in her late thirties walks in. I try to remember that she's a visitor, not yet a customer. I'm determined to turn her into one.

"You have a great selection," she comments. "I've yet to see the newest collection anywhere."

I smile. Yeah, this is what my store's unique selling proposition should be: always carrying this season's collections, not old ones. The downside? I must also sell each collection as soon as I bring it in before it becomes last season's.

"What would you like to try on? With your hair and long legs, can I tempt you with an Elie Saab dress?"

"Oh, absolutely, he's one of my favorites."

Eying her again, I decide she's a size four, and take an appropriate dress from the hanger. "How about this one?"

"Lovely. None of my girlfriends will have anything like it."

I show her inside the changing room.

"This looks gorgeous on you," I say when she comes out, parading in front of the large mirror.

"Right?" She smiles in the mirror, then turns around. Her eyes widen as she gazes at something behind me. "What is that?"

I don't even turn around to know what she means. My dresses are in that area. She picks up the train of her Elie Saab dress and hurries to them.

"These are beautiful," she exclaims, touching the fabric of a burgundy one. My stomach feels lighter than it has in days, but immediately plummets when she glances at the tag and skeptically asks, "Nadine Hawthorne? Never heard of her."

"Oh, that would be me," I murmur.

"You design?"

"Yes."

She pinches her nose. "I'd rather have something by an established designer. No offense, but I can't show up at a charity gala wearing a no-name outfit, even though your dresses are pretty."

I feel like someone punched me in the gut. Sure, I expected this to some degree, which is why I store many big-name designers. But having someone throw in my face that my work is less valuable because I'm not famous is still unpleasant. How can I be known if no one buys my designs? What came first, the chicken or the egg?

I plaster on a smile. "Should I pack the Elie Saab for you?"

"Yes, please do that. I'll tell my friends about your store. It's pretty."

I feel a bit more encouraged as she leaves. If more people come, some will *eventually* buy my designs too. But that "eventually" will come after a long time. Pippa arrives before closing time on Tuesday to pick up the dresses for the girls. I leave her alone in the front while I bring the packages from the back room.

"How's business?" she asks when I return.

"Not much happening."

"Well, obviously. No one knows about your gorgeous dresses."

"Exactly," I say miserably. "A customer told me to my face that she likes my dresses, but she can't buy them because she's never heard of me."

To my astonishment, her smile grows wider. "Things will change after Summer's gallery, if you want them to."

"How?" I ask suspiciously.

"I can invite some established fashion bloggers."

"Pippa, I appreciate it, but—"

"You're stubborn and think that my pulling some strings will give you an unfair advantage, and somehow undermine your efforts."

"Something along those lines." Not to mention I'm terrified at the prospect of fashion bloggers seeing my babies. What if they hate them? I suppose the downside of preparing twelve years for one dream is that when you're finally living the dream, you're afraid anything you do might ruin it.

Or maybe I'm overanalyzing this, and the simple explanation is that I'm a coward.

"You and I both know how the world works. You can have the best products, but if no one's aware of them, you won't sell. I'm not promising you anything. The bloggers might decide the dresses don't suit their style, but at least they'll see them."

Now I'm downright panicking. What if the bloggers *do* hate my dresses? I try to reason with myself. She's right. After all, my dream isn't an empty store, but people walking in and happily walking back out.

"Okay, thank you."

"So, I have your permission?" she asks.

"Yes."

"Thank God, because I already invited them."

With that, Pippa winks and heads out, leaving me smiling. Then I realize my dresses will be under the bloggers' scrutiny in a few days, and I'm right back to panicking.

***

Logan

"You're distracted," Max remarks. I'm sitting in my brother's office in London, and I've spaced out a couple of times in the last two hours. I'm wasting both our times because I'm not at the top of my game.

"Sorry, still have a bit of jet lag."

"Let's grab dinner. We can come back afterward."

We walk to the steak restaurant across the street where we eat every time I'm in London. The waitresses greet Max as if he's an old friend. He regularly spends his evenings at the office, which irks me. Sebastian and I work long hours too, but he's overdoing it.

"We can discuss sales—" I begin after the waitress takes our order, but Max shakes his head.

He raises an eyebrow. "No business talk during dinner."

"You're awfully strict about that rule, considering you're almost sleeping at the office."

"I have my priorities." He smiles, reminding me of Dad. Our father always insisted that dinner is family time. "How's Summer? Stressed out about the next gallery?"

"As always." We continue to talk about our baby sister until the food arrives.

"What's this I hear about someone named Nadine?"

I put my fork down. "I see the Bennett rumor mill has no problems crossing the ocean."

Max shrugs. "Man, there's no escape from the mill when talking to Summer."

"Nadine and I are dating, and it's going great."

"Good," he says between bites. "It was about time." His tone is final, and I know he won't ask more; my brother's not one to pry. And thank fuck for that, because there's enough meddling going on from the rest of the Bennett clan. Christopher was in Hong Kong when Sylvia and I broke up, but Max was still in San Francisco. He was my drinking partner of choice because he can down whiskey with me, while keeping his mouth shut. Sebastian would always follow that whiskey with some ridiculous advice. Blake and Daniel are even worse. "I want to find a replacement for myself, here in London. I want to come back home."

I stare Max down, then nod. "Sure. Do you have a timeline in mind?"

Sebastian and I had hoped the twins would stay overseas for about ten years, but it was obvious from the very beginning that neither was thrilled by the prospect of spending so much time abroad. We'd prefer to have someone from the family lead foreign operations, but I can understand his wish to return.

"No, but I'm already searching for someone to take over here."

"Let me know if I can help. Does Christopher also want to return home?"

"Haven't talked to him about it lately, but I think he'd like to hang out in Hong Kong for a few more years."

"I—"

That's when a group of holiday carolers enter the restaurant and start singing "Carol of the Bells" at the top of their lungs. Since there are three weeks to go until Christmas, the city's already in holiday mode. Out the window, I notice the light decorations up and down the street. I was so engrossed in business matters that I hadn't paid attention before. If Nadine were here, she would've made me pull my head out of my ass and admire everything. That woman loves her Christmas decorations. Her shop gives Santa's workshop a run for its money. The only things missing are elves.

I can't wait to return to San Francisco. I miss her and knowing she'll be home, waiting for me when I arrive, makes me even more eager to return. I can't convince her to stay with me every night because she insists I need my space, even though I've repeatedly told her it's bullshit. But on the nights she *is* with me, everything feels right.

On a whim, I snap a picture of the singers and send it to Nadine.

Nadine: They're adorable, but I was half-expecting a nude pic.

Logan: That'd raise a lot of eyebrows, considering I'm in a restaurant. But you're welcome to send me one.

Nadine: No can do. Too busy fretting over my lack of customers.

Logan: Relax.

Nadine: Have to go. Someone entered the store. I'm one step closer to world domination.

I imagine her enthusiastic smile as she greets her customer. I couldn't have timed this business trip worse—Nadine must be a wreck. In a stroke of genius, I realize what would make her day better. Lucky I have the chocolate shop on speed dial.

I convince Max to move the after-dinner business talk to his apartment instead of his office.

Later that night, when I collapse in my bed in the empty bedroom, I still can't shut my mind off, thinking about Max's return to San Francisco, and finding the best replacement for him here in London. Then my mind slides to Nadine, and that makes me smile. Actually, it makes me fucking grin.

Sebastian and I started Bennett Enterprises with one goal in mind: to make sure our family would be well taken care of. It didn't cross my mind that Nadine would have a similar goal behind her dream. My woman rocks, and I couldn't be prouder of her. If she thinks I'll let her go, she hasn't been paying attention. Yeah, she's an independent woman who doesn't like to rely on others and all that, and I respect that. But I'm her man. I'll do everything in my power to help her.

I only have to be careful not to cross the line and become overbearing—Pippa's favorite accusation— while I'm at it.

Chapter Fifteen

Nadine

Logan sends me a box of chocolate on Tuesday and on Wednesday too. The problem? I don't want chocolate; I want Logan. I miss him like crazy.

When the delivery guy brings the chocolate box on Thursday at lunch, I decide to tease Logan. I ask the guy if it's okay to take a picture of him. He's happy to pose for me.

I text the pic to Logan.

Nadine: Can I consider this hottie part of your gift too?

I don't expect to receive an answer right away because it's very early in the morning in London. But Logan surprises me.

Logan: Be careful. Elf on the Shelf is watching you.

Nadine: What are you talking about? I didn't buy Elf on the Shelf.

Logan: I did. In fact, I'm surprised you didn't discover it already. He's my spy, makes sure you behave.

My eyes widen as I clutch the phone, inspecting the shop. Sure enough, I find an elf sitting on one of the shelves in the back.

Nadine: How did this get here?

Logan: I have my spies.

Nadine: Pippa brought it, didn't she? When she picked up the dresses?

Logan: Bravo, Sherlock.

I turn the elf so his back is facing me, snap a picture, and send it to Logan.

Nadine: He can't see me anymore. I can be as naughty as I want with the chocolate man.

Logan: Are you trying to make me jealous?

Nadine: Is it working?

Logan: Yes.

Nadine: Great. Jealous enough to return one day earlier?

Logan: No can do, though I'll make sure to tell the shop to send someone else with the delivery tomorrow. Have to go to a meeting right now.

Nadine: *sad face*

Logan: Before I forget... Don't wear panties at the gallery. I'll just rip them apart.

Oh, my.

***

I am very optimistic on Friday, for several reasons. The first: Logan returns tonight. He'll meet me at Summer's gallery. No matter how the bloggers react to my dresses, it appeases me that Logan will be there.

The second reason for my optimism: I have three more customers. When I close for the day, there's a dance in my step all the way to Logan's. I do my hair and makeup meticulously, and put on the same dress I wore to the theater. I've lived in New York, so I'm aware this is a fashion no-go, but I can't afford to waste another one of my dresses on myself. In the cab to the gallery, I force myself not to chew my lip so I don't wipe away the lipstick. The venue is at the base of the Twin Peaks, and it's already buzzing with visitors and press. *Okay, here goes nothing. Fingers crossed.* I exit the cab.

Logan waits for me a few feet away from the entrance. He grabs my waist, pulling me away into a shadowed corner, kissing me hungrily.

"I've missed you," he says. "Even if you gave me a bruise."

"I've missed you too, and I don't believe I gave you a bruise."

"I'll show it to you as soon as we're alone," he says seductively. "Now, let's go inside before I change my mind, and steal you for myself for tonight."

"Mmm, impatient, aren't you?" I tease.

"You have no idea. I've fantasized about your sweet little body for days." He cups my jaw, rubbing his thumb across my skin.

"I'll give you something else to fantasize about." I drop my voice to a whisper. "I'm not wearing panties."

His eyes darken, and his grip firms on my jaw. "Woman, you want to drive me crazy?"

"You told me not to wear any, and I thought it was an excellent suggestion. I'm all commando down here. You're welcome to check."

He drops his hand, taking a step back. "Go inside." His voice sounds a lot like a growl, which makes me smile.

"Not going to join me? Going to keep lurking in the shadows? Fantasizing about the commando situation?"

He chuckles. "I'm hard. I'll walk this erection off 'in the shadows,' and then I'll join everyone inside the gallery."

I catch my breath, not daring to lower my gaze, and leave him to walk it off.

I walk into the gallery and notice the three Bennett sisters plus Ava posing for pictures in front of a group of people with cameras.

"There's the woman we've all been waiting for," Summer says. Alice pulls me to the group. "Meet Nadine Hawthorne, the genius behind these gorgeous dresses we're wearing."

"These are the bloggers," Pippa whispers in my ear as we're asked to pose for another photo. Pippa wasn't entirely truthful. She didn't invite just a few blogger friends—she invited a dozen.

After the group photo, we spread out. Summer takes the press on a tour of her paintings while the bloggers assault me with questions.

"Could we come by your shop?"

"Do you have more pictures?"

"Is Pippa's dress available in a smaller size? I'd love to buy it. No? Shucks."

I chat with them for what feels like hours, and my anxiety decreases bit by bit. These women seem to genuinely like my dresses. Not only the ones in sight tonight, but also those from the portfolio I have on my phone. A few times, I catch Logan's eyes. He stares at me with a smile from across the room. A proud smile. Butterflies roam around inside my belly.

Toward the end of the evening, the bloggers leave, promising to send me links to their posts in the coming week. Two even promise to post during the weekend. I'm ecstatic, but the moment they leave, tiredness hits me, almost giving me whiplash. I find Logan, but he's talking to Summer, and I decide to wait until they finish. Summer confided in me that her expos don't get easier, even though she's done many, and her family is her rock for each one.

"Ms. Hawthorne, is it?" a man's voice sounds from behind me as I admire a painting. I swirl around.

"Yes." I size him up and down.

"Archer Daring. Nice to meet you." We shake hands. "I happened to notice that you're in the garment industry," he says.

"I am."

"So am I. I have a chain of boutique stores in Europe: Paris, London, Milan, and Barcelona. Why don't you tell me a bit about you? Judging by what I see here tonight, your style fits ours. I'm always on the lookout for up-and-coming designers."

The words *up-and-coming* fill me with pride. Exuberant, I tell him about my store, and he inquires more about my designs. Just like I did with the bloggers, I also show him the pictures on my phone. At the end of the conversation, we exchange business cards. When he tells me, he'll contact me about the possibility of selling my designs in his stores, I nearly faint.

"Also, I'd love to get to know you better, on a personal level. Maybe we can grab a coffee sometime?"

Wow, that was smooth. I hope his offer of collaboration wasn't just a way to get in my pants, but if it was, he can shove it up his ass.

"I'm dating someone," I reply, "but let me know if you're interested in my designs."

He presses his lips together. "Of course. You'll hear from me soon." Then he leaves.

***

"Can I kidnap you now?" Logan whispers in my ear a while later.

"I barely had time to admire the paintings." I'm standing in front of one right now.

"I can sum them up for you: My sister's a genius, they are great."

"Won't she miss you if we leave?"

"The place is swarming with Bennetts: siblings, cousins, adopted Bennetts. One less won't matter."

"I disagree, I think you matter the most."

"Mmm. . . You're biased, though."

"A bit." I hold my thumb and forefinger together, smiling. "Let's do a small round so I can at least say I've seen all the paintings, and then we can go."

"You can never straight-out agree with me, can you?" He shakes his head, smiling.

"Where would be the fun in that?"

"Indeed. Okay, let's stay for a while." Pushing a strand of my hair behind my ear, he gives me a quick peck on my lips. "At any rate, I can finally show off my girlfriend at my arm. I spent the evening admiring you from afar. You were very professional." There's an edge to his voice, and I know what's causing it. "Who was the guy you talked to forever?"

I smile. *Bingo.* "Are you ready?"

He raises an eyebrow.

"I might have my first partner. That guy has a chain of boutiques in Europe, and he'd like to showcase my designs too."

"What's his name?"

"Archer Daring. Don't laugh."

"How about if I say it as Daring Archer. Can I laugh then?" Logan immediately bursts out laughing, of course.

"Fine, laugh. I'm excited, though."

"What did he say exactly?"

I recount the conversation quickly. I expected him to share my exuberance; instead, his expression is grim.

"People don't go around offering partnership deals like that."

"Well, he didn't say it's a done deal. Just hinted he's interested."

"Be careful, okay? I want you to keep me informed of every step you take."

I look at my toes. "Why? You don't trust my judgment enough to let me decide on my own?"

"That's not true, Nadine. I want the best for you."

"Fine, I'll keep you informed. But you stay out of this."

Logan remains silent.

"Promise me," I press.

"Fine, I promise."

I debate whether I should tell him that Archer asked me out on a date. I go for honesty though he'll dislike Archer even more.

"He also asked me out," I confess.

Logan's jaw ticks. "Okay. I'll stay out of it right after I punch him. Where is he?"

"Nothing like some jealousy to take the gentle out of gentleman, and bring the cave in," I mutter to myself. "Relax, Logan. I told him I'm seeing someone."

"Doesn't make me want to punch him any less."

"It's your fault for giving me naughty ideas," I say coyly. "He probably felt the sexy vibes from my commando situation."

"That's it." His eyes glint with desire as he steps closer, eying my mouth. I lick my lips to egg him on. The air between us instantly charges with sexual tension. Logan steps closer, and my knees weaken as his warm breath caresses my lips. "You're mine, Nadine. Every inch of you is mine. Now, let's go home and I'll show you."

This time, I don't argue.

Chapter Sixteen

Nadine

On Saturday, Logan and I head to the shop to finish setting up the back room, where I'll keep my inventory. For now, I've only brought half of the boxes stacked with expensive designer dresses from my apartment. I'll bring the rest after we finish today.

We're done by late afternoon, and then drive Logan's car to my place so we can load the boxes.

When we arrive in front of the building, it's clear we won't be able to park nearby, and Logan says, "Why don't you go in and start preparing everything? I'll come up after I find a place to park."

"Sure."

I exit the car, heading inside with a dance in my step. My fingers tingle with the temptation of checking my email, to see if any of the bloggers wrote about my designs already, but I keep myself in check. I'm ridiculous. They all must have better things to do on a Saturday. Still, the temptation is here, and it's nearly irresistible.

My euphoria takes a nosedive once I open the door to my apartment. On a sigh, I make my way between the boxes.

I'm in the process of counting the boxes when all hell breaks loose. A fire alarm rings loudly. My stomach gives a painful jolt as I swirl on my heels, facing my closed door. I've lived in many shitholes in my life and experienced false alarms more than once. Something tells me it's not false this time. The hairs rise on the back of my neck.

Without hesitation, I open the front door and head out into the corridor. At first glance, nothing is wrong. But then I peer over the railing, looking down then up the staircase. There is thick gray smoke on the floor above me. My heart sinks, my pulse quickens. In case of fire, one shouldn't use elevators. Right. I'm on the fourth floor. With the deafening alarm ringing in my ears, I skid down the stairs.

Rushing downward, I exert the muscles in my calves until they burn. I don't slow down until I reach the first floor, where it's crowded with the rest of the residents, all trying to get out. When I glance up the staircase, a knot forms in my throat. There are flames in sight, and the smoke is thick, which can kill as viciously as fire does. Covering my ears, I rise on my toes, trying to see what's keeping us from escaping. To no avail. We don't have much time. The air grows hotter, thicker. Every breath brings more torture than relief. My eyes water, and the crowd isn't moving. Suddenly, dust falls on us, thick and suffocating. I turn my eyes up and freeze.

The staircase will collapse on us.

***

Logan

"What do you mean, I have to remain calm?" I ask the police officer through gritted teeth. "That building's on fucking fire. There are people inside." Nadine is inside.

"The firefighters will be here any minute now, and they will do their best," he replies. His voice is so calm and robotic that it makes want to smash his nose.

I ball my hands into fists. The top floor is in flames. "This building will burn to the ground in a few fucking minutes. Where the fuck are the firefighters?"

"Sir, I will ask you to step back and calm down," he says in the same robotic voice. I back up, panic replacing my anger as flames engulf the fourth floor as well. My pulse quickens and my mind turns blank except for one thought: *I am powerless, and I might lose the woman I love.*

Someone shoves me hard in the back, and I realize there's a crowd behind me that wasn't here before. From the fleeting comments I catch, they live in the neighboring buildings.

"The firefighters are here," someone from the back of the crowd calls, and some of my sanity returns. They're not *here*, per se, but I can hear their siren.

They arrive within seconds, followed by ambulances. Jesus. Ambulances. My blood goes cold.

I watch as if in a nightmare as the firefighters rescue the residents, and hand them over to the paramedics. I make my way through the crowd, desperate to see Nadine. She must be okay. *Please, dear God, let her be okay.* I cannot lose her. I *will not* lose her.

"Everyone was evacuated," someone yells through the crowd as I finally reach the ambulances.

My heart constricts when I see her, covered in dust and whatnot. Her eyes are wide and fearful as she peers around her frantically. She only calms down when she sees me walking to her.

I step inside the ambulance and hug her as the paramedic scribbles something on a piece of paper. Nadine molds into my arms, fisting my shirt. She's trembling slightly, and so am I. The relief of having her with me again is overwhelming. "Nadine, are you hurt?" My voice quivers.

She opens her mouth, but no words come out, so she shakes her head.

I hug her tight again, caressing her hair. "Is she hurt?" I ask the paramedic.

"Physically, no, but she might be in shock. I suggest you take your wife to the hospital to have a thorough checkup."

"Wouldn't it be safer to take her with the ambulance?"

The paramedic shakes her head. "She doesn't need to ride in the ambulance, and we're needed here for first aid."

I nod, licking my lips. "I'll take her to the hospital right away."

"Please, Logan," Nadine murmurs. "I want to go home. I want to sleep."

"I'm taking you to the hospital. I'm not negotiating on this."

Without waiting for her reply, I lift her in my arms. She rests her head against my chest without arguing. We ride to the hospital in a cab instead of my car, because I can't concentrate on anything until a doctor tells me she's one hundred percent okay.

Chapter Seventeen

Logan

I can't fall asleep, even hours after I put Nadine to bed. The doctors checked her at the hospital, assured me she's in perfect health, but exhausted, and still in shock. I brought her home, put her on the bed, and prepared her a bath. When I returned to the bedroom, she was already asleep. I didn't have the heart to wake her up, even though she still smelled of danger: smoke and burnt wood.

I try to sleep, but it evades me, so I simply lie next to her, her small body nestled against me. If I'm honest, I don't want to sleep; I have the irrational fear that something will happen to her if I don't watch over her. I've never been more afraid in my entire life, from the moment I saw the smoke until the doctors cleared her. The minutes I waited for Nadine to come out were paralyzing. I wanted to go in and save her, and no one would let me. I was powerless to protect her, and I hated it.

Nadine shifts, draping an arm and half her body over me. I wrap both arms around her, holding her as tight as I can, hoping I won't wake her up. Some things I can't control, but I'll control everything else I can. This woman is mine, and I won't let anyone or anything harm her again.

**

Nadine

I know something's off the second I open my eyes. I stink. That's when I remember: the fire, the hospital, and Logan.

Logan… I bolt upright.

"Morning, gorgeous," he says from a recliner in front of the bed.

"Not so gorgeous today." I point to my clothes, then at the disheveled bed. "Oh, my God, I made a mess out of your bed."

"We'll wash the sheets." Rising to his feet, he walks over to me, putting one knee on the bed. Cupping my cheeks, he kisses my forehead. "I'm so glad you're awake. How are you?"

"Much better now after a full night's sleep." To be honest, I still don't feel completely okay. I have never been more scared in my life than I was yesterday. The fear seems to have seeped into my bones, and I think it'll remain there for a while.

Inspecting him, I notice he has deep circles under his eyes. "But you're tired."

"I couldn't sleep all night."

"Why?"

Logan smiles. "I couldn't let you out of my sight. I just wanted to look at you and be sure you're okay."

Speechless, I smile back.

"Come on, let's clean you up." Logan takes my hand and leads me to the bathroom, where he proceeds to undress me. He's done this many times before, taking off my clothes gently or with passion, but now it's different. He moves as if he's afraid he might damage my skin by undressing me.

"I'm all right, Logan. I just stink."

He frowns as he removes my last piece of clothing. "The doctors said you might still be in shock."

"I'm not," I argue, even though I suspect that the lingering fear might be related to shock. I step into the shower and Logan watches me while I wash, his eyes never leaving mine. There is nothing sexual in his gaze; it's raw and powerful, and brings me a sense of safety as I try to wash off the fear.

When we step into the living room a while later, the full impact of what happened last night hits me as Logan shoves a cup of coffee in my hands.

"Was anyone hurt?" I ask in a strangled voice, fighting to keep the panic away. Logan seems to have noticed the shift in my mood. In a fraction of a second, he sits next to me on the couch.

"No. The firemen evacuated everyone before the staircase collapsed, but the building burned down."

I swallow hard, lowering my eyes to the cup in my hands. "Define 'burned down.'"

"Everyone will have to relocate, and nothing inside could be salvaged. All your boxes burned up, Nadine."

"No." The word comes out in a single strangled whisper. "That was half of my inventory." The very expensive inventory I paid for upfront. I didn't have renter's insurance. I couldn't afford it. One of the reasons I chose this building was because they didn't require such an insurance. "This is going to ruin me for good." Not daring to look up, I try to run the numbers in my head, grasping at straws for how I can make this work.

Logan puts his hand under my chin, trying to lift my head. I stubbornly keep my stance.

"Nadine—"

"I can't lose everything again. Not this time." There is no way I can make this work with half the inventory gone. Starting from zero again is unthinkable. Another thought chills the breath in my throat. Last time I lost everything, Thomas bolted. Losing Logan? That would break me for good.

"Nadine—"

"After all this," I whisper.

"Nadine. Stop."

I wince.

"You're not alone, Nadine."

At this, I eye him, baffled.

"I'm the man who loves you, and I want to take care of you. I won't take no for an answer. I made an appointment with a friend of mine at the bank. We're seeing him first thing on Monday morning about a loan so you can make up for the burned inventory. Also, as of now, you're officially living with me. We should go shopping so you can replace whatever clothes you still had in your apartment. Mind you, I'd love for you to go around naked all the time, though I'd rather you don't go naked outside."

He says all this with a determined smile on his face.

I'm still hung up on the first part of the sentence. "You love me?" I repeat slowly.

"Yes." Logan looks at me expectantly, but I remain silent for a long minute. Or maybe several long minutes as I process everything. Logan loves me, and not only won't he leave me, but he also wants to fight through this with me and help me. He's not like Thomas, or Dad. Part of me knew this, of course, but another part suspected that if things got awful, he'd bolt.

"If you're not going to say anything, things will get really awkward, really fast," Logan says in a light tone, though I detect unease in it. "No pressure or anything."

I burst out laughing, tearing up slightly. "I love you. Of course I love you. Hearing you say it just felt so surreal."

"I can say it as often as you wish. Don't do the silence thing again. It freaked me the hell out."

I climb in his lap, straddling him on the couch. He leans back, settling his hands on my hips. I move a strand of hair from his eyes, caressing his chest. I want to touch him everywhere.

"Ah, Logan Bennett, afraid of something. Who would've thought?"

"I was afraid last night," he says in a low voice. "I don't want anything to ever happen to you. While I couldn't sleep, I thought of various ways to keep you safe. One of them was to have you with me at all times."

I grin. "That's not caveman behavior at all, you know."

"I don't care, as long as you're safe."

"I'm safe now, with you."

He pulls me into a kiss. As his lips capture mine, it dawns on me that he doesn't only make me feel safe, but also cherished and appreciated. This man is perfect, and I can't believe I was lucky enough to find him.

"I need to be inside you, Nadine," Logan growls. He peppers my neck with kisses, his hands on my thighs.

"I need you too."

A bolt of heat courses through me, from my chest to my groin. My whole body needs him with desperation. We won't make it to the couch. I know this because he undoes the cord holding my bathrobe together, then pushes said robe to the ground. When he lets his gaze roam over my breasts, I feel more naked than ever. After this morning, there is no part of me Logan hasn't seen. He has seen me at my best, and at my worst, yet here he is, worshiping my body with kisses.

Not for the first time, I believe Logan can read my thoughts. He can see through me. Cupping my face in his hands, he says, "I don't want you to ever think you're alone again. Whatever happens, I'm with you. I'm your guy."

"You're my guy," I whisper back.

Desperately wishing to touch his body, I pull his shirt over his head, baring his perfect chest and hard abs. I lick my lips and run my hands over his taut skin, from his nipples down to the button of his jeans. He flashes a wicked smile while I unbutton his pants, clumsily pushing them past his ass, together with his boxers, freeing his gorgeous erection. He pulls my upper body to him, hugging me tenderly, burrowing his head into my neck. Abruptly, he stands up, and I wrap my legs tightly around him. His erection presses against my clit and the length of my entrance, sending delicious shivers along my nerve endings. I'm about to commend him on his self-control for wanting to lead us to the bedroom when he puts me on my back on the couch. My hips surge forward, but he shakes his head.

"Not ready yet."

Rising to his knees on the couch, he parts my legs, exposing me further to him. Under his heated gaze, a rush of wetness pools in my already slick center.

He caresses the skin on my thighs while he peppers my sternum with kisses, deliberately avoiding my breasts even though my nipples are hard buds from the anticipation. He lingers on my navel, his tongue nuzzling around. Need spears through me; I arch my back involuntarily as it overtakes my body.

When I can't stand it anymore, I whisper, "Please."

"Please, what?"

"Touch me."

"Show me how you want me to touch you, Nadine."

My eyes widen, heat rushing to my cheeks. I drop one hand to my mound, keeping the other one around my breast.

"You're beautiful," he says in a deep baritone voice. "So beautiful. I won't ever let you go, I promise."

"I love you." The words are binding and liberating at the same time.

He watches me with a hungry expression, his eyes growing darker by the second. His breathing becomes more labored as he rips the foil of a condom package and rolls the condom on.

I expect him to lose control any second now, and make love to me hard and fast. My entire body needs his unrestrained passion. But when he touches me, his fingers tread lightly and carefully, as if he's afraid of hurting me. *Time to show him I'm in perfect condition.*

As he positions his erection at my entrance, I push myself against him without restraint. Breath whooshes out of me from the impact.

"Nadine." He grips my hair, tilting my head back, gaining better access to my neck. Logan makes love to me unrestrained and uncontrolled, sliding out of me and slamming back in again and again.

On a moan, he pushes his hand between us, circling my clit. It drives me crazy, igniting a need for release. I spread my legs even wider, frantically moving to meet his wild thrusts. The tension inside of me builds to an impossible high before I explode, clinging to him. His grunts of relief fill the air seconds later, and then he shifts off me before collapsing on the couch.

We remain silent, lying on our backs, for several long minutes before a ring at the door startles us. Hurriedly, I put on my robe.

"Are you expecting someone?" I ask. "Your family?"

Logan leisurely rises from the couch, putting on his jeans and shirt. "No, it's Pippa dropping off some things for you."

"I'm not following."

"I texted Pippa while you were sleeping, asked her to go shopping for you."

I narrow my eyes. "You said *we* were going shopping."

"Did I say that?" The corner of his mouth lifts, mischief dancing in his eyes. "What I meant was I asked Pippa to shop for you."

Crossing my arms over my chest, I tap my foot, trying very hard to feign being upset with him. "You did that before talking to me?"

"Guilty." He puts up his hands in mock surrender. "I'm sure you'll like what she bought for you."

Unable to contain my smile, I shake my head. "You're awfully self-assured, you know that?"

"That's my middle name."

He gives me a quick peck on the cheek before rushing to the door. He returns a few seconds later with about a million shopping bags.

"Errrr... I swear I told Pippa to buy you only essential things. She went way overboard," Logan says.

"She's a lot like you, then. Why didn't you ask her to come inside?"

"I asked my family to back off today. After I told them about the fire, they all wanted to drop by to make sure you're okay. I insisted they shouldn't even call you today."

"Why?"

Logan strides across the room, closing the distance to me. When he's right in front of me, he says, "I want to have the whole day just for us."

Chapter Eighteen

Nadine

On Monday morning, at seven o'clock sharp, we're at the bank.

"Thank you for meeting us on such a short notice, Finn," Logan says after the introductions are out of the way.

"Anything for you, Logan," Finn replies. "What are friends for?" Turning to me, he states, "I understand you need a loan large enough to pay back the debt you incurred to buy the inventory that burned, as well as to replace that inventory?"

"That's correct."

"I will analyze your financial documents as soon as possible, Nadine. I'm sure we'll find a way to grant you the loan."

"It's a big loan," I say.

"He'll find a way," Logan reassures me, putting his hand over mine. I suspect he'll all but coerce poor Finn into finding a way. After fighting alone for years, having Logan here with me, supporting me, feels surreal.

I appreciate that he didn't offer to outright pay my loan, which I wouldn't accept on principle alone, but letting him help me won't change anything between us. I hope.

"Thank you," I say. "To both of you."

***

The rest of the day is crazy. With Logan's ban on calling lifted, all the Bennetts call me within half an hour in the morning. Three of the bloggers have already posted about me over the weekend, and I'm over the moon. They have glorious shots of the girls and the address of my shop.

Within the first hour of opening the store, I have three customers. One of them specifically asks to see *my* designs. Mine. I nearly trip over my own feet trying to impress her.

"I'll try this one," she says. "I'm so lucky that Flirty Flo featured you. She's my go-to blogger."

I'm the lucky one. I help her put on the dress, which hugs her curves gorgeously, but it needs something more to achieve perfection.

I fetch the magic weapon and, holding it up, I say, "You'd be even more stunning if you put this bra beneath it."

Smiling, the woman takes it from me. Several minutes later, she steps out of the changing room. "You were right. I'll buy them both. You have a real knack for this."

"Thank you."

"My sister told me to let her know if your stuff is as good as it appeared in the pictures. I'll tell her it's even better. Expect her sometime this week."

I grin as she leaves. This was my dream, to see people leave my shop with smiles on their faces, feeling a little more fulfilled than they did before they walked in. The customer keeps her promise—her sister pops into my store the next day, buying a dress too.

I sell nine of my designs over the course of the week. I won't take over the world anytime soon, but I'm beyond happy. There are people out there wearing my stuff. People I've never met before.

On Friday afternoon, Pippa calls me. "How's our superstar?"

I chuckle. "I'm hardly a superstar, but I'm doing pretty damn good if I can say so myself."

"I've read every blog post. They loved you."

"Yeah." I can still hardly believe it. "How are things on your end? Is the show driving you crazy already?"

"Funny that you're asking. Things are not so great."

"How come?"

"I fired the designer who was supposed to dress our models."

I gasp. "But the show's one week away. Why did you fire her?"

"He was being a diva and was driving everyone nuts, trying to boss us around. I wanted to be fair, but I'm not stupid. It's our show, not his. His dresses are the background drop for our jewels. He was acting as if this was his private show."

"What are you going to do?"

"Depends on you. Our fate is in your hands."

"Not following."

"We're in desperate need for a new designer for the show."

"Okay, but how—OH." *Oh. Wow, no way.* "Pippa Bennett, are you asking me what I think you're asking me?"

"I believe I am."

I can practically hear her smile on the other end. It takes me a few seconds to process it. "Yes, yes, yes."

"Wow, you're so enthusiastic, you'd think I asked you to marry me."

"What do you need from me?"

I write down everything Pippa requests. I was lucky none of the dresses I designed burned up, just the ones I bought. Well, lucky because Logan stepped in to help me out with the bank. I haven't heard from Finn yet, but I hope he calls soon and that my loan will be approved, because I need to make some payments to cover my old debt right away. I went back to see the building, and it's a lost cause.

Not in a million years did I want to rely on a man again. Then again, I didn't expect Logan to stick around either. He proved me wrong, and it felt *so* right.

"Can you come by the office after you close the shop?" Pippa asks.

"Sure, but won't it be too late for you?"

"It's show week. Everyone's practically sleeping here."

"All right. See you in a few hours. Thank you so much, Pippa. I'll find a way to make it up to you."

"No need. But you can make it up to Logan. He was the one who told me that you might be a perfect fit for us months ago. I just didn't want to be unfair toward our current designer, but he asked for it."

"He did, huh? Anything else Logan's done without telling me?"

"If you're referring to my shopping spree…"

I can imagine her grinning ear to ear at the other end. I didn't touch this topic when she called to check on me on Monday.

"You have fantastic taste," I say. "I know both of you meant well. I just don't like other people deciding things for me."

"Yeah, my brother sometimes does that for no reason. Or, well, I'm sure he *does* have a reason, but it's not understandable to us. The whole 'guys are from Mars, women from Venus' thing is true. This time, though, I'm on his side."

I laugh softly. "Of course you are. See you later."

I almost pinch myself after I hang up. My dresses will be in the Bennett show. I feel like I'm flying. As Pippa said, it'll be *their* show, not mine, but this is more than I ever dreamed of achieving in such a short time.

I have two more customers until closing time, and then I receive a call from Archer.

"Nadine, how have you been?"

"Great." I decide to keep the fire incident to myself, but I want to brag about my good news. "A few minutes ago, I was informed that my dresses will be used in the Bennett show at the end of the week."

"Congratulations. That's fantastic news."

"I still can hardly believe it."

"Why not? Hard work pays off," he says good-naturedly. I smile.

"What can I do for you?"

"I spoke to our buying managers in Milan and Barcelona, and they'd both be happy to carry some of your models."

I nearly drop the phone. "Seriously?"

"Yes. I can forward you the email with the designs they're interested in. Could you have them ready for shipment in two weeks?"

"I… Wow. You're quick. Send me the email and I'll look into it. Archer, thank you."

After I hang up, I call Logan to share the good news.

"Hello, handsome," I tell him.

"Hello back."

"I wanted to share some great news with you. Archer called, told me he wants to send a shipment to Milan in two weeks."

"Be careful, Nadine."

I sigh. I knew this was going to be his reaction, but I still wanted to share the news with him.

"I am. Didn't give Archer a definite answer yet. I can handle myself; don't worry. And don't get involved. Please."

"I won't."

Telling him about Archer isn't the only reason I called. I also wanted to thank him for Pippa's invitation but decide against it at the last moment. I'll surprise my man today. After I hang up, I open Archer's stores' website, to do a background check.

***

Logan

"What do you mean, the loan wasn't approved?" I yell into my phone.

"Her financial situation wasn't deemed good enough for such a large loan. The bank can re-evaluate if we receive new information, but that can take a while, and she'll default on her old debt if she doesn't repay it soon."

"Fuck this," I say through gritted teeth. "Pay her old debt from my account."

"I'll need her permission for that."

"No, you don't. We're friends. Do me this favor, and I'll tell Nadine about it." She will not take this well, I know it in my gut, but I won't sit back and see my woman endure hardships.

"Fine, but you have a week max to tell her before she'll find out anyway."

"Done."

I finish the conversation and look at Blake's amused face. He sits across from me in my office. He was here when Finn called and heard everything since I had my phone on loudspeaker.

"Solving everyone's problems again, brother?" he asks.

"None of your concern," I reply in a clipped tone. "Why don't you tell me why you came to see me?"

"I've started planning Sebastian's bachelor party."

"Let me get this straight. Sebastian's wedding is six months away, and you already want to plan the bachelor party?"

Blake nods, stifling a yawn. It's very late, and almost everyone on my floor has left already. I stare at him in disbelief. My brother, the ultimate spur-of-the-moment guy, who doesn't even plan one month ahead, is suddenly planning six months ahead.

"Yeah. Our big brother is getting married. It'll be the first bachelor party in our family," he explains. "I'm not leaving anything to chance. The wedding's for the women; the bachelor party is for the men. It's hard to bring together a dozen people—"

"Who have actual jobs? I can't imagine."

Blake narrows his eyes. "Daniel and I are the PR representatives of the company."

"You mean showing up at collection shows and bragging? That's not a real job."

"Don't start. I'm not in the mood for a lecture."

"You never are, and I still give them. But I'll let it slide today."

My relationship with Blake and Daniel can be summed up by the following conundrum: I want to strangle them on a daily basis, while also making sure no one else does.

"Back to the party," Blake says. "I plan to send our big brother to marriage jail in style."

"What do you have in mind?"

"Vegas."

I scoff. "That's your idea of style?"

"Yeah. Don't worry, your bachelor party will be in some fancy-ass place where you can wear your cufflinks, and not look ridiculous."

I'm not sure how I feel about Blake already thinking about my bachelor party, so I focus on Sebastian.

Leaning back in my chair, I say, "Maybe Vegas isn't such a bad idea."

"I wasn't expecting you to give in so easily." Blake eyes me closely, as if he's suspecting I'm setting a trap.

"Why the hell not? If there's a time for Vegas, it's then. Not sure how happy Ava and Nadine will be about it, though."

Blake picks up a crystal panther I have on my desk, inspecting it. I received it when we struck our first deal with a luxury chain distributor, and it's been on my desk for more than a decade.

"Pippa tells me Nadine will be the designer of the next show." He says this without taking his eyes off the panther, blatantly ignoring my woes at the girls' disapproval of Vegas.

"Yeah, I'm very proud of her. It'll be splendid exposure for her. Summer's gallery helped a lot too. She made connections. Some good, some dubious."

"What do you mean?" He puts the panther back on the desk, training his eyes on me.

"There's this guy, Archer Daring." I tell him quickly about the offer to Nadine.

"Archer Daring," Blake sneers. "Even his name sounds suspicious. Did you run a background check on him?"

"No, Nadine asked me to stay out of it."

"So?"

"So I'm staying out of it."

There is a pause, and Blake raises his eyebrows. "Oh, you're serious. I was waiting for the punchline—something like, 'I've already got my men on it.'"

"I meant what I said."

"You just paid a loan she didn't ask you to pay. Since when are you keeping out of other people's business?"

"I'm working on improving that."

"Who are you, and what have you done with Logan?"

"I'm trying not to be overbearing."

Blake chuckles, crossing his arms over his chest. "Well, well, well. The mighty *have* fallen."

"I see this as progress."

"We never really agree on anything. Except Vegas. Can't believe Sebastian is getting married in six months, and you're in love. It's scary."

It's my turn to chuckle. Blake shuns commitment, whether commitment means a stable job or a steady girlfriend. Maybe a woman wouldn't be so bad for him; she could bring him on the right track. I should put Pippa on it. Though, knowing my sister, she's probably already made a shortlist of potential candidates for him.

"You have the girl; now make sure you keep her."

"What's that supposed to mean?" I stare down at him.

"As someone who's mastered the art of screwing up relationships, I'm just saying be careful. Also, not judging you, but you've screwed up plenty of times before."

Since I cast so much judgment on him, it's fair that I take some in return.

"Those weren't exactly screw-ups. I wasn't interested in making those relationships last."

"I see."

Blake opens his mouth, but a knock on the door interrupts us.

"Come in," I call out.

The door opens, and Nadine comes in, wearing an elegant cardigan... And two seconds after stepping inside, she drops the cardigan to the floor. She's stark naked underneath it.

Then she notices Blake.

"Oh, my God," Nadine exclaims. Hurriedly, she covers herself with the cardigan again.

"I haven't seen anything," Blake says, turning to face the wall. Judging by his grin, he took an eyeful. The bastard.

Nadine's blushing, Blake's biting his fist to keep from laughing, and my dick's twitching. *Perfect.*

"I thought you were alone, Logan," Nadine says, mortified. She clutches the collar of her cardigan with both hands. "The security guard said all the employees on your floor have left."

"I'm not an employee," Blake chimes in. "He wasn't there when I came into the building. Anyway, I'm leaving now."

Nadine flattens herself against the wall as Blake heads to the door. She stares at a spot on the carpet the entire time. He doesn't wipe off his smile, but at least he has the decency not to joke about it in front of her.

Nadine covers her face with her palms after he leaves. "I'm never going to be able to look Blake in the eyes again."

I walk up to her, lying through my teeth. "He didn't see anything."

She peeks at me between her fingers. "You're lying."

"Fine, I am. Let's forget about him."

"I can't believe this. The first time I was in this building, I soaked my dress and shoved my boobs in your face, and now—"

"Shh," I say, fighting not to laugh.

When she still doesn't take her hands off her face, I kiss her forehead softly. She smells like oranges, as usual. I've never had her smell in my office. It feels good. "I appreciated the view very much. Both times." I lower my fingers to her collar, but Nadine slaps my hand. Taking a deep breath, she looks up at me. She's adorable.

"I'm not ready to be naked in your office right now."

I grin. "Okay. I want you to be comfortable."

I walk over to my desk, slumping in my seat. She glances around the office with curious eyes, finally joining me behind the desk, leaning against the counter. Knowing that she's naked underneath the cardigan makes me so aroused I can barely think straight.

Still, I try.

"How come you decided to visit?"

"Pippa called me today asking if she can use my designs for the show, so I brought the dresses, and wanted to surprise you."

"That was definitely a surprise."

"I saw pictures of the new collection. The jewels are so beautiful, the sapphires especially."

Sapphires would suit her; they'd match her blue eyes. I file that information in my mind for later.

Nadine smiles, her usual seductive spirit overpowering her lingering embarrassment. About time, because I'll explode in my pants otherwise.

"Thank you for putting in a good word for me with Pippa, by the way."

"Mmm." Unable to resist anymore, I pull her in my lap and run my thumb across her lower lip. She takes it in her mouth. Jesus, this woman will kill me. Somewhere in the back of my mind, I know that I should talk to her about the bank situation, but I don't want to spoil the moment. In fact, I'll wait until after the show. She has enough on her mind as it is.

"I thought you'd be difficult." Her tone is playful as she shifts over the bulge in my pants.

"What are you talking about?" I manage to ask.

Her eyes widen. "You have a very strict 'no sex at the office' rule. Ava told me about it."

I pause in the act of opening the belt of her cardigan. I do have that rule, but I haven't even thought about it. The office has been my sanctuary for years. I never brought women here. But Nadine belongs here, just as she belongs in every area of my life.

"You make me want to break all the rules. Or at least change them. My office. My rules. Strip." I kiss her passionately, enjoying her soft lips.

I won't mess this up.

Chapter Nineteen

Logan

The opportunity to mess things up presents itself two days later, in the form of a call from Blake.

"I have info about Archer," Blake says instead of good morning. "I ran a background check on him."

"What? Blake, Nadine specifically asked—"

"*You* to stay out of it, yeah. But I'm not you— thank God, by the way. Not sure I could handle so many cufflinks. She didn't forbid me anything, so I did some digging."

"Are you trying to kill me?" Gritting my teeth, I rub my forehead. I'm in my office and have a million things to do.

"Actually, I'm trying to be of service to my older brother. I don't expect a thank you, don't worry."

"I suppose you wouldn't call if you'd found out he's the Dalai Lama."

"That's my brother. I knew there must be some truth to the rumor that you're smart. And you're right, I wouldn't have called."

"What did you find on him?"

LAYLA HAGEN

Blake has nothing good to share. Archer Daring is a scam artist. He's doing it smartly, which is why his stores have operated for years, leaving a trail of scammed designers in his wake. There are many roads to success, but crushing the other people in your way is the lowest one to take.

"I can dig up more dirt," Blake finishes.

"No need, I'll have one of my men in Europe do it."

"By the way, now I finally understand your desire to commit. Nadine is hot."

"If you ever mention that again, I will punch you."

"No deal. I'll gladly take the punch to see your annoyed face. You'll never hear the end of it."

"Very mature, Blake. Thank you, by the way. For helping with this Archer business."

"Welcome. See you at the show."

"Bye."

I make a few phone calls to some people I know in Europe, requesting a full background check on Archer. The report comes at the end of the day, and I find out how he operates down to the dirtiest detail. It's all I can do not to smash the guy's face, or ruin him. That's what he deserves. He ruined countless unsuspecting designers starting out, and now he's after Nadine. But he's in for a nasty surprise. He won't hurt my woman, not on my watch. I've been in the business world a lot longer, and I know all the shades scam artists come in. She doesn't, but I'll protect her from it, even if she doesn't want me to.

I can crush the bastard and his business in a matter of days.

***

I'm mapping out the best course of action when my phone rings.

"Hi, Dad."

"Hi, Logan. Everything all right, son?"

"Sure. We're busy with the collection launch, but that's not news." Dealing with Archer is news, though. An idea strikes me—Dad always gives good advice. "Do you and Mom mind if I stop by for dinner tonight?"

"Sure. We'd love to see Nadine as well."

"I'm afraid that won't be possible." I chuckle. "She's with Pippa and Ava in Creative, setting the finishing touches for the show on Friday. They'll be here until midnight."

"All right."

"See you in a few hours."

"Okay—Wait, your mom is asking if you want her to cook something specific."

"N—actually, yes. Tell Mom I want apple pie."

"Order taken," Mom's voice sounds in the background.

"See you two later."

***

Somehow, with only five hours' notice, my mom cooked roast beef, turkey, and pie.

"Mom, you know it's just me, right?" I ask, surveying the full table in my parents' living room. "Not the entire clan?"

Dad shrugs.

Mom beams at me from her seat. "I wanted to make soup too, but your father convinced me there was enough food."

Dad and I avoid each other's eyes. Mom is a great cook... most of the time. But somehow, making soup completely escapes her. Dad never had the heart to tell her, and neither did the rest of us.

Over dinner, they tell me their plans to refurbish our old ranch, and turn it into a bed and breakfast. The ranch was all my parents had many years ago. My father built it with his own hands. When Sebastian asked them to sell it and hand him the money so he could set up Bennett Enterprises, they did it without blinking. It was a huge gamble, but we all trusted Sebastian. It paid off.

Last year, the ranch was up for sale, and Sebastian bought it back and gave it to my parents as an anniversary present.

"It'll give us something to do, running the B&B," Mom says happily.

"It's a great idea," I say. My parents don't need the money, but I understand where they're coming from. They are used to hard work, yet the second Bennett Enterprises turned a profit, Sebastian and I took care of all their financial worries, basically forbidding them to work. It seemed like a good idea to us at the time, but it wasn't the best for our parents.

"I'll leave you boys to talk," Mom says after we finish the pie. My puzzlement must register on my face because she adds, "You always request pie when you want to talk to your dad."

"I do?" The things parents notice will never cease to amaze me.

"Yes," she confirms, leaving the room with a smile.

"Spit it out, son," Dad says.

I tell him everything about the situation with Nadine and Archer. That I discovered Archer's a bastard, and that Nadine asked me not to get involved, but it's hard for me not to step in and flat-out ruin that son of a bitch.

"Son, you were always overprotective. When you were young and were watching Blake and Daniel learning to walk, you were hovering around them, catching them every time they were about to fall."

I raise my eyebrows. My memories don't go that far back. The only memories of Daniel and Blake I have from our childhood are that Sebastian and I pranked them to no end. When they grew up, the twins pranked our asses off as revenge. They got much better at it than Sebastian and I. But I trust my dad to have a more extensive memory of those early days.

"You know what happened?" he continues. "It took them a lot longer to learn how to rise back up on their tiny feet after falling because you were constantly keeping them from doing so. You've always been protective, and it's commendable. Sometimes, though, it's good to let people make mistakes so they can learn from them. "

"Are you suggesting I let Archer scam Nadine?" My words come out harsher than I intended.

"No, of course not. Not in this case. What I meant was that you always try to solve everyone's problems, and it's not always for the best. Sometimes, all you have to do is be by their side while they solve their problems, giving them your counsel. What I suggest is you tell her what you know and let her handle it. The secret to a happy marriage is honesty."

I open my mouth to say Nadine and I are not married, and then it hits me. I *want* to marry this woman. I've never been more certain of anything. While I digest this epiphany, my dad goes on and on about him being honest with Mom.

"Dad," I interrupt. "Drop the act. You went behind her back when you covered for Blake and Daniel at school."

"Well," Dad says. "Your mother can be very stubborn sometimes, and a man's got to do what a man's got to do."

I chuckle. "So, the secret to a happy marriage is to be honest, except those times when you're not honest."

"You're twisting my words, son."

"I believe I'm just summing everything up. Did you ever tell Mom about covering for the twins?"

"No. And I'd appreciate it if you wouldn't either."

"Don't worry, Dad, I wouldn't want to incur Mom's wrath. But I did understand your point."

"You love this woman."

"I do," I affirm.

He pats my shoulder. "We're happy for you, son. After everything that happened with Sylvia, we feared you were going to swear on being a bachelor."

The mention of Sylvia no longer brings the sour taste it used to. Nadine wiped that away too.

"We want you to be happy."

"I know. Thanks, the talk helped. Now I have a plan."

Like Dad said, a man's got to do what a man's got to do.

***

The pre-Nadine Logan would have done things the following way: I would've ruined the bastard's business with a few phone calls, and stormed into his office to tell him to stay away from Nadine.

The current Logan will wait until after the show to talk to Nadine, and then decide together what the best punishment for this asshole is. I still hope to convince her that wiping his business out is the best thing.

But I *am* still going to his office to warn the moron to stay away from Nadine. I walk into his office the day before the show. His office is in a slimy neighborhood. Fits him, I guess. His secretary inspects me in surprise. No shit. My suit is more expensive than everything in this room.

"Logan Bennett," I say before she opens her mouth. "I'm here to see Archer Daring."

"Do you have an appointment, sir?"

"No."

"Then you—"

She breaks off mid-sentence as the door to her right opens, and Archer fucking Daring himself comes out.

"Logan Bennett, what a surprise," he says.

So he knows who I am. Perfect.

"I will make this quick. I ran a background check on you and found out all about your scam business. Stay away from Nadine, or I will destroy you."

"You're all talk," he says through gritted teeth.

"I can close your miserable stores with one phone call."

"Archer. . ." the secretary pleads. At least she has the decency to worry.

"You son of a bitch," Archer spits. "You and your family run around, thinking you own the world because you have more money than me? You think that makes you better?"

"I never screwed anyone over. No one in my family has. *That* makes us better than you." I roll my palm into fists, fighting to keep my control.

"I screwed plenty of people, and I'm not sorry. Give me a few more weeks, and I might literally screw Nadine too. She seems stupid enough."

"You have a death wish." I lose my last shreds of self-control. My punch connects with his jaw. Taken by surprise, he stumbles backward. I throw in another punch, aiming to give him a black eye, so the moron has something to remind him how stupid he is when he looks in the mirror tomorrow. He hits me back with a vengeance, and we don't stop until the secretary steps between us, her eyes wide and fearful.

"Mr. Bennett, please, leave," she pleads.

"Don't worry, I'm done here," I tell her. Turning to Archer, I say, "Stay away from Nadine."

At that, I stomp out of the office. The chilly air cools my nerves on the way to my car. Once inside, I inspect my reflection in the mirror. I bear no signs of a fight, except for my very prominent split lip. Damn it.

When Nadine asks me about it, I'll have to do the one thing she asked me not to: lie to her. Coupled with the bank story I still haven't told her about, I'm treading on dangerous territory.

Chapter Twenty

Nadine

"Okay, everyone, we're done. Let's all go home," Ava says. We're in the ballroom, where the show will take place tomorrow, having just wrapped up the very last rehearsal. Everyone is exhausted. Pippa tells me that they usually have the last rehearsal at least one week before the show. Since they replaced the designer with me, the schedule became even crazier.

"I can't believe it's midnight," I tell Pippa.

She yawns as we head to the door. "I'm glad the show is tomorrow. I'll sleep for a week afterward."

"Me too," Ava says.

"Let's rest for a few hours tonight," I suggest.

We step out of the venue and find Logan propped against his car, waiting for me.

"Someone won't sleep tonight," Ava tells me. She winks and leaves with Pippa.

"How long have you been standing here?" I ask Logan.

"Not long. Pippa texted me fifteen minutes ago that you were about to be done."

Stepping closer to him, I notice his lip is split. "What happened to your lip?"

"I cut myself on a nicked glass."

Before I can ask anything more, Logan pulls me into a kiss. I immediately give in, opening my mouth, welcoming the possession, craving it. My body flattens against his, needing more points of contact. I always need more when it comes to Logan.

"We won't get very far if we continue like this," Logan says when we pull apart.

"We're going somewhere?" I tilt my head up, moving my focus from his full lips to his dark eyes. "Besides home?"

"Yep."

He opens the door of the car, gesturing for me to step inside.

"Where are we going?" I ask once he's inside too.

"To have a little private celebration because you're going to see your designs on a runway."

I yawn. "Can't we do that tomorrow? I'm so sleepy."

Gunning the engine, Logan shakes his head. "No can do. You'll be a star after tomorrow night. Everyone will want to interview you. Tonight, you're only mine."

"Oh, that reminds me. I decided to throw a pseudo-opening party for the store in two days."

"Huh?"

"Pippa and Ava said there will be reporters from influential magazines at the Bennett show, and that it'd be good if I threw a party right after the show and invited them."

"It's a good idea," he says thoughtfully. "But more work. Hence, more power to my argument. We need to celebrate tonight."

"So, you're kidnapping me?" I ask coyly, curiosity overpowering my tiredness.

He confirms it with a nod as the car speeds through downtown.

"You still didn't tell me where we're going," I remind him.

"Now, it wouldn't be kidnapping if I told you, would it?"

"Okay." I wait patiently as he drives out to the edge of the city and up one of the hills. The car comes to a halt in a curious place: a patch of woods where the lights of the city are visible in all their glory. We exit the car and sit on the hood. It's one week before Christmas, but the weather is remarkably warm, and there is almost no wind.

"What is this?" I ask.

"Few people know about this place. At least, I've never run into anyone here. I like to come here and think. The first time, it was after Sebastian and I signed a big contract. It was the most crucial deal in our 'go big or go home' strategy. I made a promise to myself that no matter how things turned out, I'd always remember my roots and take care of my family. By then, I'd seen what money could do to people. It can turn them into selfish shells, or bastards. I didn't want to be one of them."

He says all this while glancing at the lights in the distance. I try to gauge whether he's sending me a message because tomorrow is my big night, but I realize he's simply Logan. Very self-aware and grounded. I realize something else too, something even more important. He's allowing me in, and that's worth even more than whatever success the show will bring me tomorrow.

"I can't wait to bring my parents to San Francisco," I confess. In response, he squeezes my hand, and it's all the support and reassurance I need. "This is your special place," I say brightly. "And you brought me here. That makes me feel special too."

"You are, Nadine." Turning to me, he cups the back of my neck, bringing me inches away from his lips. "You've invaded every facet of my life, and I love it."

Logan's mouth covers mine, his kiss a testament of both our desperation. In a haze, I sense him pushing himself over me. I let myself lie with my back against the hood of the car, my hands roaming over the taut tendons of his arms.

"You're mine." His tone drips of determination. Nodding, I lean in for another kiss, but he denies me. "I want to hear you say it out loud."

"I'm yours. Only yours."

His dark eyes probe me for a few seconds, then he leans in and gives me the sweetest of kisses. Needing more of him, my fingers fist in his hair, demanding passion and relief. When we pull apart for breath, his hair is mussed, his eyes hooded. *My man is incredibly sexy.* On a sigh, I feel myself getting slicker.

His hand cups between my legs over my jeans, as if saying that's his too. I become slicker still. Arching into him, I seek the release only he can give me. His palm presses straight on my clit. I rasp out his name along with a deep, guttural moan.

"I want you." His low voice does dangerous and delicious things to my body. He dips his hand in his back pocket, retrieving a condom, and placing it right between my breasts. Desperate for him, I unzip his jeans, pushing them past his ass. I slip my hand in the waistband of his jeans, palming his hot and hard length.

Logan's breath comes out in short, fast bursts as I move my hand with urgency. He makes quick work of pushing my pants down, and there's just our underwear between us. He kicks off his boxers, and I roll the condom over his erection. He doesn't bother removing my thong; instead, he pushes the fabric to one side, entering me in one swift move.

We both groan at the connection. As Logan moves in and out of me, my senses are overwhelmed by him. I hitch my legs around his waist, giving him better access. The contrast of the cold hood of the car against my ass, and his hot body over mine becomes almost too much. His thumb circles my clit, driving me crazy. Anticipation builds inside me with a vengeance, and I become insatiable.

My nails dig in his ass as my hips move in sync with him. He fills me utterly and completely until my orgasm hits hard. I ride the wave of my climax alongside him, pulsing around him, crying out against his mouth. As he captures my pleasure, he gives me his release, wild and sweet at the same time.

***

The day of the show is surreal. I wake up at five o'clock and am in a frenzy the entire day in my shop. I would've preferred to be at the show location, even though there's nothing for me to do there. Pippa messaged me during breakfast, letting me know she has everything under control, and I don't have to worry about anything. I can't help it, though. Every time something good happened to me, it was followed up by something bad that completely obscured my happiness. The show is one of the best things ever to happen to me, and my experience has taught me that good things come at a price.

The afternoon is unusually quiet, with only a few customers. Struggling to keep my mind from imagining scenarios of my doom, I answer my emails when the store's empty. I leave a certain email from Archer until the very end. I was supposed to give him my answer two days ago, but it completely slipped my mind, what with the show preparations and everything. I type up a long reply, and then delete it. No, it's best if I call him. He doesn't pick up. Weird. He used to answer my calls after the first ring. Maybe he's upset I haven't called him before, but I had my reasons. I insist, and he picks up after the third try.

"Hello, Archer. Do you have a few minutes?"

"Make it quick." His tone is brisk and cold, very different from his usual friendly demeanor. He is upset I didn't call him in the time frame he gave me. Well, he's making this easier.

"I know I was supposed to call you and tell you my decision, but I—"

"Your boyfriend made your decision clear."

"What are you talking about?" I rub the back of my neck. The skin there prickles as my stomach constricts with foreboding.

"He made the message pretty clear when he gave me a black eye."

"I don't…" My words falter as I remember Logan's split lip. No, that must be a coincidence. Logan told me he hurt his lip on a glass. He wouldn't lie to me. Would he? "What are you talking about?"

"Logan attacked me yesterday. He told me to stay away from you. You can consider my offer for cooperation invalid. Don't call me again."

I clutch my phone, stunned. What is going on? Archer must be lying. This can't be happening. Logan would never lie to me.

***

I arrive at the Bennett show with my heart in my throat, an hour before it's set to begin. Pippa leads me to hair and makeup, instructing the personnel to turn me into "a star." I'll be wearing one of my dresses, of course, a red bandage one. When the prep team is done working their magic on me, I resemble the models who'll be wearing my designs.

Pippa whistles when she sees me. "Logan'll have a heart attack when you come onto the runway with me at the end."

"Where is he now? I need to talk to him."

"No can do. The girls will start walking on the runway in five minutes." Pippa's exuberant smile falters. My apprehension must be visible on my face because she adds, "Is everything all right with you and Logan?"

"No idea," I say in a small voice.

"Right. You can tell me all about it after the show, and I'll help you kick my brother's ass, but right now—"

"How do you know I'm not the one who should have her ass kicked?" As usual, being around Pippa makes me smile.

She puts her hands on her hips. "Call it sixth sense. Also, I know Logan. He has this excellent talent for making me want to strangle and hug him at the same time. I have a hunch you just discovered that." Stopping one of the servers, she says, "Bring Nadine a cupcake from the buffet outside, please." After he takes off, she winks at me. "When men mess up, cupcakes make everything better."

While munching on my cupcake a few minutes later, I have to admit there is some truth to Pippa's words. She waits for me to finish, puts my plate away, and takes me by the shoulders.

"This is your night. Enjoy it. You can deal with my brother later."

Smiling, I nod.

Pippa and I remain backstage during the show, doing the last checks on each girl. At the end of the show, Pippa always walks out on the runway. Whenever a new designer provides the clothes for the show, he or she walks with Pippa at the end. This year, I'll be joining her. My palms sweat just thinking about it.

After the very last piece of jewelry is presented, Pippa takes my hand. "Ready?"

"Not really." I say this with a grin on my face. The atmosphere is infectious. The models are loud, laughing and joking, waiting to walk outside one last time, led by Pippa and me. Drawing in a deep breath, I announce, "Now I'm ready."

Praying not to stumble over my own feet, I step on the runway with Pippa by my side. The crowd erupts in applause. The deafening sound has the unexpected effect of calming my nerves. I realize I was chewing the inside of my cheek. Carefully, I put one foot in front of the other. I can't make out any faces because the spotlight blinds me, so I wave in the general direction of the crowd, smiling brightly and whole-heartedly.

When we return backstage, my legs begin to tremble.

"Oh. My. God! My legs have turned to Jell-O."

"That's adrenaline," Pippa explains. "Listen, quick instructions. There will be reporters wanting to speak to you. Just be calm and be yourself."

"Noted."

"Don't forget, there are plenty of cupcakes out there. If you feel down, grab one."

"Only you could give that advice with a straight face, sister." Logan appears from behind us, taking both Pippa and me by the waist. "You two were stunning out there."

"This is my cue to leave before becoming a third wheel," Pippa says. She gives me a knowing look as she leaves.

Logan loses no time, pulling me in the now-empty hair and makeup section. Hairspray clogs the air, and breathing becomes a chore.

"I wanted to kidnap you from that stage," he says in a low, seductive voice. "Since we'll both be busy with reporters tonight, I wanted to give you a quick—or not-so-quick—kiss before the mayhem begins."

I take a deep breath, unable to meet his eyes.

"Is something wrong?" he asks.

"What *really* happened to your lip?" I blurt out.

Logan takes a step back, remaining silent for almost a minute. Finally, jamming his hands in his pockets, he asks, "You spoke with Archer?"

"Yes."

I fold my arms over my chest, looking at him expectantly. "I asked you not to get involved."

"The guy is scamming designers, Nadine." Running a hand through his hair, he sighs in frustration.

I bite my tongue, digesting this new piece of information. "I did my own research and thought something wasn't right. He wouldn't give me the contact information of any designer he's worked with. That was a big red flag. I wasn't going to go into business with him anyway. Why did you do all this behind my back?"

"I was going to talk to you about it after the show. I didn't want to spoil this for you." Taking a deep breath, he adds, "Since it's confession time, I should also tell you that the bank didn't approve your loan, so I paid your old debt."

I gasp. "You. . . Oh, Logan."

"Nadine, I just want to protect you. You know that, right?"

"I do, but you... Oh, God. We don't have time to talk about this right now. I need to go outside to the reporters."

"Of course. We can talk later, at home."

"We'll both be tired and angry, and that's not a good combo for a talk."

Logan straightens his shoulders. "Okay. We'll sleep and talk tomorrow."

"I think I should sleep at Ava's tonight."

"What?" Logan stiffens.

"It's that... I won't be able to sleep at home knowing you're next to me, and we still have to talk about this. I'll sleep at Ava's, and tomorrow I'll come home. We'll be both be rested and we can talk. I just need a good night sleep, that's all."

He runs a hand through his hair. "Okay, I'll pick you up."

I nod as Pippa steps into the room, throwing her hands in the air. "Here you are. What are you doing?" Watching Logan and me, she adds, "Looks like I need to kick your ass, brother. However, this is bad timing. Reporters are waiting to interview you. Nadine, too."

Logan nods and leaves the room. Immediately, Pippa hurries to me, putting an arm around my shoulders. "I have a feeling cupcakes won't cheer you up. This is tequila territory."

Despite myself, I laugh. Then I draw in a deep breath. "I'll need to crash at Ava's place tonight. I'll talk to Logan tomorrow."

"You can stay with me," Pippa says. "Now, I need you to smile and charm reporters. There are people from *Vogue* and *Elle* who want to talk to you."

"Bad timing," I mumble to myself.

"Unfortunately, life tends to be a series of badly timed events," Pippa responds. "Go get them. This is your night."

I hug Pippa. "Thank you for everything."

Chapter Twenty-One

Logan

I wake up the next day with my head pounding as if I have a nasty hangover. The truth is I barely slept.

I check my phone and find a text from Nadine.

Nadine: I went to the store early. Can we meet there instead?

I'm about to reply when the doorbell rings. Maybe she decided to come here instead? I open the door and find Sebastian and Blake bickering. Interesting.

"What are you doing here?" I ask them.

"Sebastian called and told me to meet him here. I obeyed," Blake answers with a smirk. "And I brought breakfast." He holds up a bag from Wendy's.

"Fast food?" I ask as I let them in.

"Best hangover burgers," Blake says.

"No one's hung over but you, Blake," Sebastian retorts.

Blake shrugs. "Not my fault you two skip the best part of the Bennett show after-party: cocktails."

"I'm starving, so the burgers will do," Sebastian says. He and Blake exchange glances as they sit on my couch. Suspicious glances.

"You're plotting something against me," I tell them both.

"*Against* isn't the right word," Blake remarks, grabbing a burger himself and handing one to Sebastian. "But Pippa told us about the situation with Nadine, so…"

"So, what?" I challenge.

"So, what are you going to do about it?" Sebastian asks. Burger in hand, he paces by the large window overseeing the city.

"I'll talk to Nadine today. I'm supposed to pick her up in an hour."

"What's your strategy?" Sebastian inquires.

I stare at him. "Dude, I'm talking about a conversation with my woman, not a fucking business meeting about mergers and acquisitions. What strategy?"

"He means groveling strategy," Blake says, and Sebastian nods in agreement.

I'm used to Blake being a smart-ass. What I'm not used to is Sebastian siding with Blake. Lately, alliances change faster than the wind in the Bennett family.

"She just said she needed a good night's sleep before we talk," I say with exasperation.

Blake looks at me as if I'm insane. "Do you have any idea how many thoughts a woman can have in one night? Women are masters at overthinking words, overblowing situations. You have that bank thing and the fight with Archer against you. A woman's mind can twist that into a deadly sin."

"You're overreacting, don't you think?" I ask, but now I'm starting to worry.

"It's better to be on the safe side," Sebastian says. His constant pacing around the living room grates on my nerves.

"Since when are you two experts on women?" I retaliate.

"Let's see," Blake says. "Sebastian's engaged, and I have plenty of experience. Summer doesn't call me a man-whore for nothing. What a woman wants in your case is for you to grovel: flowers, presents, and so on."

"Nadine's not like that."

"Nadine's a woman," Blake replies. "If she doesn't like flowers, you have to come up with more creative presents and strategies. I have this down to a science. There are three stages for a woman to forgive you: apologizing, groveling, and kissing the hell out of her."

I give him the stink eye, but Blake continues undeterred. "My groveling tactics have always worked. Before you repeat that Nadine isn't like other women, I'll say this. She *is* a woman, and has magnificent breasts to prove it."

"Don't go there, or I'll punch you," I warn.

Sebastian stops pacing. "Wait, Blake saw Nadine naked? Am I missing something?"

"Nadine wanted to surprise our dear brother with an office striptease," Blake explains. "I was in the office with him."

Sebastian grins.

"Not funny," I growl through gritted teeth.

"That's the funniest thing I've heard all week," Sebastian says.

"Yes, yes, let's all laugh about it," I reply without humor. "Blake, if you ever bring this up again, I will punch you. Sebastian, stop grinning."

Sebastian draws in a breath and bursts into laughter. I ignore him.

"All sorts of things can happen if you don't have a groveling strategy," Blake says.

"Like what?" I challenge. "Humor me."

"Like a new guy showing up and stealing her from you. And before you tell me for the millionth time that Nadine isn't like that, let me tell you, men are smart. First, he'll be her friend. He'll give her a shoulder to cry on. Things escalate quickly from there." Dropping his voice, he adds, "Trust me— been there, done that. It's called rebound sex."

"You're a dick," I tell him, but with less annoyance in my voice than before.

"Have you heard the saying 'a shoulder to cry on becomes a dick to ride on'?" Blake asks.

"Enough." I jump from my seat, fully intending to throttle the moron. *Younger brothers have no respect.* Sebastian steps between me and the desk.

"He was talking hypothetically," Sebastian says. "You're meeting her in an hour, Logan. No time for anyone to steal her from you."

It takes a few minutes for me to calm down, but eventually I slump back in my chair. Blake's sprawled on the couch with a smug grin.

"Do something that matters to her," Sebastian suggests. "Something that tells her you understand what she needs and will respect it, even if you're bound to occasionally put your foot in your mouth."

Finishing my burger, I mull over his words. "You're right," I tell Sebastian.

"Don't take all the credit," Blake tells Sebastian. "It's still called groveling, and I suggested it."

An idea suddenly strikes me. "I have a plan, but I need two days' time, and I need Pippa's help. God, our sister will be so smug about this."

"Is this part of the groveling strategy?" Sebastian asks skeptically.

"Yeah," I say.

"Okay, then. Go grovel," Sebastian encourages. He and Blake exchange relieved looks.

"Yeah. Go grovel. This motto will go on your grave, Logan," Blake says.

Ignoring that last part, I ask both of them, "Any tips?"

"Don't make any promises you don't mean," Sebastian says firmly.

Blake folds his arms. "Especially if she tells you to take out the trash every day. Women have a tendency to remember those promises like you wouldn't believe."

"Blake!" I throw my hands up. "I'm pretty sure that topic won't come up."

"Just saying."

"I'd still buy her a present," Sebastian says.

"Changed my mind. I don't need any tips. You're both clueless when it comes to my woman."

"I love this," Blake announces.

"What?" Sebastian and I ask at the same time.

"Watching a woman trapping my second-eldest brother," Blake answers.

Sebastian shakes his head. "Eventually, your time will come."

"In about a million years. I'm very happy with my man-whore status for the moment. Just because you two decided to stick with one woman doesn't mean I want to follow your lead. By all means, please start shooting out babies as soon as possible to keep Mom and Dad busy."

"They already gave you the talk, didn't they?" I ask. Judging by Blake's grimace, they did. "I need a ride to the airport."

At this, Blake snaps his head to me, his eyes wide. Even Sebastian appears surprised.

"Long-distance groveling?" Blake questions. "I can drop you off at the airport."

"Thanks."

"Don't scare him off," Sebastian calls after us as we head to the door.

Blake grins. "I'd never do that. I like Nadine. I'll give him more shit about the almost-striptease we both got."

Right. Blake should consider himself a lucky man if I don't throttle him on the way to the airport. Taking out my phone, I dial Pippa's number.

"Hello, brother," she greets me.

"I need you to keep Nadine busy for two days."

Chapter Twenty-Two

Nadine

"This dress is gorgeous." A redhead in her thirties stands in front of a mirror, admiring herself in one of my dresses.

"It brings out the best in your figure," I say brightly, even though my mind is somewhere else. I keep checking the phone in my hand. Logan isn't replying. Why isn't he replying?

"And that bra," she whispers conspiratorially. "It's fantastic."

After she leaves, I fall into a funk. Still no news from Logan. I did a lot of thinking last night, and I know what I want to say to him. Right now, I just want to see him, though. I need him. I missed his warmth last night, his arms around me. My man is stubborn, but so am I, and I love him to pieces.

I glance up from my phone when the door opens, hoping to see Logan. Instead, Pippa, Ava, and Alice surprise me.

"Hey, superstar," Pippa says.

"What are you all doing here?"

"Kidnapping you," she answers nonchalantly.

"Am I about to receive the promised tequila?" I ask her. I'm about to add that it's bad timing, yet again, when she smiles devilishly.

"Not exactly. We thought you deserved a few days at the spa," Pippa answers. "With Ava and me, of course. There's no better way to relax than by having a mani, pedi, a facial, and a massage. Hot guys are giving said massages too." Pippa rubs her palms excitedly.

Alice throws Pippa a dirty look. "Hot guys aren't the point."

"Hey, I was trying to sell her on the trip," Pippa replies.

"Wow," I interject. "Girls, I'm meeting Logan today, and I need to organize this party. I can't go anywhere."

"Yeah, about Logan," Ava says. "He had to go on an urgent business trip. He'll return in two days."

"What?" I ask.

"Urgent business. Last minute," she explains.

Pippa and Alice aren't meeting my eyes. *What is going on?*

"Alice and Summer can take care of the shop, and organize the party while we're gone," Pippa informs me.

I turn to Alice. "But you have the restaurant. And Summer has to paint."

Alice waves her hand as if that small detail doesn't matter. "The restaurant won't crumble if I take two days off, and Summer says she lacks inspiration right now."

"What's the use in having so many Bennetts, if not to help each other occasionally?" Pippa puts an arm around Alice's shoulders.

"Summer and I will have everything under control," Alice assures me. "You need a few days off to clear your head."

"You three will have an answer to every objection I raise, won't you?" I ask.

"You're a fast learner," Pippa says, as Alice and Ava both give me a thumbs-up. "I went to Logan's apartment and already packed a bag for you so we can go from here."

This isn't just kidnapping. They're ambushing me. *All righty. Time to get my ducks in a row.*

"Alice. You're doing the catering, so you already have the schedule for that. There's also—"

Alice holds her hand up, stopping my ramble. "I meant it when I said everything is under control. You sent me your schedule and to-do list two hours ago, so I'm already up to date with everything regarding the organization. Summer will handle the customers, and she'll do fine."

"You thought this through," I say. The three women nod, clearly proud of themselves. Without warning, the corners of my eyes start burning, tears forming. I look away from them, pretending to search for my bag.

Ever since I moved here, my life has changed radically. I was used to doing things on my own and taking care of everyone else, not having others to do things for me. Certainly, I wasn't expecting the girls to drop their jobs and interrupt their routines for me. I'm not used to having people do nice things for me. The Bennetts and Ava changed that.

My bag in my hands, I point to the door. "Okay, let's go. When will Summer be here?"

"She's stuck in traffic, but she should be here in ten minutes," Alice answers. "Go, I'll wait for her here."

***

"How is it all right that the two of you took off?" I ask Ava and Pippa once we're in the car. Pippa drives, Ava claimed shotgun, and I have the backseat all to myself.

"Sebastian was a bit grumpy, but he got over it. As if Bennett Enterprises would collapse if we weren't there." Pippa rolls her eyes in the rearview mirror, but she also smiles. "Don't worry; with the collection launch behind us, this is a free period for Ava and me. Logan and Sebastian, on the other hand, have their hands full. This is an intense negotiation period with new buyers."

My heart constricts at the mention of Logan. "Logan didn't go on this business trip to avoid me, right?"

Pippa's eyes widen. "Absolutely not. He just had an urgent matter to take care of."

"Very urgent," Ava adds. These girls are hiding something. I can feel it.

Pippa peeks at me in the rearview mirror then elbows Ava.

Ava whispers to her, "Stage one completed. I think she's ready for stage two."

"Wait, what?" I ask. "What exactly do you girls have planned?"

"You'll see," they say at the same time.

***

Ava and Pippa keep me hostage for two days. Turns out the second phase of their plan was tequila. The third was heart-to-heart talks about men over our mani-pedi. I passed all stages with flying colors, particularly the second one. I had a headache the next day to prove it.

I miss Logan terribly.

"This was fun," Pippa states as she parks the car a few feet away from my shop.

"It was," I admit. "Except we should've come back earlier. The party starts in one hour." I try to keep the panic out of my voice. We stopped by Pippa's apartment, where we got dressed. Pippa had a hair stylist and makeup artist from the show work their magic on us, insisting this is too monumental a night not to have professionals pep me up.

"Alice and Summer have everything under control." Ava winks at me. The three of us leave the car and walk side by side toward my shop.

Inside, Alice orders the servers around, and she's doing it with severity and tact at the same time. She did a great job transforming my small foyer into a space that can easily fit the number of guests we're expecting. The two armchairs and small table are gone; in their place are tall, slim cocktail tables. There are small plates with finger foods on each table, and there is a bar in the corner. It's tiny, but I'm sure it's well stocked. When Alice told me she'd bring in a bar, I told her there was no way she could fit one in the foyer. She said she had exactly what I need. Looking more closely, I realize she also pushed the mannequins from the foyer farther into the shop.

"Here are my girls." Alice hugs us briefly. "I love you all, but you're standing in everyone's way."

"Alice, you can relax now and hand the reins over to Nadine," Ava tells her. When Alice merely raises her eyebrows, she adds, "Since it's her party."

"Which is why she'll be talking to a lot of important people, and leave the organization to me," Alice replies sweetly.

"I didn't realize your catering services came along with organization, but I'll take you up on this. Thank you." Alice saved me. I'll have to talk to plenty of people. Three reporters from national magazines will be here, along with four bloggers.

"Oh, they don't usually. Only for family."

"Thank you, Alice."

In the next half hour, Sebastian and Summer arrive. Summer's wearing a floor-length yellow dress I know only too well.

"I know that dress," I say conspiratorially.

Summer giggles. "I couldn't help it. I stayed in here after closing one evening, trying on all your dresses. I bought three more, including this one. I hope you don't mind."

"Mind? I'm over the moon."

"I loved taking care of your shop," she whispers to me. "I'm *super* inspired right now to paint again."

I adore her energy. The door opens again, and my palms sweat as I scan the small crowd walking in. Logan's parents, Blake, and Daniel have arrived. No Logan, though. My heart constricts. *Isn't he back from his trip?*

I want him here tonight. There is no one else I would rather share this night with. I wouldn't be celebrating anything if it weren't for him. Yes, I worked hard, but he helped me. He was there for me every step of the way.

More guests arrive, milling around the foyer. Blake glances around and grabs a glass of champagne without waiting for an invitation.

I eye him suspiciously, because he seems even more arrogant than usual. Walking over to him, I ask, "Why so smug?"

"I have my reasons." He holds up his glass then takes a sip.

"Is Logan coming tonight?"

He grins. "I'm not allowed to say anything."

"This is a Bennett-wide conspiracy, isn't it? The kidnapping, Logan's trip?"

He doesn't reply, just winks.

The bell at the door rings again, alerting me that new guests have arrived. I swirl on my heels, intending to head to the door and greet them, but I freeze in place. Mom and Brian are inside my store. I told them about the opening, of course, but the notice was too short for them to be able to take time off from work, and the plane tickets were expensive. *What is going on?*

They wave at me from the doorway, as though they're unsure if it's okay to come in. I hurry to them.

"Mom, Brian, what are you doing here?"

"We've come to support our daughter at her opening party," Brian says. Speechless, I kiss both of them on their cheeks. Mom pulls me into a tight hug. After letting me go, she looks around with wide eyes.

"This place is so fancy," she whispers, as if she can't quite believe it.

"I'm so happy you're here. I can show you around. We still have a bit of time until the rest of the guests arrive."

The tour takes longer than I anticipate because Mom touches every shelf and decor piece. Once or twice, she makes a grab for a dress, and then quickly retracts her hand, as if she's afraid she'll damage it.

"You did this all by yourself?" Mom asks.

"The Bennett family helped me a lot. I'll introduce you to them as soon as we finish the tour."

"Oh, we met Logan," Brian says casually.

"What? When?"

"He came to our house to talk to us," Mom explains, and the pieces in the Bennett conspiracy start falling into place. "He's a very nice man, and he loves you. He said you'll be having important people here tonight, but what would make you truly happy would be if we were here too."

I swallow hard, my eyes watering. "He's right."

"He also explained to us how hard you worked and how far you've come," Brian says.

"We're very proud of you, dear," Mom continues.

"I... Wow. I still can't believe you're here. "

"That young man seemed to be ready to do anything to see you happy, including dragging us here if we said no." Brian winks at me.

Mom chuckles. "He didn't say that last part out loud, but it was very apparent from his body language how fiercely he feels about you. I have no idea what he said to our bosses, but neither of them objected when we said we needed to take a few days off." Taking my hands in hers, Mom leads me a few feet away from everyone. "Nadine, hon, I want to thank you."

"For what?" I ask, not really following.

"For taking care of me all those years. I've never said this out loud, so thank you, and I'm sorry I never did take care of you the way I should have. You've always been strong, Nadine. But even the strongest can't do it all alone."

"Mom—"

"I'm happy you ran into this family and their wonderful son."

"Me too."

She pulls me into a tight hug, and I welcome her warmth, patting her hair. I love her perfume. She smells like oranges. As a kid, I longed for her hugs, but between her illness and our hardships, they were hard to come by. Still, she was always Mom. Pippa said being around her mom makes her feel like she's sixteen again, but I feel like I'm six. I'll never be too old for a hug.

As the door opens again, I see a few reporters arriving, and then Logan. He smiles my favorite smile: wide and heartfelt. He points at the reporters, as if saying, "They're all yours."

***

The party lasts until the early hours of the morning. It's easily the best night of my life, surrounded by the people who matter most to me: my parents, Ava, and the Bennetts. One Bennett specifically. It was all I could do not to drag Logan in the back room, but I knew if I did that, we wouldn't come out anytime soon. The Bennetts and my parents are the last to leave. Logan stays behind, watching my every move as I bid everyone goodbye.

The second we're alone, the air charges with our sexual tension. I take my time to appreciate Logan fully for the first time tonight. He's wearing a suit that highlights his strong, imposing figure. I then dim the lights until it's dark, so no one from outside can see us.

Turning to him, I say, "Hi there."

"Hi back." Logan's gaze travels over my body slowly.

I join him by the bar. "Business trip, huh?"

His lip curls into a delicious smile. "Yeah, I got lost in the airport and somehow ended up at your parents' house."

"Thank you for bringing Mom and Brian."

"They are quite a pair."

"You went to them, and brought them here." My voice is filled with emotion and gratitude. "Thank you."

"I want you to be happy, Nadine. Always."

Logan pulls me to him, wrapping an arm around my waist. After days apart, being this close to him is intoxicating. His cologne, his scent—all man—clouds my mind, ensnaring my senses.

"I missed you," he says.

"I missed you too."

Logan tilts my chin up. He kisses me hard, first sweeping his tongue over my lips, then slipping it inside my mouth. He fists my hair, deepening the kiss. A bolt of heat courses through me, right through my center.

"Let's talk," he says after we pull apart.

"Mmm, I liked that kiss. But you're right. Let's get the words out of the way first."

"I'm sorry I got carried away with Archer and the bank," he begins. "But I will always want to protect you, love you, and make sure you are safe and happy in every way. It's who I am."

His speech steals my breath away. "I wouldn't have it any other way." I know he did everything to protect me, and it's time for me to accept that allowing the man I love to watch over me isn't a vulnerability. Trusting him is a strength.

"I'm your guy, remember?"

I laugh softly. "You're my guy."

"So, I'm forgiven?" he asks.

I smile against his cheek. "You are. But you have to promise me you won't keep things from me anymore."

Logan adopts a serious demeanor. "I was advised by a certain brother not to make promises I can't keep. So, I can only promise I'll *try* to do that." Pushing a strand of hair behind my ear, he drags his fingers down my cheek. "I can make a different promise, though. I promise always to love you and make you happy. How about that?"

"Works for me," I whisper.

Throughout this conversation, he hasn't kept his hands off me. He touches my lips, dragging his fingers down my neck and my cleavage.

"You're beautiful tonight, Nadine."

My breath comes out in quick exhales, desire overtaking me. "People can still see inside the store if they try hard enough."

Logan chuckles, though his eyes are hooded with desire. "I won't make love to you here. I want you all to myself. It's bad enough Blake saw you in my office; I don't want to give any late-night lunatics a peep show. I will take you home and make love to you the entire weekend."

"What now?"

Logan smiles. "Now, we go home."

We leave the store and walk all the way to his apartment hand in hand. Once inside, I take in the familiar sight with a smile, grateful to be back here with him.

"Did you have fun with Pippa and Ava at the spa?" Logan asks.

"Oh, we had too much fun. It involved tequila, and massages," I tease.

Logan pulls me to him, wrapping his arms around my waist. "Do I want to know more details?"

"Depends. Don't you have anything better to do than questioning me about the escapade with the girls?"

With a mischievous smile, Logan lifts me off my feet. He carries me in his arms all the way to the bedroom, laying me on the bed. He lies next to me, propping himself on an elbow, and cupping my cheek with his other hand.

"I want you with me every day of my life, Nadine. I want to hear you sing obnoxiously loud in the shower in the morning, and see you scratch the headboard when we make love."

"I only did that once."

We look in unison at the scratched headboard and laugh.

"You make me a happy man, and for that I love you."

My heart leaps in my chest. "I love you too, Logan Bennett. For knowing the importance of chocolate, laughter, orgasms, and for always being here for me." Grinning at him, I lean into him, searching his lips. "Now, make me scratch that headboard."

Chapter Twenty-Three

Nadine: Two Months Later

"Where are we going?" I ask for the millionth time. Logan came to pick me up from the store today. After I entered his car, the man *blindfolded* me.

"I'm not telling you. Even if you keep asking another twenty times."

"This is ridiculous," I inform him. I drum my fingers on my knees in my anticipation, while we drive and drive and drive. I can't be sure if the trip actually *is* long, or I'm just impatient, but it seems that an eternity passes until the car slows down. Logan takes off my blindfold without any words. I see he's parked the car in front of a beautiful, two-story villa.

"I don't understand," I say. "Are we invited here?"

He chuckles. "No, we're looking at it as prospective buyers."

I swear to God my heart stops. "What?"

"The backyard has an old oak tree."

"Logan," I whisper. "I told you about my dream house during our first date."

"Exactly," he declares proudly. "I searched for months for a house that came as close to your description as possible."

"But you love your pad, and being in the middle of the hustle and bustle," I state.

"Well, this is close enough to downtown. Come on, let's check it out."

I'm speechless as I get out of the car. When I look at the house again, I see it with different eyes than before. It's perfect, with large windows, allowing in plenty of sun.

"I'll give you a tour," Logan says with excitement in his voice. As we walk toward the main entrance, I inspect the porch. I can already picture decorating it for Halloween and then for Christmas. Logan unlocks the door, pushes it open, and takes my hand. A smell of something new welcomes me inside, and I adore it. The walls must have been painted recently. The house is empty on the inside, but in my mind I already see what kind of furniture and matching carpets I would bring in.

"The house has an electric fireplace," Logan says when we reach the enormous living room. "We can have it changed to a real one. Do you want to see the kitchen?"

"Maybe we can go upstairs?" I ask excitedly.

"Ah, I see someone won't spend much time in the kitchen."

"You barely let me cook, anyway."

Logan winks, taking my hand and leading me up a large, wooden spiral staircase. I run my free hand on the balustrade. There are five rooms upstairs, and we peek quickly inside the first four before reaching the last.

"This can be your small workshop," Logan announces when we step in the fifth room, smiling brightly. "You have a direct view of the backyard. We can put your sewing machines by the window."

I step closer to the window, glancing outside. The backyard is perfect; we can easily fit in a table and some lounge chairs. The oak tree is old and massive. I wonder how many generations it has witnessed living in this house. I'm glad no one cut it down.

"I love you, Logan."

He walks up behind me, takes me in his arms, and kisses my neck tenderly.

"I love you too."

I turn to face him, caressing his cheek. "This is such a nice surprise."

"First, I wanted to buy it directly and surprise you that way, but then I thought we should decide. . . You know. Together."

"Very thoughtful of you." I grin. "When can we move in?"

"As soon as you want to."

"I can't wait to bring my sewing machine in here. I still have so much work to do on Ava's wedding dress, and on the bridesmaids' dresses."

"Speaking of Ava, on a scale of one to ten, how upset would she be if you weren't her maid of honor?"

"One hundred. In what universe would that happen?"

"In a universe where we'd marry before Ava and Sebastian."

"Did you—" My voice is so coarse, I have to clear my throat. "Did you just propose to me?"

"I guess I did."

I'm speechless for an entire minute. Or longer, it seems, because Logan crosses his arms, raising his eyebrows.

"You're doing that silence thing again. It's freaking me out."

"Yes. Of course I want to marry you." I lean over him and give him one hell of a smooch. Logan loses no time, wrestling me to the ground, kissing me back with passion. I end up on my back on the floor, him over me.

"I'll tell you a little secret. The day I flew to your parents, it wasn't just to bring them to your opening party. I also asked them for your hand."

"That's so sweet. Wait, why did you wait two months to propose to me?"

"I still wasn't supposed to do it now, but it felt right. In case you didn't notice, I didn't give you a ring. I don't have one."

"You own a jewelry company."

"Yeah, but I don't want just any ring for you. You have no idea how many designs I'm making Pippa do."

"You're adorable, and you're making me feel good about myself."

He traces my lips with his thumb. "I can make you feel *very* good." He winks then wiggles his eyebrows.

I laugh, fisting his shirt, pulling him closer to me. "There's no bed."

Logan pats the floor beneath me. "We do have the habit of not making love on a bed the first time. Let's make that a tradition."

Epilogue

Nadine: Four Months Later

"Let me get this straight," Logan says. "We're going in chronological order for this matchmaking thing?"

Ava and Sebastian's wedding is one week away, and Logan and I asked them to come to our new house for dinner. We're in the garden, under our big oak tree, bickering about which Bennett we should concentrate on next.

"If you're going to mock us, Logan," Ava starts, "you'd better stay out of here. We're excellent matchmakers on our own."

His gaze slides to me, but I hold up my palms. "What Ava said."

"I'm not mocking you," Logan responds patiently. "I'm trying to understand the bigger picture."

Ava sighs. "No, we're not matchmaking in chronological order, we think it's Pippa's time now."

"I was hoping you'd concentrate on Blake next," Logan says.

"Nah, it's Pippa's time now," Ava insists. "She deserves to have her happily ever after."

"You might be right," Sebastian chimes in, and I narrow my eyes. Men don't do things like matchmaking. I'm one hundred percent sure that Sebastian and Logan want in on this only so they know what we plan for their sister. Not that I'm complaining. If they're on our side, they won't try to scare away any potential suitor.

"Alice agrees with us," Ava says, eyeing the two men.

"I can't believe we're taking a page out of Pippa's book and using it against her. What's she going to think about this?" Logan asks. "Won't she find it weird that she's not matchmaking anyone?"

"Oh, she *is* matchmaking someone," I reply with a grin. Logan and Sebastian look crestfallen. Having insider information feels *so* good. "As a matter of fact, she's planning Alice's downfall as we speak."

"And you're planning it with her, aren't you?" Logan accuses.

"I am," I state proudly. Ava gives me a thumbs-up.

"Wait," Sebastian says. "You're planning a move against Alice with Pippa, and at the same time a move against Pippa with Alice?"

Ava confirms this with a nod, and Sebastian whistles loudly.

"That's a dangerous game," Logan says.

"What can I say? Ava and I like to live on the edge." I rise from my chair, announcing that I want to replenish the juice can. When I return, both Logan and Sebastian seem to have made up their minds.

"Fine, we're in. But Sebastian and I want to have the last word on any potential candidates. *Before* you tell her about them."

Ava leans toward me. "I like our men when they're so pretentious." She says this loud enough for them to hear it. Sebastian raises his eyebrows, and Logan drums his fingers on the table.

"If you play nice, we *might* let you know when we have a candidate for Pippa," Ava teases.

"What about Alice?" Sebastian asks. I take a good look at him to make sure he's not pulling my leg. Nope, he genuinely has no idea. Men can be *so* oblivious. Alice has been pining for one of Sebastian and Logan's oldest friends since she was in high school.

Judging by the glances that he gave Alice at the last meeting with the wedding planner, he's done some pining too, or at the very least lusting. The wedding will be an excellent opportunity for these two to… explore each other.

"We'll see," I say vaguely. Ava warned me that Sebastian wouldn't take this lightly. His best friend is a heartbreaker. "Let's concentrate on Pippa first."

Ava's phone beeps. She checks it quickly then groans, turning to Sebastian. "The wedding planner wants us at the location ASAP."

"Since when do you say ASAP?" Sebastian teases her.

"She actually wrote that to me. Come on, let's go, and let the lovebirds enjoy their new house." Ava sighs, hugging me goodbye. "A word of advice: run away to Vegas and marry. Skip the reception. Preparations are a nightmare, even with wedding planners."

"Aww, it's not so bad." I hug her back.

"Don't overwork yourself this week. You're my maid of honor, and I require you to be in top shape."

"Yes, ma'am."

Honoring her request won't be all that easy, however. My shop is booming. I'm now selling my designs mostly, and I'm on the brink of signing contracts with big department stores. Several boutique shops in New York carry my dresses, and I can barely keep up with demand. I had to hire two seamstresses. Archer disappeared. Logan and I agreed that he shouldn't be allowed to scam anyone anymore, and Logan informed me that he'd take care of it. He was quick too; Archer's website disappeared a week after that. I'm not even sure I want to know how everything went down.

"Ava is right," Logan says after they leave.

"About what?" I sit in his lap, running my fingers through his hair and admiring my engagement ring. Logan finally gave it to me two months ago. It's gorgeous, made of white gold with a large sapphire in the center. I sneak glances at it all the time, even in meetings, when no one's paying attention.

"We should elope to Vegas."

I open my mouth then close it again, my stomach dipping. "I… We… No. Your parents—"

"Will still have Ava and Sebastian's wedding to enjoy."

"Mom would kill me if she didn't see me in a white dress, and I can't do this to Ava, even though I do find the idea tempting."

"Fine, but I want to set the date already."

"What's the rush?" I ask.

He wiggles his eyebrows. "I have big plans with my future wife."

"Wanna share those plans?"

"Only after the wedding, so you can't run away."

I narrow my eyes. "Sounds dangerous."

"You and Ava *did* say you like to live on the edge."

"Speaking of which, I forgot about Alice."

I fish my phone out of my pocket. With Logan peeking over my shoulder, I text her.

Nadine: Your brothers agreed to our plan for Pippa. We can start with the first stage already.

My phone chimes with a new message a few short seconds later.

Alice: Game on.

***

THE END

***

Dear Reader,
If you want to read Pippa's story,
Your Forever Love, you will find pre-order links here:
http://laylahagen.com/books/the-bennett-family-

series/your-captivating-love/
It will be published mid-summer.

Description:

Logan Bennett knows his priorities. He is loyal to his family and his company. He has no time for love, and no desire for it. Not after a disastrous engagement that left him broken-hearted. When Nadine enters his life, she turns everything upside down. She's sexy, funny, and utterly captivating. She's also more stubborn than anyone he's met. . .including himself.

Nadine Hawthorne is finally pursuing her dream: opening her own clothing shop. After working so hard to get here, she needs to concentrate on her new business, and can't afford distractions. Not even if they come in the form of Logan Bennett. He's handsome, charming, and doesn't take no for an answer. After bitter disappointments, Nadine doesn't believe in love. But being around Logan is addicting. It doesn't help that Logan's family is scheming to bring them together at every turn.

Their attraction is sizzling, and their connection—undeniable. Slowly, Logan wins her over. What starts out as a fling soon spirals into much more than they are prepared for.

When a mistake threatens to tear them apart, will they have the strength to hold on to each other?

***

Dear Reader,

If you want to receive news about my upcoming books and sales, you can sign up for my newsletter HERE: http://laylahagen.com/mailing-list-sign-up/

Author Contact
Website: http://laylahagen.com/
Email: author@laylahagen.com
Facebook: http://facebook.com/LaylaHagenBooks/
Twitter: @laylahagen

***

Other Books by Layla Hagen

The Lost Series

Novella Lost

Lost is a FREE is a prequel novella to Lost in Us and can be read before or after.

Whatever might help him forget his past and numb the pain, James has tried it all: booze, car races, fights, and then some. Especially women. College offers plenty of opportunities for everything. . . Especially when you have a trust fund to spend.

Serena spirals deeper and deeper into a hurricane of pain. But no matter how far she falls, there's no redemption from the overwhelming guilt. Two souls consumed by their pasts fight to learn how to survive. But all hope seems to be lost. Until they meet each other.

Available as a FREE Ebook download. You can find the links to all retailers here: http://laylahagen.com/books/lost-series/lost/

***

Lost in Us: The story of James and Serena

There are three reasons tequila is my new favorite drink.
- One: my ex-boyfriend hates it.
- Two: downing a shot looks way sexier than sipping my usual Sprite.
- Three: it might give me the courage to do something my ex-boyfriend would hate even more than tequila—getting myself a rebound

The night I swap my usual Sprite with tequila, I meet James Cohen. The encounter is breathtaking. Electrifying. And best not repeated.

James is a rich entrepreneur. He likes risks and adrenaline and is used to living the high life. He's everything I'm not.

But opposites attract. Some say opposites destroy each other. Some say opposites are perfect for each other.

I don't know what will James and I do to each other, but I can't stay away from him. Even though I should.

AVAILABLE ON ALL RETAILERS. You can find the links HERE: http://laylahagen.com/books/lost-series/lost-in-us/

***

Found in Us: The story of Jessica and Parker

Jessica Haydn wants to leave her past behind. Hurt by one too many heartbreaks, she vows not to fall in love again. Especially not with a man like Parker, whose electrifying pull and smile bruised her ego once before. But his sexy British accent makes her crave his touch, and his blue eyes strip Jessica of all her defenses.

Parker Blakesley has no place for love in his life. He learned the hard way not to trust. He built his business empire by avoiding distractions, and using sheer determination and control. But something about Jessica makes him question everything. Not only has she a body made for sin, but her laughter fills a void inside of him.

The desire igniting between them spirals into an unstoppable passion, and so much more. Soon, neither can fight their growing emotional connection. But can two scarred souls learn to trust again? And when a mistake threatens to tear them apart, will their love be strong enough?

AVAILABLE ON ALL RETAILERS. You can find the links HERE: http://laylahagen.com/books/lost-series/found-in-us/

***

Caught in Us: The story of Dani and Damon

Damon Cooper has all the markings of a bad boy:
• A tattoo
• A bike
• An attitude to go with point one and two

In the beginning I hated him, but now I'm falling in love with him.

My parents forbid us to be together, but Damon's not one to obey rules.

And since I met him, neither am I.

AVAILABLE ON ALL RETAILERS. You can find the links HERE: http://laylahagen.com/books/lost-series/caught-in-us/

***

Standalone USA TODAY BESTSELLER
Withering Hope

Aimee's wedding is supposed to turn out perfect. Her dress, her fiancé and the location—the idyllic holiday ranch in Brazil—are perfect.

But all Aimee's plans come crashing down when the private jet that's taking her from the U.S. to the ranch— where her fiancé awaits her—defects mid-flight and the pilot is forced to perform an emergency landing in the heart of the Amazon rainforest.

With no way to reach civilization, being rescued is Aimee and Tristan's—the pilot—only hope. A slim one that slowly withers away, desperation taking its place. Because death wanders in the jungle under many forms: starvation, diseases. Beasts.

As Aimee and Tristan fight to find ways to survive, they grow closer. Together they discover that facing old, inner agonies carved by painful pasts takes just as much courage, if not even more, than facing the rainforest.

Despite her devotion to her fiancé, Aimee can't hide her feelings for Tristan—the man for whom she's slowly becoming everything. You can hide many things in the rainforest. But not lies. Or love.

Withering Hope is the story of a man who desperately needs forgiveness and the woman who brings him hope. It is a story in which hope births wings and blooms into a love that is as beautiful and intense as it is forbidden.

AVAILABLE ON ALL RETAILERS. You can find the links HERE: http://laylahagen.com/books/withering-hope/

Cover: http://designs.romanticbookaffairs.com/

***

Acknowledgements

There are so many people who helped me fulfil the dream of publishing, that I am utterly terrified I will forget to thank someone. If I do, please forgive me. Here it goes.

First, I'd like to thank my beta readers, Jessica, Dee, Andrea, Carrie, Jill, Kolleen and Rebecca. You made this story so much better!!

I want to thank every blogger and reader who took a chance with me as a new author and helped me spread the word. You have my most heartfelt gratitude. To my street team. . .you rock !!!

Last but not least, I would like to thank my family. I would never be here if not for their love and support. Mom, you taught me that books are important, and for that I will always be grateful. Dad, thank you for always being convinced that I should reach for the stars.

To my sister, whose numerous ahem. . .legendary replies will serve as an inspiration for many books to come, I say thank you for your support and I love you, kid.

To my husband, who always, no matter what, believed in me and supported me through all this whether by happily taking on every chore I overlooked or accepting being ignored for hours at a time, and most importantly encouraged me whenever I needed it: I love you and I could not have done this without you.

Table Of Contents

Made in the USA
Middletown, DE
08 February 2018